For Catrin, who kept the secret.

Ottilie Colter and the Narroway Hunt
first published in 2018
this edition published in 2021 by
Hardie Grant Children's Publishing
Wurundjeri Country
Ground Floor, Building 1, 658 Church Street
Richmond, Victoria 3121, Australia
www.hardiegrantchildrenspublishing.com

A catalogue record for this
book is available from the
National Library of Australia

Text copyright © 2018 Rhiannon Williams
Design copyright © 2018 Hardie Grant Children's Publishing
Cover illustration by Maike Plenzke
Cover design by Jess Cruickshank
Typeset in Fournier MT Std 13/17pt by Eggplant Communications

Hardie Grant acknowledges the Traditional Owners of the country on which
we work, the Wurundjeri people of the Kulin nation and the Gadigal people
of the Eora nation, and recognises their continuing connection to the land,
waters and culture. We pay our respects to their Elders past, present and
emerging.

Printed in Australia by Griffin Press, part of Ovato, an Accredited
ISO AS/NZS 14001 Environmental Management System printer.

7 9 10 8

The paper this book is printed on is
certified against the Forest Stewardship
Council® Standards. Griffin Press holds FSC®
chain of custody certification SGS-COC-005088.
FSC® promotes environmentally responsible,
socially beneficial and economically viable
management of the world's forests.

RHIANNON WILLIAMS

BOOK ONE *of* THE NARROWAY TRILOGY

Ottilie Colter
AND THE
Narroway Hunt

Hardie Grant

CHILDREN'S PUBLISHING

— 1 —

The Lightning Song

Ottilie skipped and stumbled. 'Gully, wait!'

Her skirt was caught on a branch. Panicking, she tugged hard and lurched backwards into the mud, drenching her legs and peppering her back with muddy spots all the way up to her neck. As she clambered to her feet, cold water trickled down her bare ankles into her boots.

'Gully!' she called again, tripping through the scratchy scrub. He was only six – nearly two years younger than she was. It was *supposed* to be Ottilie in charge, but Gully always led the way.

'Ottilie, what are you doing?' said Gully, bounding back towards her.

'I fell.'

Gully's face broke into a grin. 'You're all muddy.'

'It's not funny, Gulliver!'

'Did your leg get cut?' Gully squatted to check, and his own familiar scattering of scabs stretched over his kneecaps. Ottilie sometimes thought they looked like a cluster of islands marked on a map.

'It's just my skirt,' said Ottilie.

'Come on, we're nearly there.' Gully pulled her forwards.

Ottilie and Gulliver Colter were an odd pair. They were little, scrawny even. Both had unruly hair, small ears and crooked teeth, but as far as similarities went, that was about it. Ottilie was pale, with a fat trail of freckles across her nose. Gully's nose, and the rest of his face, was bronze like the square coins they passed around in Market Town. His large eyes reminded Ottilie of a midnight sky.

Ottilie didn't know why she and Gully were so different. She supposed that was just the way things were. Everyone was different. She even knew one boy with hair the colour of ripe oranges. Peter Mervintasker was his name. Old Moss once told her that Peter Mervintasker had hair that colour because his mother ate too many carrots before he was born, but Ottilie had stopped believing that years ago. Carrots didn't grow around the swamps, and Mrs Mervintasker didn't have any money to buy them. *No-one* Ottilie knew had any money for carrots.

'You know where we are now?' said Gully, pushing through the ferns at the fringe of Longwood Forest.

'I know the way to the sunnytree, Gully!'

She didn't really. The thing about always following was it made it hard to remember the way to anywhere.

It was worse in Longwood. Ottilie struggled to think straight in that eerie forest, and it was only when they cut into the field that she recognised where she was. Fine krippygrass, greener than green beans, tickled her elbows and her feet sunk a little into the mushy soil with every step.

The tree was in sight. Gully released her hand and charged ahead. This was their favourite place in all the world. Standing alone in the grass, the sunnytree had pale, twisted branches. It was leafless, but enormous golden flowers blotted its stark frame with light. They smelled awful, like muddy metal, but you could only smell them if you shoved your nose right into the petals, and Ottilie had learned to keep her distance since her face had puffed up after last time.

The sunnytree was the best tree to climb, but they hadn't really come to play. They had come to count their treasure.

'*Crunch, thud, dig deep down, pay for what you've done,*' Gully chanted under his breath.

'Stop it, Gulliver, that's not even the words.' Ottilie hated the lightning song.

'It is the words!'

'No, it's *sleeper comes for none.*'

'Peter Mervintasker says it's *pay for what you've done.* Because you called the storm with the song, so you get struck by lightning.'

That was what everyone said about the lightning song. Ottilie had never believed it, but she didn't like the song all the same.

'It doesn't matter anyway,' she said. 'Come on, let's dig it up.'

Their treasure chest was a narrow wooden box buried beneath a low branch of the sunnytree where Ottilie had carved an X. It only took a minute to unearth it with their hands. After wiping the mud on her skirt, Ottilie slid her blackened fingernails under the lid and prised the box open.

'*Flash, smack and crackle, lightning knows the spot. Hiss, flick and sputter, three will mark it hot.*' Gully was swinging from a forked branch, singing again.

Ottilie ignored him. She was counting the box's contents to make sure nothing was missing. There were several duck feathers, a star-shaped pebble, a silver button that they really should have tried to sell in Market Town, a scrap of cloth stitched with little yellow moons, and other precious bits and pieces they had collected over the years.

'*Wail, whine, dinnertime, no more rest for Mum. Crunch, thud, dig deep down, pay for what you've done.*'

'That's not the words,' said Ottilie, pressing the lid closed. 'It's all there.' They had been checking and counting every few weeks since Peter Mervintasker had found their old hiding place and made off with some of their treasure.

'It's going to rain again,' said Gully, his face tipped skyward.

Sure enough, dark clouds were rolling in. Ottilie sighed. Her clothes were already ruined, but she supposed there was no point in Gully getting all wet. Clothes took so long to dry around the swamps.

There was a sudden horrible boom. Ottilie felt as if the ground was shaking beneath her feet, and her teeth rattled in her mouth.

Gully laughed. 'It's going to storm!'

Lightning flashed, and the grass was veiled in shade as the angry clouds swallowed up all the light.

'I didn't even sing it loud!'

'It's not because of the song! Come on,' Ottilie said, turning her back.

'I want to watch the lightning!' Gully swung his leg onto a branch.

'We have to go home!' Ottilie grabbed his shirt and pulled.

He shook himself loose. 'I want to stay.'

5

Lightning flashed again. Ottilie squeezed her eyes closed, but it was as if someone had painted the insides of her eyelids a bright, shining white. 'Please, Gully, I don't like it.'

Gully looked at her for a moment. She could see he wanted to laugh at her. She could almost hear him say, *Ottilie, you're scared of everything!* But he didn't say it. Instead, Gully took her hand and turned his back on the sunnytree. He stomped his feet as they trekked back through the krippygrass, but he kept hold of her hand all the same.

As if from nowhere, a gust of icy wind nearly knocked them down. Thunder rumbled and lightning followed immediately after. The storm was right on top of them. Just as Ottilie squeezed her eyes shut, Gully yelled, 'Oh no!' and pulled away, charging back towards their treasure chest.

They hadn't buried it properly.

'Gully, wait! It doesn't matter!'

There was yet another grisly boom from the sky and Ottilie lost her footing from fright. Lying tangled in the krippygrass, she gazed up in horror as a spear of lightning plunged from the roaring skies and struck right through the heart of the sunnytree.

Ottilie smelled burning wood, heard the sizzle of flame on damp grass. Finding her feet, she flew away from the light and, stumbling through the ferns, she disappeared into Longwood.

No thought crossed her mind but escape. She didn't feel the bramble thorns pull at her skirt, nor the branches snatching at her arms. She just pushed on and on, deeper and deeper into the forest. Finally she stopped. Breathing hard, she pressed against the scales of a tree fern and, hiding beneath its giant fronds, she wrapped her arms around her knees.

It took a few moments for her vision to return to normal. She became aware of her surroundings. She was alone in Longwood. No, that wasn't the problem. There was something far worse – Ottilie had left Gully behind.

She had to go and find him. She had to bring him back. Ottilie knew it was right. She knew it was her job, but she couldn't move. She commanded her arms to release her legs. *Move*, she thought. *Move*!

Branches thrashed and whirled above, and wind howled through the alleys between tree trunks. The minutes hurtled past, but still she could not move.

Ottilie heard something from far away. Eyes wide and wet with tears, she glanced up.

'Ottilie!'

Someone was calling her.

Ottilie opened her mouth to respond, but nothing came out.

'Ottilie, where are you?'

He was closer.

'Here!'

It was a mere squeak but at least she'd made a noise. She couldn't seem to make another. She could hear leaves crunching and twigs breaking. She focused on the sounds of his approach until there he was, standing right before her. Gully pushed forwards and kneeled next to her, resting his hand on her knee.

'I wanted to come get you. I was going to,' said Ottilie, arms still firmly wrapped around her legs.

'That's all right,' said Gully. 'I came to get you.'

— 2 —

The Swamp Hollows

Five years later …

Their hollow was empty.

Ottilie picked at the smallest of many holes in her mother's only blanket. The bed was untouched, the woollen blanket pulled tight and tucked in at the sides. Stretching to stand, Ottilie winced. Her entire left side had stiffened overnight, and all for nothing – she need not have slept on the floor. Their mother's health had been in slow decline for as long as she could remember, and Ottilie had given up her scrap of a mattress weeks ago so that Freddie could layer one on top of the other. Now Ottilie felt lopsided, and more than a little annoyed.

Freddie's absence was not a big surprise – but where was Gully? He hadn't been home when Ottilie went to sleep, although this was not unusual, but he was always there in the morning. Ottilie crouched awkwardly on the smooth limestone floor. Her own threadbare blanket was wrapped tightly about her shoulders as she frowned. Was it too early to worry?

No.

She launched herself off the ground, pulled the nearest moth-eaten coat over her nightdress, forced her bare feet into soggy, mud-crusted boots and unlatched the door.

The Colter hollow was one of the few in their quarter with an actual door. The Swamp Hollows were a series of caves and tunnels on the edge of the Brakkerswamp, managed by a man they called the keeper.

The caves had been deserted for years before the squatters settled in. No-one knew who originally built the doors to section them off. The central chamber even had window shutters covering the holes in the cave walls. Freddie said the keeper's hollow had window shutters too, but Ottilie had never been inside.

The Hollows were a last resort, shelter for those without means to live elsewhere. Ottilie was what they called 'Brakker born and bred'. She had lived there for nearly thirteen years.

She pressed the door open a smidge, just wide enough to slip through. It was a noisy old thing and she was wary of making a disturbance so early in the morning. In the Hollows there were neighbours everywhere. Old Moss and Mr Parch slept in the tunnel just outside. Tiptoeing past, she averted her gaze. Mr Parch always slept with his eyes open. It gave her the shivers, probably because he was old as dirt and it was hard to tell the difference between sleeping and dead. Shivers aside, she liked that they were always there. Freddie was so often absent, and with Old Moss and Mr Parch just outside, Ottilie never felt alone.

She stopped at the wash grotto to splash her face and take a gulp from the fresh running spring. She had thought the place deserted, but something shifted in the shadows. Ottilie froze. It was little more than a whisper, but she heard it – a bare foot stepping on wet stone.

'Gully?'

No-one spoke.

But for the steady dripping of stalactites over the pools, the grotto was silent. This was just like her brother. He was going to jump out any second now and tackle her to the ground.

'Gul–'

This time she definitely heard something – a breath, just feet away. Someone was around the corner, breathing beyond the spring. It wasn't Gully. That wasn't how Gully breathed. It was wet. Wet breath. She didn't want to know who was there, not anymore. Without another thought, Ottilie bolted.

After a clumsy drop into the lower tunnels, Ottilie slowed. Pressing her cheek against the cool stone wall, she closed her eyes. It felt as if someone were trying to pull apart her ribcage.

She needed a plan. Freddie was the obvious place to start. She would find Freddie and see if she knew of Gully's whereabouts.

'Gurt!'

Ottilie fluttered impatiently in front of the mouldy old curtain that was the entrance to Gurt's hollow.

'Just a minute!' called a mucusy voice.

'Is my mum in there?'

'Eh? Oh. Yuh, Freddie's here.'

Ottilie felt a lump form in her throat. 'I'm coming in.'

'Hold your trotters –'

There came a loud crashing and clanking from beyond the mouldy veil. Ottilie wrenched it aside and was overwhelmed by the sharp stench of old bramblywine.

'Oi, careful there, nearly took my eye!' Gurt stumbled backwards, tripped over one of many empty bottles, and fell to the floor. With a crackling sigh, he rolled himself into a jumble of knobbly bones. 'What can I do you for, little Ott?'

'Freddie.' The word came out more like a growl than Ottilie intended. She had always hated how Gurt called her *Ott*.

'Over there.' He jerked his head. 'Sleeping.'

Ottilie glanced over to the corner. Visible somewhere within a pile of crusty clothes and blankets was Freddie Colter's thinning mop of grizzled hair.

'You didn't give her your stuff again?' said Ottilie, tears welling in her eyes.

'Course I did. Best brewed bramblywine in the swamps.'

'Yours always makes her sicker. You don't know how to make it right.'

'What would you know? You ever even tasted it, little Ott?'

'No,' said Ottilie, her anger mounting.

He reached for the nearest bottle, checking to see if it was empty. 'Here, I'll find you a bottle half pri–'

Ottilie ignored him. 'Mum.'

Freddie didn't move.

'Mum!'

The greying mop shifted back and forth like an old possum sifting through a pile of garbage. Ottilie squatted down beside her and pulled the covers away. Freddie groaned and rolled over.

Ottilie could never be sure how much she really resembled her mother. Her own hair was long and wildly curled; Freddie's was lifeless, thin and greying all over. Ottilie's eyes were a swampy grey-green; Freddie's were empty and dark. And where Ottilie's face was plump and heart-shaped, Freddie's had been growing looser and thinner with every passing season.

Her mother was beginning to look like the old paintings in the empty tunnels above the central chamber – paintings of stick figures with wide mouths and feathery crowns. Old Moss said the ancient markings were lost stories from the Lore. The feathery crowns signified fiorns, chosen children of the god Fiory, lord of the raptors. But they were fearsome, magical creatures, and Freddie was about as far from fearsome or magical as Ottilie could imagine.

'Ottilie, it's cold,' Freddie mumbled. Her breath reeked of vinegar and rotting gums.

'Mum, did you see Gully last night?'

'Last night?'

'When did you last see him?'

'Yesterday ...' Freddie's eyes were half-closed and caked in yellow crusts. 'In the morning.'

'But did you see him after?'

'Mm. That's when I saw him. He's always getting lost.'

Ottilie felt the colour rising in her cheeks. 'No, Mum, he's never lost. Not ever.'

'Check the swamp. He likes the swamp.'

Her heart sank. '*I* like the swamp. Gully hates the swamp.'

'Oh.' Freddie closed her eyes.

'You don't think the Laklanders got him?' said Old Moss, narrowing her pouchy eyes.

'No! There are no Laklanders around here ...' said Ottilie.

Laklanders were old enemies of their kingdom. Ottilie liked to think they were completely gone, extinct, like the ancient giants and their scaly steeds whose bones had been found in the dunes of the north island. But of course, Laklanders were far more recent, and far more real. Whispers of their wicked deeds sent shivers down her spine, and they always featured as imaginary villains in Ottilie and Gully's most exciting games.

Ottilie turned to Mr Parch. 'There are no Laklanders here,' she repeated. 'Are there?'

'Course not,' said Mr Parch, glaring at Old Moss.

Ottilie had looked for Gully everywhere, asked everyone she could find. Most of them said the same thing: 'He's an adventurous boy – he'll make his way back.' But Ottilie knew him better. He would never disappear, not for this long, not without a word. He would never leave her behind.

Finally, when afternoon met evening and everything slowed, Ottilie had headed for home.

'Why do people say that? About the Laklanders?' said Ottilie.

Mr Parch had taught her almost everything she knew, except how to read – Old Moss had taken on that responsibility. Moss was the proud owner of one single book: *Our Walkable World, Volume Six: The Usklers and The Laklands*. It was very valuable, made from real parchment. Not like the ones in Market Town with pages made from compressed old rags.

The book was her most treasured possession. Mr Parch's most treasured possession was his pair of eyeglasses. Both refused to sell either for anything, not even food or better lodgings, and their stubbornness on the subject was a perpetual point of contention between the two.

'It's just a story, Ottilie. No truth to it,' said Mr Parch.

'But where did it come from? It's just about boys, isn't it? The Laklanders take boys. But what for?'

'They chop them up and feed them to the birds.'

'Moss!'

'They creep around at night and snatch little boys for bird meat,' said Moss.

'No truth,' said Mr Parch, shaking his head.

'But boys do go missing?' whispered Ottilie.

'People of all kinds can go missing,' said Mr Parch. 'It's the way of the world, but it doesn't happen very often and it's nothing for you to worry about.'

'Little boys more than others,' Old Moss said. 'Every year or so a couple vanish from around the Hollows or the villages nearby – but plenty more disappear from more populated areas. My horrible sister, may she *not* rest in peace, lived in Wikric Town and she said common as corn, the disappearances are. People treat the stories like they're real. Makes you wonder.'

Ottilie didn't want to wonder.

'Moss, enough! You're scaring the girl,' said Mr Parch. 'Don't listen to her, Ottilie. Tell you what, if he still hasn't turned up by nightfall I'll go see the keeper about it.'

Old Moss snorted loudly. 'What do you think that slimy old chomper's going to do about it?'

'Moss –'

'He probably sells them off!' said Moss, hooting with laughter.

'Moss, will you shut up!'

'Don't you tell me to shut up!'

'I will tell you to shut up if I want you to shut up, you insensitive old tortoise!'

Moss let out a wheezy roar, grabbed her walking stick and pointed it at Mr Parch like a spear.

'Moss!' Ottilie wrenched the walking stick from Old Moss's surprisingly strong grasp.

'Oi! Ottilie, you pass that back!'

'No. You can't threaten people with walking sticks, Moss.'

'I wasn't going to touch him!'

Ottilie was feeling panicky and irritable, and she'd had enough. 'I'm taking this.' Without another word Ottilie marched away, Old Moss's walking stick tucked safely under her arm.

<hr />

There was only one place left to look. Ottilie took the back way to Longwood, skirting the edge of the swamps. The Brakkerswamp was a funny place and Ottilie liked it a lot. There was no point in searching there, though – Gully never went into the swamps. But Ottilie would have loved to venture out. She knew exactly where to step along the mushy, hidden paths. She liked clambering onto mossy islands, crawling along slippery fallen gum trees, and stirring deep puddles with forked sticks the way ancient sea witches had stirred their rock pools.

Probably most of all, Ottilie loved balancing on the low branches of the freshwater fig trees that grew up out of the water, holding fast and leaning out, waiting to catch sight of lights glowing far down in the deep.

There was a crunching noise up above. Ottilie swung around. Her ribs locked, and her shoulders curved in defence. She took a breath; the feel of Old Moss's walking stick tucked beneath her arm offered a scrap of comfort. The Hollows stretched up behind her, dotted with fissures and small holes that led to tunnels no-one could reach. Gully was always trying to get up there.

'Gully!' she called, sure someone was nearby.

There sounded a faint scuffle, followed by a quiet sigh.

It wasn't Gully. That much she knew. For one thing, the sound came from the opening high up above. No person could get up there.

Ottilie clutched the walking stick so tightly her fingers turned white, and pushed herself onwards. As the wetlands thinned and the ground grew firmer beneath her feet, her heart began to race. She hated Longwood. Hated it! The temperature dropped and she hugged herself in the cold.

She had heard rumours of secluded Laklander camps buried in the deepest corners of Longwood – but Ottilie had never really believed them. It was Longwood itself that spooked her. There was something about the air in the forest. It whispered dark words to her senses, raising the hairs on her neck and setting her jaw so that her teeth ground together.

She wasn't the only one. Despite the wealth of wood, nuts, fruit and plump birds that Longwood had to offer, people stayed away. Even the poorest of the Swamp Hollows folk only ventured into the forest when truly desperate for a meal, or something to trade to pay their monthly boarders' toll to the keeper.

The moss-covered trunks grew thicker and closer, and the light began to fade. She took a deep breath and tried to speak.

'Gully.' It was little more than a whisper.

Ottilie shivered. It was like being trapped in a nightmare, fighting with weak limbs and feeble fists and crying out with voiceless screams. Ottilie screwed up her face, not quite closing her eyes. This was not a nightmare. Of course she could speak.

'Gully!' Her voice was perhaps a little higher than usual, but perfectly loud.

There was no answer.

Knees quaking, she took a step backwards. She had to get out.

It was growing too dark to see her feet in front of her, and by the time she made it back to the Hollows the stars were in full bloom. Breathing hard, she rushed back through the tunnels.

'Any sign, Mr Parch?'

'Sorry, Ottilie.' Mr Parch shook his head. 'I'll talk to the keeper first thing.'

'Can I have my stick back?' snapped Old Moss.

'No.'

Ottilie slipped into her hollow and pulled the door shut with a thump. Leaning against the chipped wood,

Ottilie closed her eyes and made a wish. She wished harder than she had ever wished before. She wished that when she turned around she would see Gully asleep in his bed. She wished that he had slipped past Old Moss during her afternoon nap, and that Mr Parch had missed him because Old Moss knocked his eyeglasses off last week, and they didn't fit on his big nose anymore. She wished that Gully was exhausted from his adventures and had fallen asleep before sundown.

Ottilie counted to three. She turned around. She opened her eyes.

Their hollow was empty.

— 3 —

Bill

Ottilie's eyes flicked open. Something was different. It was after midnight, she was sure. Freddie was absent. Gully hadn't returned. She should have been all alone, but there was a new smell in the air, a scent like puddles and rain-soaked bark. There was something else, too. She was only halfway home, one foot still in a dream, but slowly it came – the subtle but sure sense that someone unfamiliar was in the hollow.

Ottilie lay stiff as a board, one thought spinning round and round in her mind.

Laklander.

That was when she heard it. That strange, wet breath from the day before. Heart battering against her ribs,

Ottilie sat bolt upright. She could see a shape in the dark, bending over Gully's empty bed.

At exactly the same moment she and the Laklander leapt up, emitted yelps of surprise, and scrambled to opposite sides of the hollow, breathing in panicked unison. Ottilie grabbed Old Moss's walking stick and held it aloft.

She took a breath, wide eyes fixed on the dark shape cowering against the wall. It occurred to her that the Laklander was afraid of her. It didn't make sense. A scream surged up through her body, but just before it escaped she clenched her jaw shut.

'What are you doing over there?' she demanded, walking stick in hand, ready to swing.

'You frightened me,' he said. The voice was strange, like he had a winter chill. It was throaty but wet, and somehow blocked.

'I frightened *you*?' Ottilie jabbed the stick in his direction.

She squinted at him. There was something strange about the way he was standing, even his smell. She couldn't be sure, but Ottilie was fairly certain that this intruder wasn't human – which meant he couldn't be a Laklander after all.

'What are you …' Realising that she may have been asking a very rude question, Ottilie added, 'doing … in … here?'

He swallowed audibly. 'I was just seeing.'

Ottilie could only just make out his silhouette against the wall. 'Seeing? Seeing what?'

'Seeing if the boy was in his bed.'

She gripped the walking stick very hard. 'What?'

'My head gets muddled. Sometimes I remember something from long ago and forget where the memory belongs.'

'What do you know about my brother?'

'That's just it,' he mumbled. 'I wasn't sure. I had to see.'

'Don't move,' said Ottilie. She pointed the walking stick at him like a sword and backed out of the hollow. Old Moss and Mr Parch were sleeping soundly. Ottilie slipped past. With a shaking hand, she pulled a flaming torch from the nearest wall-bracket and hurried back.

She pushed the door open with her shoulder and entered the hollow, flame first. A bead of sweat trailed slowly down her neck as she studied the intruder.

She did not know what to make of him. He was the strangest creature she had ever seen. His strangeness came not from the differences, but the similarities he bore to a human being.

The creature was taller than Ottilie, and rather thin. He was dressed in an old grey shirt and trousers with a cracked leather sack slung over one sloping shoulder. His skin was very unusual. In fact, it was – well, she thought it might be … fur. It was very short and thin and sleek, like how she imagined the shiny hair on sea creatures. The colouring was pale and pinkish like human skin, but there was a distinct grey tinge.

He had a narrow nose and his eyes were very close together, framed by spidery eyelashes, which were a muddy colour to match the fine hair atop his head — beneath which poked two blunt horns. He shielded himself from the flame, and Ottilie could see slight webbing between his long, knobbly fingers.

Ottilie narrowed her eyes and took a breath. 'What — I mean, who are you?'

'No-one … *bad*,' he said, his eyes darting back and forth between Ottilie and the flaming end of the torch.

Ottilie squared her shoulders. She was determined to look much braver than she felt. 'Why were you looking for my brother?'

'I wanted to tell … about the boy. But I got muddled and had to be sure …' He squinted away from the light. 'That the swamp picker got him.'

'The who?'

'The swamp picker takes boys from the villages along Longwood and around the Brakkerswamp.'

Ottilie felt like someone had placed a sack over her head. 'Takes them *where*?'

'Down through the tunnels under Wikric Town. That's as far as I've ever followed.'

Wikric was the largest town in the west. Why would anyone take Gully *there*?

'How come you saw?'

'I live nearby, in the caves up there.' He pointed awkwardly upwards.

Ottilie followed his finger, staring up at the craggy ceiling of her hollow. 'How long have you lived up there?'

'I can't remember.'

'But – how old are you?' He didn't look much older than she was.

'I never kept count.'

Ottilie gazed at him. His small, dark eyes were stretched wide in distress. He seemed genuine. She was regaining control over her breath and something clicked into place. 'You were following me yesterday,' she said, finally lowering the torch.

Relaxing his arms, the creature freed an uneven sigh of relief. 'I was trying to figure out … if there used to be two of you.'

'There did.'

His eyes widened as he sucked in a long, wet breath. 'Oh dear. That's no good. I was afraid of that.'

'My brother. He's missing.' Ottilie was surprised by how steady her voice had become. 'I don't know what to do,' she added, more to herself than him. Mostly what she wanted to do was sleep. She had a sudden overwhelming urge to lie down and close her eyes.

Ottilie realised the creature was still leaning away from the flame. She took a step back. He seemed to relax a little more, but his webbed fingers wound together and he started shifting from foot to foot.

'Can you show me where they took him?' That seemed the obvious thing to ask.

'Oh no. No ...' He stared at the floor. 'I ... I could tell ...'

'No, I need you to show me.' She would follow after him. It was all she could do. 'I don't know anything about the Wikric tunnels and I don't have time to get lost. *Please*. Please, I need your help.'

He blinked hard and rubbed his nose. 'Alr– no – ye– yes. I can show you part of the way.'

'Thank you.' Ottilie frowned, thinking hard. This was it, wasn't it? It was the only thing to be done. Her attention was all off-kilter. She couldn't think far ahead. There was only the immediate – only the now. Gully was gone. This creature knew where. It was enough. This creature ...

'What's your name?'

He looked confused. 'I just call myself *me*.'

She blinked. 'Someone must call you something. I can hardly call you *me*.'

'The birds call me Bill.'

'The *birds* call you Bill?'

He nodded.

'You can talk to birds?'

'Can't you?'

'No.'

'Oh.'

There was a rather long pause.

'All right, Bill it is — and you can call me Ottilie.'

4

The Duck Door

Ottilie packed quickly. She had already lost an entire day, and she wanted to get to Gully before they took him too far. She didn't pack much: a waterskin, two apples, a chunk of stale bread, some shrivelled beans, and a handful of pale gold brakkernuts she and Gully had collected from Longwood a few days before. She was careful to leave enough in their food chest for Freddie. She didn't know when they would be back, and without Ottilie and Gully Freddie would have to survive on what she could afford to buy, which was almost nothing. It was more likely she'd settle for the scraps the keeper handed out.

Ottilie considered taking Old Moss's walking stick as a weapon, but she didn't have the heart to leave her without it any longer. Instead, she took Freddie's only knife and tucked it carefully into her pack. Just in case. She really would have preferred the walking stick.

Hoisting the pack over her shoulder, Ottilie gazed about the hollow, searching for something she might have forgotten. It felt strange, even … good. In the space of a blink, she felt a prickle of excitement.

The door creaked ominously as Ottilie pulled it shut. She was just about to place Old Moss's walking stick back down beside her when Bill lunged backwards, stumbling into her and causing her elbow to hit the rock wall with a crunch.

She swallowed her growl and hissed, 'What!'

Bill gestured to Mr Parch, who was lying on the floor in a cocoon of blankets, his eyes wide open. 'Sorry,' whispered Bill. 'But I think … I think he's dead.'

They both stared. Mr Parch snorted and rolled over, snoring loudly.

Ottilie rubbed her elbow and glared at Bill. 'That's just how he sleeps.'

'He should put up a sign,' said Bill. *Sleeping. Not dead.*'

Ottilie had to clap her hand over her mouth to keep from laughing. It was the first time she had smiled in hours.

'Where do we go?' she whispered.

'There's a shortcut, but you won't fit. We'll have to go out your entrance and take the road for a bit.'

'What do you mean I won't fit? You're bigger than me.'

'I sort of … fold.'

Ottilie looked him up and down in the dark. 'Right.'

Market Town was the furthest Ottilie had ever travelled. Once or twice a month she and Gully travelled south, down the winding dirt road, to see what they might get for whatever useful things they had managed to collect. Krippygrass was quite good for weaving, and there were always waterfigs and brambleberries in the warmer months. They used to sell a bit of firewood, but two seasons ago they had sold their barrow to buy a remedy for Freddie, and now they had no way to transport anything heavy.

Ottilie and Bill crossed the River Hook at Drifters Bridge and marched down the bumpy road, winding through a meadow of krippygrass and up the slope of the grey and pointy Brakkerbend Hill. There shone only the thinnest sliver of a moon. The darkness was thick as smoke, and the ground below was uneven. They passed over the peak and Ottilie slowed her pace. She knew there was a steep drop somewhere to her left, but she couldn't see the edge.

'Here,' said Bill, pulling a jar from his sack. 'You have water?'

Ottilie passed him her waterskin. Bill uncorked the jar and filled it to the brim. A light flickered, and another and another, until what appeared to be three feeble twigs glowed with a bright greenish light.

'Glow sticks,' said Bill. 'From the swamp.'

Ottilie remembered the lights in the water – bright eyes winking in the deep. She held the glow sticks aloft like a lantern to navigate the rocks and craters ahead.

Ottilie had never seen the road empty before. On market days the way was usually dotted with faulty peddlers, birds tethered to their wrists and floppy hats pulled low, offering their allegedly magical wares. There was no end of potential customers. The road was always busy with folk from the nearby villages: pulling weighty barrows, leading black goats with curled horns, lugging barrels of silver salt from the River Hook, passing stories and gathering the latest news from Wikric, the biggest town in the west.

The king and his company ruled their kingdom, the Usklers, from four main towns. All Kings' Hill, in the east, was the king's primary residence. But there was also Rupimoon Rock in the north, Stavey Bay in the south, and Wikric Town. If these pickers were using the tunnels under Wikric, did that mean that the king knew what was happening?

Ottilie didn't know much about the king. To her, he was no more than a fairytale character – albeit one she knew to exist. Any rumours about the king were no more real to her than whispers of witches or legends of Laklander mischief.

'Who took him, Bill? Who are the pickers?' She didn't understand. What was it all for?

Bill shook his head. 'I don't know … I only know they take boys from everywhere, all across the Usklers, and they all come through Wikric. I think they must take them further west.'

'But we *are* west. The only thing more west than Longwood is –' Ottilie gulped. She knew what lay beyond the western border. 'The Laklands.'

A fresh wave of unease washed over her. Could this have something to do with the Laklanders? But there couldn't be many of them left. The Laklands had been destroyed over a century ago. The Usklers had flattened them and left their home uninhabitable. At least, that's what she'd been told.

'But why go there?'

Bill shrugged. 'I don't know why. I do know your Swamp Hollows keeper gives the pickers lists of boys to take.'

Ottilie felt ill. She didn't know the keeper very well and had never much liked him, but for whatever reason, he had always looked out for Freddie, letting her skip payments and giving her food whenever things got desperate. Tears gathered in Ottilie's eyes.

'But they're usually older than your brother,' Bill added.

'Gully just looks young,' said Ottilie, sniffing forcefully. 'He turned eleven at the beginning of spring.'

Bill shook his head. 'I think they're usually about thirteen.' He pointed a webbed finger towards Longwood. 'We have to get off the road now.'

'We're not going in the forest?' said Ottilie, her voice a little higher than she expected.

'N– uh – no ...' Bill shuddered, 'not – never go in there. Just that way until we meet the river again. Then under – there's a tunnel. You'll get there by first light, just before, if you're quick.'

'First light!' Ottilie gawked up at the sky; daybreak was hours away. 'But what if we miss them?'

'They'll hold them in cells under Wikric until the pickings from the north arrive. I heard them talking.'

Ottilie narrowed her eyes. 'I thought you couldn't remember.' Bill was an odd creature. She didn't know if she could trust him.

'I did hear. I just thought I might have heard a long time ago, but now I know it was now and not another time, because you lost your brother now.'

'I don't think that makes sense,' she said.

'It probably does.'

Bill took hold of her sleeve and pulled her off the road, onto a stretch of moss and smooth stone by the river. Longwood lay just beyond, but the barrier of flowing water kept Ottilie's nerves at bay. She looked down, away from the trees, and for the first time she noticed Bill's bare feet.

'Bill!'

He stopped abruptly and Ottilie walked straight into him. 'What?' said Bill, steadying her.

'Don't your feet hurt, on the road? And aren't they cold?'

Bill looked perplexed. 'Yes. But I don't have any shoes, don't need them in the caves.'

'You don't have any … but here, let me see …' Ottilie squatted down and inspected Bill's feet, holding the glow sticks close. His furry skin was strangely dull in the moonlight. He almost seemed to blend with his surroundings. 'Bill, this one's all cut up!' she said, taking his ankle in her hands and forcing his webbed foot off the moss. His anklebone seemed oddly soft, not like bone at all – more like a bendy green twig, or whatever human ears were made of.

Bill wobbled and had to hop to regain his balance. 'It's just from the rocks on the road. It's all right, the moss is nice.'

'No, here – wear mine for a bit!' said Ottilie, pulling at her left boot.

'They won't fit. It's fine.' Bill took her sleeve again and they moved on.

Ottilie couldn't stop thinking about his poor battered feet. 'Thank you,' she said, 'for telling me about Gully, and showing me the way.'

He nodded.

'Bill.'

'Mm?'

'I'm quite scared.'

Bill looked at her for a moment. His kind eyes crinkled and Ottilie had the sudden feeling that he was much older than he looked.

'I'm always scared,' he said.

She didn't find his words particularly comforting.

The stretch of green came to an end and they reached a series of wide, smooth rocks a yard or so from the river's edge. Bill stopped, turned on the spot, and bent down to run his long fingers over a stone.

Ottilie hurried over to see.

'Is that a –'

'Hatch,' said Bill.

The hatch was made of a circular slab of stone, with thick rusty hinges at the edge. There were strange markings outside the circle, but an ordinary duck was carved into the centre.

'A duck?'

Bill ran his fingers around the edge of the circle. 'There,' he said, his fingers slipping into a subtle groove between the rock and the hatch. His arms strained as he eased it open.

Ottilie stared at him. 'How do we get down?'

'I – we?' he croaked.

'You're not coming?'

'Well … was … I thought – home …' He pointed east.

'Home is that way,' said Ottilie, pointing north. 'Please, Bill. Show me the tunnels. Just a bit further?'

Bill's arm twitched as he gazed about, clearly a little lost. 'I – yes, a bit further.'

Ottilie peered into the tunnel. She couldn't see anything except for an old ladder leading down into the depths. Bill went in first. When she had lost sight of his head, Ottilie pocketed the glow sticks and placed one boot on the first step. It seemed sturdy enough, though her legs were wobbly with nerves. She descended carefully, and then eased the hatch over her head with an unpleasant scrape.

5

The Swamp Picker

One foot after the other, the hours dragged on. The air in the tunnel was thick, and Ottilie couldn't shake the thought that this was how the inside of a coffin would smell – like rotting leather, bone dust, and hundred-year-old dirt. She shook her head, trying to clear all thoughts of death and small spaces. Aside from the ladder and the hatch, there was nothing man-made about the tunnel. Here and there it forked, or a shadowed opening would appear on one side. It was like a passage in a rabbit warren, only much bigger, as if the earth had been forced apart by a wandering hippopotamus.

Bill led the way. He was beginning to breathe harder and harder, wet breath catching in his throat, but still he pushed on. Ottilie had a sneaking suspicion he was only sticking with her because he couldn't remember he had wanted to go home in the first place.

'So you've come all this way before?' said Ottilie. Her voice sounded oddly muffled, as if the heavy air was smothering her words.

'Once,' said Bill. 'I saw them take a boy from the squatters' cavern, and followed.'

Ottilie was horrified. Another Swamp Hollows boy. She racked her brains for anyone she knew who had disappeared. People came and went from the Hollows all the time. 'Who did they take?'

'He was just passing through. Staying in the Swamp Hollows for a few nights by himself. I followed, saw the swamp picker take another boy around Balding Village. I followed them all the way to Wikric, where other pickers brought more boys from far away.'

Ottilie frowned. 'But you didn't tell anyone?'

'I listened, I heard a lot … it's a dangerous business. Once you get your brother, I don't think you can stay near the Brakkerswamp. They won't leave you be, not now that you know.'

Her stomach performed a somersault. 'But I don't know anything.'

'As much as you do know is too much already.'

She felt herself begin to panic. 'First we have to get Gully,' she said, her voice weak. 'How much further?'

'Not far. We need to start being quiet, I think.' Bill's voice was very unsteady.

She buried the glow sticks in her pack. 'How are your feet?' she whispered.

'They're fine,' muttered Bill.

They rounded a corner and lantern light spilled into the curving passage ahead. Bill gasped at the sight of it, making Ottilie jump. 'Don't do that!' she hissed.

'Sorry.' He pressed all ten fingers over his mouth, then through his hands he mumbled, 'The cells are around that bend.'

'I'll go and see if Gully's there,' said Ottilie. 'Then we'll figure out how to sneak him out.'

'Nuh – n– no. Stay back,' he said, pulling her away. 'I can – I'm better at looking.'

'You're *better at looking*?' She raised her eyebrows.

Bill took a long, furtive step forwards. Ottilie grabbed his arm. Shaking her head vigorously, she pointed at her chest. 'I'll go.' She wanted to see Gully, just to catch a glimpse of him and see that he was all right.

'You're easier to see,' Bill whispered. 'They'll catch us if they see you. I'm good at it.'

'Stop saying you're good at it!'

Bill pressed himself against the tunnel wall. He was right; with his grey clothes and strange fur he was almost impossible to see in the darkness. Ottilie stood still and focused on breathing quietly as Bill slipped around the corner.

It felt like an age had passed when a clammy hand wrapped around Ottilie's in the dark. She nearly yelped in surprise. Silently, Bill led her backwards, away from the light.

'They're in a sort of cage. There's no guards, but something's wrong …'

'What do you mean? Did you see Gully?'

'No, and there's hardly any boys, less than twenty. I think that's about half as many as there should be.'

Ottilie's throat constricted and she felt her blood drain all the way to her toes. She grabbed his sloping shoulders.

'Where is he?!' she hissed.

'That's what I'm saying,' said Bill, carefully prying her fingers off his shoulders. 'Something's wrong. I think some of them have already moved on.'

She finally understood. 'You mean we're too late? We missed him?'

'I think so.'

Ottilie couldn't breathe. She began pacing back and forth. 'What am I going to do? I don't know where he's gone! How am I supposed to find him now?' Tears flooded her eyes.

'But these ones will move on too,' said Bill. 'You could follow them.'

At that, a horrible thought struck Ottilie. What if it was all a trick? What if Bill had led her there to get caught? He had said Gully would be there – and he wasn't. What if there was no such thing as the pickings and Bill was leading her into a trap?

Eyes narrowed, Ottilie took a step towards him.

'Argh!' Bill hopped on the spot. She had accidently stepped on his foot.

Ottilie looked down. She couldn't see them in the dark, but she remembered very clearly his torn and battered feet. Of course it wasn't a trick. No kidnapper would walk barefoot across a rocky road to deliver his pickings. That would be ludicrous. A kidnapper would wear shoes.

'Sorry,' said Ottilie. 'I couldn't see you properly.'

'That's all right,' said Bill.

'I need to see for myself if Gully's there.'

Slowly she slid along to the corner and peered towards the light. She could see shadows ahead. It took her a moment to move again.

Ottilie growled quietly to herself. She would have control of her feet. She would move closer. She inched nearer.

The tunnel widened and forked at the end with an enormous ironbark door blocking one of the passageways. Ottilie could see a cell with figures inside. It stretched out from the wall just yards from where she stood. The thick bars reached high, not quite touching the ceiling. It stretched longways, long enough to fit at least thirty people. Another cell ran along the opposite wall. It was empty. There was no sign of the so-called swamp picker, or anyone guarding the cell at all.

Ottilie crept closer. Two flaming lanterns hung low from chains along the wall on either side of the cell. She could make out the figures within, a group of boys, all bigger than Gully.

She froze. One of the boys was looking right at her. Cool bubbles of sweat rose to the surface of her skin. The boy scanned her slowly with glassy eyes. Holding her breath, she placed her finger to her lips.

He didn't react.

Exhaling in relief, Ottilie crept closer. There was something odd about him – and the others, too. They all seemed half-asleep. Some of them actually *were* asleep.

Scanning at top speed, she took them all in. Gully wasn't there. She was sure of it.

Voices sounded from beyond the door. Ottilie slid back into the shadows just as somebody pushed it open. She felt her spine crunch into the wall with each silent, heaving breath. For a moment she thought she might actually be sick.

'I was rightly on schedule, as you can see.'

A thin figure stepped through the doorway. His scraggy auburn hair was flecked with grey and a reddish goatee curled just below his chin. Ottilie knew that man. She had seen him around the Swamp Hollows. He had stayed in the squatters' cavern many times.

'*My* job's done,' he was grumbling. 'Should've been off home yesterday.'

'What's the problem?' This second man Ottilie did not recognise. He was dressed in a uniform, with thick plates of shiny armour over his shoulders and chest. The swamp picker looked very raggedy in comparison, with his brown moth-eaten trousers and discoloured coat.

The uniformed man seemed an official sort, a Wikric guard perhaps. But if a Wikric guard was meeting with a picker, what did that mean? Maybe this really was Uskler business. Or maybe not. Could the guard be a traitor?

'The problem is, we got word the northers are a day behind schedule,' said the swamp picker. 'And it's *their* turn to take them on to the border gate.'

Ottilie held her breath. The border gate ... that confirmed it. They were taking them further west. But *why*?

'I sent some of the troublemakers off with the group last night. Good sign that – I'm told they need a good bit of fight in them where they're going,' he said. 'But this lot here, and the pickings from the north, won't be able leave till tomorrow morning. Like I said, day behind schedule – they won't like that.'

Ottilie screwed her eyes shut. Troublemakers. That had to be why Gully wasn't there – because they had sent him away early.

She was too late.

'So I'll be wanting some food, if you please,' added the swamp picker. 'Didn't bring provisions for an extra day of waiting.'

The uniformed man nodded. 'I'll have something sent down.' He headed for the door. 'Do not send for me again.'

Careful to make no sound, Ottilie slipped back to Bill. 'Did you hear?' she whispered.

'Your brother's already gone,' said Bill. 'What are you going to do?'

Ottilie scrunched her eyes closed, thinking hard. 'You were right. They're crossing west, over to the Laklands. I don't think I can risk it.'

'Risk what?'

'Getting caught, before I can get to Gully. Even if I managed to sneak in, I don't know what the Laklands are like ...' Ottilie couldn't believe the words coming out of her mouth. What was she talking about? Crossing borders? Leaving the Usklers? This couldn't be real.

'So what can you do?' said Bill, wrapping his fingers around one of his horns.

Ottilie stared at her feet. She knew the answer. She could say it. The words were easy. 'I have to go with them.'

Bill looked at her as if she were mad.

'I can pretend to be a captive and they'll take me right to Gully.'

Would she actually be able to do this? There was no way she would be able to do this.

'B-but, no. Ottilie, it's too dangerous –' Bill wound his webbed fingers together, twisting them as if moulding clay between his palms.

'I have to.'

It was as if she, Bill and Gully were playing a game. It was one big game of make-believe and Ottilie was make-believing that she was brave enough to do this.

'But Ottilie,' said Bill, 'the other captives are all *boys*.'

6

A Gift from Gurt

Bill didn't approve, but he didn't leave her, either. He and Ottilie took turns spying on the swamp picker. The way she figured it, the best time to sneak into the cell would be after the handover, when the northers arrived and the swamp picker was gone. They didn't want to risk him recognising Ottilie from the Hollows.

She had a plan, or at least the makings of a plan. 'I'm going to have to climb over the top to get in there with them. I just have to wait until they're all asleep and then –'

'Then hope you don't break your head.'

'– hope no-one hears me jump in. And that none of the boys give me up. I don't think they will. One of them saw me before and didn't say anything.'

'One saw you already? But then he'll have seen your hair's long already.' Bill held out a strand of his own hair. 'You can't go.'

'I don't suppose it matters if *they* know I'm a girl.'

'I think it's better if everyone thinks you're a boy,' said Bill. 'You don't know where you're going, or what will happen.'

Ottilie knew he was right. She would have to keep her true identity a secret. Luckily she was wearing trousers, not a skirt, but her hair was a problem. 'We should get it over with.' She gripped the small knife she had brought as a weapon, the one she and Gully used to cut lengths of krippygrass to sell in Market Town. 'Have you ever cut hair before?'

'No,' said Bill.

'Oh well,' said Ottilie. She was trying not to think too hard about it. It was just hair, after all. She had never taken much pride in it. Having long hair wasn't a skill. It just hung there. No-one had ever paid much attention to her hair before. She could remember Gurt calling it pretty once, and she had some distant memory of Freddie grumbling about the knots, but that was about it. Why did girls always have long hair anyway? She had never thought to ask.

'Just hack it,' she said.

It was a painful process, so very different to when Mr Parch trimmed her hair with freshly sharpened scissors. Ottilie could tell Bill was trying to be gentle, but the knife, along with his nervous hands, made things difficult. He had to pull at chunks of her hair and saw into them one after the other. It felt more like a feather-plucking than a haircut.

As Ottilie's hair fell strand by strand into her lap, she felt the strangest need to cry. Screwing up her face, she focused on Gully. She would do this for him, there was no question, and as her head grew lighter, her courage grew.

Bill released a long, uneven breath. Placing the knife shakily onto the ground, he said, 'I think that's the shortest I can do it with a knife.'

Ottilie ran her hands over her skull. Her wild, curly hair was gone and in its place were soft, short strands no longer than two or three inches.

'Perfect,' she said.

***

Hiding the evidence, Ottilie and Bill gathered the severed strands of her hair into the sack before making their next move. They crept around the corner – past the swamp picker, who was lying on the floor with a red scarf over his face, paying absolutely no attention to his captives – and slid into a fracture in the wall just out of the light. It was a comfortable enough place to be, just wide enough for Ottilie to sit with her legs stretched out. Now it was time to wait. She passed the minutes by trying to eat the last of her food as quietly as possible. She wasn't sure if the captives were being fed or not, and she figured it was important to keep her strength up. As it turned out, she found taking tiny nibbles of brakkernuts oddly calming.

'You should save some of those. You can put them in your pockets.'

Ottilie nodded, holding the brakkernut up to her bared teeth like a mouse with a crumb. 'Do you think it's Laklanders taking them?' She couldn't get the idea out of her mind. 'People are always saying *never trust someone with Lakland blood*, aren't they?'

It had been over a century since the war, but whenever there was trouble Laklanders were still the first to be blamed. These days, even people with distinctly fair hair, similar to the rare, almost bluish Lakland hue, were eyed with distrust. Ottilie thought these waves of serial kidnappings could be the work of a secret group of Laklanders. But then again, that guard had been wearing a Wikric uniform …

'Or do you think that the pickers could be working for the king –' Ottilie froze. 'Do you hear that?'

Something had disturbed the drowsy silence. It was far away, but there was definitely movement. She could hear the shuffle and scrape of well-wandered boots.

Ottilie and Bill barely breathed. The northers moved slowly, and it seemed an age had passed when they finally breached the dark. But there they were, three pickers with maybe thirty sleepy-looking boys, all fastened at the waist to a single rope.

Something was wrong with them, and for the first time it clicked with Ottilie. They moved sluggishly, if they bothered to move at all. She had taken it for exhaustion, but the fact was, they looked like Freddie and Gurt after too many bottles of bramblywine. They had all been dosed with something – some draught to keep them quiet.

Ottilie thought of Gully, pictured him being pulled by a rope, drifting along as if asleep. She felt sick. But he had caused trouble, hadn't he? That was what the swamp picker had said. Some of them had fought back.

'Well about bleeding time!' the swamp picker hollered, hauling himself off the ground.

'Pipe down, Mr Sloch,' said the oldest-looking picker.

'I want out of this stinking dungeon,' said Mr Sloch, gathering his things and pulling a scrappy roll of parchment from his pocket. 'Here's the wester list.'

Ottilie grabbed Bill's wrist. 'Oh no,' she breathed.

'Hang on a minute, there's twenty-odd names on here,' said a picker with a fat blond moustache. 'D'you lose some, Sloch?'

'Right, I forgot I sent seven in already. Troublemakers. Here, I'll scratch them off. One was, uh … Murphy Graves … and there was Gulliver Colter –'

Hearing Mr Sloch utter his name, Ottilie felt as if she had been punched in the chest.

'There you go,' finished Mr Sloch, handing back the parchment. 'There's a record of every kid in that cell.'

'That's not good,' whispered Bill. 'You can't go.'

Ottilie ignored him. 'Bill, we have to get that list.'

Ottilie hated bramblywine. She had held a grudge against the drink for as long as she could remember. Bramblywine made Freddie sick. Worse, bramblywine made Freddie absent. Not just absent from the Colter hollow, absent in general. Whatever creature was walking around wearing Freddie's skin, it wasn't her mother anymore.

So Ottilie hadn't thought she would ever be glad to see a bottle of bramblywine. Not until the moment Mr Sloch pulled a familiar squarish green bottle from his satchel.

'Here gents, take this to get you through the night,' he said, tossing it to the young picker. 'Got it from a fellow up the Brakkerswamp. Nasty stuff. Nearly burned a hole in my tongue.'

'Generous of you, Sloch,' said the young picker, narrowing his eyes. He pulled the cork with his teeth, spat it aside, and took a hearty swig.

A fellow up the Brakkerswamp. This was very good. One bottle of Gurt's noxious brew would have the pickers sleeping in no time. Ottilie watched them gulp it down and thanked her lucky stars for the stupidity of adults.

When the pickers had been snoring for nearly an hour, Ottilie hovered anxiously by the crack in the wall. With barely a sound, Bill crept over, retrieved the list from the nearest picker's coat pocket, and darted back in a flash.

Ottilie gripped Bill's damp, furry arm in excitement. Her relief was short-lived, however, when she thought about what needed to be done next. It was up to her now. She had to jump into that holding cell. Bill would be gone, and she would have to do the rest on her own.

'Are you ready?' said Bill.

'Wait,' she said, her nerves getting the better of her. She took the parchment from Bill and unrolled it. There were two sheets; the northers had brought one with them, and the other was Mr Sloch's. At the top of Mr Sloch's page, *Wester Pickings* was scrawled in black ink, with *Gulliver Colter, age 11,* right underneath it.

There was something about seeing his name scribbled out that sent a chill down her spine. It was just what she needed – a reminder. This was all for Gully.

She would be all right. There was no record now. Bill would keep the lists with him and burn them when he had the chance. No-one would be able to prove that there was one more boy with the pickings than there should have been. All she had to do was pretend to be a captive until she found Gully and then they would find their way home together.

'I'm ready,' she breathed.

To Ottilie's surprise, climbing the wall was the easy part. Bill had riddled it out in a matter of minutes, and she followed his every instruction. The trick was knowing which stones to grab, and where to slot your foot. Before she knew it she was perched directly above the holding cell. A few of the boys gazed up, staring without really seeing. None of them made a sound.

This was it.

Ottilie looked over at Bill and waved gently. She had been so focused on memorising his instructions and ignoring his doubtful mumblings that she hadn't remembered to say a proper goodbye. It seemed so little, just a wave, but it was too late for anything grander. It was hard to see, but she was sure he was waving back.

Ottilie looked down. The ground seemed very far away. What if she really did break her head? Trembling with fear, she glanced back at Bill one last time.

It was time to jump. Once she was in that cell, her feet wouldn't belong to her anymore, not for a while. She was to be herded west, into the unknown. Ottilie braced to drop at least four times, but still she did not move. She stared fixedly at her target below.

Gully always knew the way. Gully always came to get her. It was her turn.

She squeezed her eyes shut, bent her knees, and jumped.

7

Off the Edge of the Map

There wasn't much to remember, but Ottilie would remember it perfectly. Every boy as silent as the grave. The pickers talking, jibing, grumbling and complaining. Tunnel after tunnel after tunnel. Her skin itching and chafing where the belt bound her to the rope. Her legs aching, back stiff, stomach growling, throat dry and heart ticking, ticking, ticking, just a little too fast.

When they stopped for a rest, the pickers made their captives drink more of the sleeping draught. Ottilie felt a wave of hot panic as the man drew near, shoving the bottle into her hand. Would he see that she didn't belong here? Would he know she was a girl?

It was a horrible, sharp-tasting drink, like a soup of eucalyptus leaves and unripe hagberries. To her great relief, thinking she was dosed like the others, the pickers paid her little attention. Never would they have suspected that she was sneakily dribbling every last vaguely violet drop down her chin.

When the tunnel finally came to an end, they were faced with a wall of rough stone. In the centre was an iron gate, solid, spiked and not at all inviting. A single guard in black and red stood in front of it. Black and red? Ottilie frowned. Those were the king's colours.

'You took your time!' said the guard. 'List?' He held out his hand.

The moustached picker reached confidently into his travelling coat. Ottilie felt herself smile as it dawned upon him that the list was not where it should be. He tried every pocket.

'Ah ... either of you remember what we did with the list?' he said, turning to the other pickers.

'You've got to be kidding me!' said the guard, smiling widely. 'A whole day late *and* you've lost the pickings list.' He laughed. 'Wouldn't stick around for that gate to open if I were you. Off with you!'

They didn't need telling twice. All three pickers turned tail and scurried away.

The guard knocked three times. There was a series of clicks and clunks, and the gate began to slide upwards.

A new guard with a spectacularly thick black beard appeared through the entrance. 'Up with you boys!' he hollered. 'You need to sleep off that draught. No good sleepwalking through the Narroway.'

The Narroway? Ottilie stared at her feet, thinking hard. Had she ever heard of the Narroway before? She was sure she hadn't.

The black-bearded guard led them up a spiral staircase, down several stony corridors and, finally, through a tall doorway into a long chamber lined with bunk beds.

'Right,' said the guard, opening a blue wooden box. Inside, Ottilie caught a glimpse of some strange bronze rings.

One by one, the guard freed the captives from the rope, slipped a flat bronze ring onto their left thumb, and guided them to a bed. Each moved like a ghost, making no eye contact, not saying a word.

It was strange; the ring seemed far too big when it passed over her knuckle, but once settled in place it was as if it shrunk to the perfect size. The metal felt cool on her skin, and a tingling sensation flickered up her arm. Either exhaustion was making her imagine things, or there was something very odd about that ring.

The guard sighed loudly, but didn't speak again. Ottilie lay on top of her scratchy blanket and tracked him with her eyes. The moment he was gone, she sat bolt upright and pulled off the ring. There was a peculiar swooping sensation in her stomach the moment it left her thumb. She ran her fingers over it. Something was engraved on the inside, but it was too dark to make out the letters. Ottilie glanced at the door. Light shone underneath from the corridor beyond. She crept over to crouch at its base. Holding the ring towards the thin strip of light, Ottilie could just make out the words *sleeper comes for none.*

Ottilie knew those words. It was the final line to the lightning song. Or at least it was in the version she knew. Gully always insisted it was *pay for what you've done.*

The sleeper was the collector of the dead. She guided the souls of the fallen through the gates to the everafter. So the phrase *sleeper comes for none* just meant *none will die*, which had never made much sense in the context of the lightning song.

Why would the guard have passed out rings inscribed with those words?

***

'Timing like this ... I have half a mind to think you arranged the rain yourself, Leo Darby, but then you always were a fortunate boy,' said the guard.

Ottilie couldn't be sure when she had drifted off to sleep. It was just before dawn when the boys had been roused from their slumber by the same black-bearded guard from the night before.

The change in the room was unmistakable. The boys were awake, *properly* awake. There were whispers, but only a few.

'What is this place?'

'What are we doing here?'

'Who was that man?'

All questions, and no-one offered an answer. Ottilie didn't know how much they remembered, but it seemed to be enough to keep them quiet. It was wide eyes and short breaths all around, and she spotted more than a few damp cheeks and runny noses.

The guard had told them to keep quiet – quite unnecessarily, as they were all tight-mouthed and shaken. 'No point in making trouble, lads, and let me warn you now. Whatever you do, don't take off your ring, worst mistake you'll ever make –'

Ottilie noticed the guard was wearing a ring identical to the one he had placed on her left thumb.

'– and it would be a foolish move to make a break for it. You're safer in our care, believe you me. You don't want to go out there alone.'

Wherever *out there* was, nobody was making clear.

The black-bearded guard had led them out to a sheltered courtyard. Heavy rain poured off the roof, forming a wall of water ahead. It was there they met a boy with reddish hair, whose name was apparently Leo Darby. He appeared to be no older than thirteen and had brown eyes and pale skin peppered with freckles. His hair was cropped short at the sides and he wore a uniform of dark green and black. Ottilie noted the two long knives, bow, and quiver of arrows slung across his back, the slingshot and dagger strapped to his torso and the cutlass at his hip. Pressed into the leather strap across his chest was a shiny bronze pin in the shape of a bird of prey.

Standing behind him were three boys who were perhaps a year or two older, and dressed exactly the same but for a slight difference in uniform. One wore green and grey, and another wore green and brown. She noticed that a couple of them also carried short spears. The dark-haired boy nearest to Leo Darby wore an identical uniform of green and black and Ottilie could just make out his pin. It was in the shape of a wolf. None of them wore rings.

'I'm not expecting any trouble. Not while this weather holds,' said Leo, raising his voice above the sound of the rain.

'Hope you boys don't mind a bit of wet weather,' said the guard, addressing the captives.

'Better wet than dead,' said Leo with a wicked grin.

The boy with dark hair cleared his throat.

Leo didn't even look around. 'Got a cough, Ned?' he said.

'Nope,' said Ned, smiling at the ground.

Ottilie had no idea what they were talking about, but a shiver ran down her spine all the same.

'Rug up, lads,' barked Leo, waving one of the other uniformed boys forwards.

The boy started handing out grey woollen cloaks, presumably to shield them from the rain. Clearly they were going for another walk. Ottilie's feet were angry and swollen, and as thrilled as she was to finally feel fresh air on her face, she thought any more walking might drive her mad. As he passed her the cloak, Ottilie noted that this boy's pin was in the shape of a horse.

'Before I forget, now that they're conscious, we need a new list,' said the guard. 'Right, I need names, ages and places of origin, one at a time,' he said, holding a blank sheet of parchment and a quill at the ready.

Ottilie caught a few of their answers. The majority of the boys were thirteen. The others were twelve. So Gully was younger than all of the pickings present by at least a year. Why had they taken him?

Anxiety stifled her questions. She was going to have to speak. Some of the boys' voices had deepened already. She had heard it. Hers would be so high in comparison.

Lost in her worries, Ottilie didn't even hear the guard.

'Boy ... boy!'

'What? Oh.' Ottilie looked up. The guard was staring down at her, not unkindly.

'Name and age?'

She wasn't thinking straight. 'Otti– ,' she coughed, her face reddening. She had been so close to saying *Ottilie* she could have hit herself. 'Ott,' she said quietly.

'Just Ott?'

'Ott Colter,' she mumbled.

'Unusual name. Where are you from?'

'The Swamp Hollows, by the Brakkerswamp.' She heard a couple of boys behind her snicker.

'That explains it,' said the guard, patting her roughly on the head. 'You get all sorts in there. Explains the height too. All that crouching in caves stunts your growth.'

More snickers. Ottilie was surprised they had so much spirit, but she was too scared to be embarrassed. What if they caught her now and sent her back? She had come so far!

'Pipe down!' growled the guard. 'Age?'

Why hadn't she thought about this? It was too late now. She had practically given her true name and where she was from; they might as well have her age as well.

'Twelve.' She used her own voice, hoping it wasn't high enough to give her away. Gully still sounded just like her, after all.

'Right. Ott Colter. Swamp Hollows. Twelve. And we're done.' He passed the list to the dark-haired boy, Ned, who tucked it safely into a pouch on his belt.

'We need to get moving if we want to get in before the weather clears up,' said Leo, striding across the courtyard into the pouring rain. 'Come on, lads. The sooner we get there, the sooner you'll find out why you're here.'

'You're lucky, boys,' said the guard. 'It's a long walk, but a rainy day's a good day in the Narroway.'

8

The Narroway

Ottilie gazed up at the mountains ahead. Behind her lay a small, sharply angled guard tower built into the cliffs, where they had spent the night. Leo was leading them across a rocky valley. Rain trickled down their cloaks to the mossy grass as, two by two, they trudged along an indiscernible path.

'Do you know what this place is?'

Ottilie jumped. The boy beside her had spoken. Calming herself, she muttered, 'No,' without looking up.

'That guard said the Narroway. Have you ever heard of the Narroway?'

Ottilie shook her head and kept her hood low. She was terrified that if he looked her in the eye he would know she was not meant to be there.

'I've never. It can't be in the Usklers.'

Despite the fact that he spoke in half a whisper, Ottilie could hear that his accent was clipped. He must have come from money. She stole a quick glance. The boy seemed harmless enough. He was lanky, with golden hair and unremarkable features but for the addition of clunky, round eyeglasses that magnified his pale eyes. That confirmed it – only wealthy people had eyeglasses. Or once-wealthy people who refused to sell them, like Mr Parch.

'I don't think we're in the Usklers anymore,' said Ottilie.

'You're Ott, aren't you? Ott Colter?'

Ottilie nodded.

'I'm Preddy, well, Noel Preddy, but everyone calls me Preddy.'

'I've heard of the Narroway,' whispered a voice from behind. The speaker was a wiry, stooping fellow with dark olive skin. He spoke his words quickly and his accent was rough and difficult to understand, even for Ottilie, who was used to rough accents.

'You have?' said Preddy.

'Don't sound so surprised,' said the boy.

'You've read about it?'

The boy let out a muffled bark of laughter. 'Can't read. Just heard it around. The Narroway used to be part of the Usklers, but they cut it off.'

'Why?' said Preddy.

'It was the way to the Laklands. There was a road running through all the way there.'

Ottilie blinked. She couldn't remember reading about the Narroway in *Our Walkable World*.

'The Laklands – the wasteland?' said Preddy.

'Wasn't always a wasteland though, was it? Got chewed up by that old war,' said the boy.

'But why would they block off a bit of the Usklers just because it leads to the Laklands?' said Ottilie. Were the Laklands not really empty?

'Beats me,' said the boy.

'Well, there's obviously a reason. Something must be going on in this place,' said Preddy.

'Must be. Otherwise, why would they bring us here?' said the boy.

'Don't you think it's strange that they've sent four boys to escort us?' said Preddy. 'That guard talked to that Leo Darby like the boy ranked above him, and he can't be any older than me.'

'How old are you?' said Ottilie.

'Thirteen.'

'Twelve,' said the other boy.

'What's your name?' Preddy asked him.

'Branter Scoot. I'm from Wikric.'

'Me too,' said Preddy.

'I'm guessing different parts,' said Branter Scoot, looking Preddy up and down.

'That seems likely,' said Preddy, somewhat sheepishly. He turned to Ottilie. 'Do you remember what happened? How you ended up here?'

Ottilie didn't know what to say. Was she supposed to remember? Did any of the other boys remember? Thankfully, Branter Scoot got in first.

'I can't remember a thing.'

'Me neither,' said Ottilie.

'The same for me,' said Preddy. 'It's odd. It was as if I could feel the time passing. I knew I wasn't home. I knew I was going somewhere else, but it all seems like a dream to me now.'

'Was like that when it was happening,' said Branter Scoot. 'You don't reckon we're all dead, do you?' he said seriously.

'Highly unlikely that boys only travel to the everafter with other boys of a similar age and no girls at all,' said Preddy.

'I guess. Anyways, I don't feel dead. Do you feel dead, Ott?'

'No,' said Ottilie. She was afraid to say too much, scared of giving herself away.

➤————————➤

The journey was long, slow and wet. Ottilie could almost track the time by the cycle of painful blisters that rose, rubbed and burst against her boots. Dense cloud and a constant drizzle of rain made their surroundings difficult to discern as they passed between the peaks of snow-capped mountains. Beyond, a blanket of mist rested over a vast lake. Preddy was panting quietly beside her and Ottilie was shivering beneath her cloak. Her sodden trousers clung to her ankles, but she was tolerably dry from the shins up.

'Home stretch, boys,' said Ned, patting Preddy on the shoulder and passing him a waterskin. 'Just over the bridge, then you can rest for the last bit.'

Ottilie thought she could see hills beyond, but the mist was so dense she couldn't be sure. Only when they came to the end of the bridge could Ottilie see six or seven timber wagons waiting for them at the water's edge. The wagons would have seemed perfectly ordinary if it weren't for the pair of antlered deer tethered to the front of each one.

'All aboard,' called Leo.

'They're docile,' said Ned, catching Ottilie staring at the bucks, their long reddish coats smoothed by the rain. 'We use them because they don't spook easily.'

She nodded, unsure of what to say, and followed Preddy and Branter Scoot into a wagon. Ned jumped up in front. Ottilie slumped onto a seat beside Preddy. The relief was immeasurable. She was too tired to even shuffle a foot. No matter how bumpy and uncomfortable the ride, sitting down was bliss.

It was still difficult to make out anything much in the way of scenery, but Ottilie could get a good enough sense of the landscape. First hills, then winding paths through dense forest. The air was thick, but fresh, and smelled of damp bark.

About an hour or so after sundown, Ottilie could see lights ahead. The mist lessened and she could make out a broad field stretching all the way to an expanse of sprawling hills with more mountains beyond. Atop one of the hills lay a stone fortress, shining silver in the moonlight.

'Wow,' whispered Ottilie. She had never seen such grandeur. How had they built towers so tall? It was as if the stones had been piled up and pressed together by giants.

Beside her, Branter Scoot narrowed his eyes. 'This is our prison then?' he muttered.

'There you go, lads,' called Leo from the wagon ahead. 'Welcome to Fort Fiory.'

Fiory? Ottilie knew that name. Fiory was one of the old gods from the Lore, the black eagle with eyes like hot coals, lord of the raptors.

'Take a good look,' said Leo. 'Most of you won't be staying long.'

'What do you suppose he means by that?' said Preddy.

Ottilie shook her head and shrugged. It didn't matter. She didn't intend to stay long.

The wagons stopped outside a high boundary wall. A solid wooden gate stretched above them, flanked by two fierce stone raptors, a steady stream of water pouring out of their open beaks. Leo pulled on a chain by the gate and a bell sounded.

'Time to get out,' said Ned, hopping down from beside the wagoner.

Ottilie's limbs had stiffened so much she felt she had aged seventy years.

'Watch out for the shepherds,' said Leo, somewhat gleefully.

'Shepherds? Like for sheep?' said Branter Scoot.

Ottilie wasn't really listening. This was it. This was their destination. That could only mean one thing: Gully was inside Fort Fiory.

The gates slid open with a great crunching and grinding, and they followed their guides inside. They trudged along a muddy track through a neatly maintained field. The lights along their path made a forest to the left just visible.

She heard a gasp from somewhere in front. The boy directly ahead of her darted to the side, knocking Ottilie backwards. She fell to the ground. Tangled in her damp cloak, she looked up in horror as a rumbling growl rolled in from above.

Staring directly into her eyes, fur black as the night that surrounded them, was an enormous wild dog, its teeth bared in a snarl. It took a single step towards her. Ottilie pictured its great jaws clamping around her neck, tearing at her throat, and wondered that she did not feel the impulse to scream. Something pulled at her elbow and she felt herself half-lifted, half-dragged, to the side.

'She just wants to pass. Best get out of her way.'

Ottilie stood up, shaking all over. She looked at the boy still gripping her elbow. It was Ned. 'You're all right,' he said, patting her on the back.

'Was that a shepherd?' said Branter Scoot.

'That's a shepherd.'

'What do they watch over?' said Preddy.

'You,' said Ned.

9

Fort Fiory

The rain finally cleared. A masked moon glowed feebly through the mist and a wash of stars blinked determinedly behind thin wisps of cloud. Ottilie was too tired to care. She barely perceived the uniformed boys roaming about or the occasional screech from beyond the turreted boundary wall.

Ottilie was vaguely aware they had moved inside. The light was dim. The floor was hard. Her eyes were tired. She hardly noticed the exchange between Leo and a man with a bright blue coat and a silver-topped cane. It was only when the man addressed the captives that she snapped awake.

'Bedtime, boys. There'll be plenty of time for talk in the morning. You can divide yourselves between these two empty bedchambers,' he gestured to two open doors, 'and I've got a few spare beds in here with the earlier arrivals.'

The earlier arrivals! Watching the man lift the old iron latch, Ottilie could barely contain her excitement. She counted down in her head. *Five, four, three, two ...*

Inside the chamber, it was too dark to distinguish features. There were twenty or so beds, many with large lumps upon them. One of those lumps *had* to be Gully.

Ottilie tiptoed over to a spare bed by a tall window, without noticing Preddy and Branter Scoot following her lead. The man shut the door with a scrape.

Pressing herself into a shadowy corner where no-one could see, Ottilie carefully peeled off her clothing and tugged on the green linen nightclothes she found at the end of the bed. It seemed silly putting clean clothing on over her sweaty, dirt-crusted limbs, but at least it was dry.

Ottilie crinkled her nose and gazed down at the plump rectangle resting like a fallen cloud at the head of the bed. She had never had a pillow before. She sniffed it. It smelled of dried lavender and old dust. Ottilie clambered onto the bed and let her head rest upon it. She didn't know what to think. It was nice, she supposed, but her neck felt strange.

Ottilie tugged the blanket up to her chin and gazed across at all the sleeping lumps. She just had to wait until the other two fell asleep and then she would find him.

It didn't take long. In less than five minutes Preddy was snoring loudly, and not long after Branter Scoot joined in with a harmony of heavy breathing and nose-whistles.

Ottilie slid out of bed, ready to scan each head for Gully's black, curly hair. She crept over to the bed beside hers, and her heart leapt into her throat. The sleeping boy had discarded his pillow, banishing it to the end of the bed. It was Gully, right there, in the bed beside hers!

A huge smile broke out over her face. She could have jumped in the air. She could have cried. There he was, unharmed and sleeping soundly as if nothing had happened at all. She had done it.

'Gully,' Ottilie whispered, her rapid heartbeat puncturing her breath.

Gully twitched in his sleep.

'Gully, wake up,' she said, a little louder.

'Go away, Ottilie,' he mumbled.

It took him a few seconds.

Gully sat bolt upright, eyes wide. Ottilie threw her hand over his mouth and pressed a filthy finger to her lips, signalling for him to be quiet. His eyes relaxed a little, and he nodded. Ottilie removed her hand.

'What … where's your hair?'

Ottilie beamed.

Gully didn't smile. 'What are you doing here, Ottilie?' he breathed, his dark eyes widening again.

'I came to get you.' Her smile faltered.

'But ... how?'

'Well. I'm pretending to be a boy. You'll have to pretend too – say I'm your brother.' Ottilie's heart rate increased. 'Gully, what are we going to do?' She felt rattled, as if her bones were coming apart at the joints. What in the world *was* she going to do now that she had found him? 'What is this place? Why did they bring you here?'

Gully shook his head. 'I don't know anything. I just woke up in a tower in a cliff with this ring on.' He held up his thumb.

'And no-one's explained?'

'Nothing. We only got here this afternoon. No-one knows what's going on. Most of them are really scared. I keep thinking about running away but I don't know where to go. They had guards watching us in the forest and I was scared of going out there alone anyway.'

'Wh–' Ottilie's voice wavered. She couldn't remember Gully ever admitting to feeling afraid. 'What do you mean?'

'I heard things on the way over, and there were shapes in the sky. There's something out there. It made me feel funny. It went away when the rain started but I ... I didn't like it.'

Gully had *never* been bothered by shadows or noises. Ottilie hadn't thought it was possible to feel more worried. 'What kind of things?' she whispered.

Gully shrugged. 'I don't know. I've never heard anything like it before.'

'People or animals?'

'Animals, I guess …'

'You guess?' A parade of fiendish beasts circled round and round in her mind. Claws shredding muscle, fangs cleaving bone …

'Ottilie.' Gully came back into focus. 'We'll get out of here. The two of us, we'll make up a plan.' He reached out and scrunched her cropped hair with his fingers. 'You look funny with short hair.'

Ottilie smiled.

───────────➤

They slept late. No-one came in to wake them until mid-morning, which was lucky for Ottilie and Gully, considering they had been up talking most of the night. She had filled him in on all of it; Bill, the pickers, the stolen lists and her new name – Ott. Ottilie hated that she was using Ott. Only Gurt ever called her Ott, and Gurt was not one of her favourite people.

'Rise and shine, boys! It's a new day,' hollered a voice from beyond the door.

Ottilie rolled over and looked around the room. Most of the other boys looked like they had been awake for a while, but Branter Scoot was yawning, eyes half-closed, and Preddy was still lying flat on his stomach, snoring into his pillow.

The door swung open and the same man from last night stepped inside, wearing the same ornate blue coat. He was thin and bandy-legged with dark curly hair, a pointed beard, and notably long fingers, which were wrapped around a black cane with a silver bird's head for a handle.

Branter Scoot leaned across his bed and kicked Preddy, who woke with a loud snort.

'That's the way. You've got a big day ahead. I suppose I should introduce myself: Captain Lyre. That's L–Y–R–E, the instrument, not the sin. I am captain of ceremonies, and one of the directors here at Fiory. Now. Down to business. You unwashed westers, hands in the air.'

Ottilie, Preddy and Branter Scoot raised their hands.

'Right, my little filthies, you'll be washing that muck off – then we've got a nice change of clothes for you. The rest of you clean boys, you can change now while I'm having some breakfast sent up.'

Captain Lyre had said two things that bothered Ottilie. The first was washing. Ottilie couldn't bathe in front of anyone without blowing her cover. The second was breakfast. She had never heard of such a thing. What did he mean he was going to have breakfast sent up? Was breakfast a good thing or a bad thing?

Captain Lyre whistled abruptly and Ottilie heard movement in the hall. She tried to keep her face neutral as, to her surprise, three girls entered the room. They were around her age, dressed simply in green dresses with aprons and pale orange napkins rolled up and knotted around their heads like headbands. Their black lace-up boots clicked on the floor as they moved about passing out piles of folded clothing.

She noted the precision of their movements and the neat way they stood with their heels together, feet forming a little triangle. Girls didn't move like that around the Brakkerswamp. Ottilie was slumping off the edge of her bed with her knees splaying out. She came closer to matching the boys' posture than the girls – which was just as well, she supposed. Still, she couldn't help wondering: were girls supposed to hold themselves differently? Why?

'Come with me, you three,' said Captain Lyre.

Crossing the room, Ottilie noticed a dark-haired girl with sharp eyes. Her gaze was intense, unnaturally so, and Ottilie couldn't comprehend what was behind it. Fearful that the girl could sense something amiss, Ottilie passed by as quickly as possible.

'The springs are down that corridor and through those doors,' said Captain Lyre. 'You go right where you're told and come back up to your room as soon as you're sparkling. We've got your names. We'll know if anyone's missing and I promise you, we know this place a lot better than you do.'

They nodded silently. Captain Lyre nudged Ottilie forwards with the silver beak of his cane. Ottilie felt like she had lost the feeling in her face. What was she going to do? How was she going to get out of this?

'What's breakfast?' said Branter Scoot as they walked down the corridor.

'*What's breakfast?*' said Preddy in disbelief.

'I was wondering that,' said Ottilie, distracted for a moment.

'Breakfast is the first meal of the day,' said Preddy indignantly. 'How do you both not know that?'

'Never heard of it,' said Ottilie.

'Then what do you eat in the morning?' said Preddy.

Branter Scoot raised his eyebrows. 'Nothing, usually.'

'You don't eat anything in the morning?'

'No.'

'Never,' said Ottilie.

'Amazing,' said Preddy.

Branter Scoot pushed the door open to the springs, a cavernous room that smelled of salt and wet bird. It had a curved ceiling, four enormous square pools rimmed with blue-patterned tiles, and several copper basins with pipes and pumps to draw water.

Ottilie made a snap decision. 'I'm starving!' she said, paying no attention to the boys already bathing. It was nothing she hadn't seen a hundred times. Back in the Hollows, the wash grotto was used by boys and girls alike. Once they reached a certain age, some of the girls used bathing gowns, but the boys weren't expected to cover up, which had never seemed fair.

'I thought you said you never eat in the morning?' said Preddy.

'But we didn't get much at all yesterday. I was hungry all night.' It wasn't a lie.

'Me too!' said Branter Scoot, poking his hollow stomach with his thumbs.

'Maybe we should just do a quick wash-off and go and eat?' said Ottilie.

'That's a thought,' said Branter Scoot.

Preddy crinkled his nose. 'Oh no, I'll be bathing. I've never been so filthy in my life!'

Branter Scoot snorted. 'I have. Though come to think of it, I never get proper baths. Might as well have a go.'

'You two go ahead. My stomach's about to start eating itself,' said Ottilie. Smiling inwardly, she hurried over to a basin, pumped the lever and began scrubbing away at her arms, neck and face with creamy soap that smelled of honey and gum leaves. It was a welcome change. Back in the Hollows they mostly used river salt to clean themselves, which was scratchy, and left her skin feeling itchy and dry.

It took longer than she thought to get clean. There were still specks of black dirt hidden among her freckles when she finally gave up.

There was just one more problem. She needed to change into the clean clothes. Where could she do that?

Without thinking it through, Ottilie headed for the exit. Once in the corridor she held her breath and, blocking all thoughts, kicked off the lambswool slippers, ripped away her night clothes, tugged on the simple green shirt, tunic and trousers and stood there, breathing hard, utterly amazed that she had managed it without being seen.

When she re-entered the bedchamber, Gully was sitting on the bed eating his breakfast with a curious expression on his face. There was another wooden tray beside him that was obviously meant for Ottilie. She hurried over and shoved an entire fistful of warm brown bread in her mouth.

'So there are girls here too,' said Gully. 'Did you know that?'

Ottilie shook her head, her mouth full. 'Vem uh first.'

'They're the first you've seen?' said Gully.

Ottilie nodded.

'Me too.'

'Th-ervants,' said Ottilie, nearly choking. Frowning, she swallowed. 'What now? Did that Lyre man say?'

'We're going up for an assembly,' said Gully.

'To explain, do you think?'

'Hope so.'

Gully sounded calm, but there was a look in his big dark eyes that Ottilie knew very well. It was the look he used to get when he was much younger and Freddie didn't come home. Confused, frightened, alone. Ottilie had always been there, but Freddie was *supposed* to be. Even at that very moment, where was Freddie? Had she noticed they were gone? She had probably noticed three times and forgotten three times. No, as usual, it was just Ottilie and Gully, in it alone.

'Morning food,' said Gully, eyeing their trays. 'Funny,' he added.

'I think it's a rich people thing.'

'What do they need food in the morning for? They've been sleeping all night.'

'I'm not complaining,' said Ottilie, shovelling a whole brambleberry pie into her mouth.

'Here, have the rest of mine,' said Gully, sliding his tray over to her.

A damp-haired Preddy trotted back into the room, closely followed by Branter Scoot. They had barely managed a bite each when Captain Lyre appeared in the doorway.

'The time has come,' he said dramatically. 'There's no turning back now.' He winked, tapped his cane twice on the door and turned, whistling for them to follow.

10

The Narroway Huntsmen

They were seated in rows. To her left, Ottilie could see Leo and Ned sitting with a group of young uniformed boys. Directly in front stood Captain Lyre, leaning casually against his cane. Three huge arched windows lay beyond, orange shutters thrown open, a stream of sunshine lighting him from above and behind. The buttons on his blue coat glowed like tiny fireballs in the light.

A boy had collected their bronze rings at the door. Ottilie felt strange without it. Her head ached a bit and she felt on edge. Somewhere above, a bell rang eleven times. It was an hour from midday.

Captain Lyre grinned. 'Let's begin.' He spun his cane, then tapped it on the stone dais beneath his feet. 'Welcome,' he paused, 'to your calling.'

'What?' whispered Branter Scoot.

'You are here, at Fort Fiory, on a very secret mission for the king.'

Ottilie felt her mouth fall open. So this wasn't part of some Laklander plot. The pickings were orchestrated by the Crown.

'You lucky boys have been specially selected for important work – the most important work any man will ever do. You are called to join the Narroway Hunt.'

Ottilie looked around. The other boys looked as confused as she felt.

'Let me start by explaining where we are. At this very moment, we are in one of three strongholds, or stations, in the Narroway – a thin strip of land that connects the Usklers to the Laklands.'

So Branter Scoot had been right. Ottilie reached back into her memory. She was trying to picture the faded map in Old Moss's copy of *Our Walkable World*. She could see the edge of Longwood, and the Laklands reaching out to the west. She thought she could remember a stretch of unnamed land in between.

'Why have you never heard of the Narroway? Because we ensured it. There is no better-kept secret than what goes on in this place, and for good reason, but

I'll get to that later.' He paused to clear his throat. 'We have people throughout the Usklers who keep a record of boys with promise. Those of you who made the cut were then collected and brought here.'

Ottilie's insides churned. *The keeper*, that's what Bill had said. The keeper had been watching Gully, decided he had promise, and given the order for the swamp picker to snatch him.

'We apologise for the manner in which you were removed from your previous circumstances, but we are confident, as always, that you will forgive us, and be willing and happy to stay.'

Ottilie screwed up her nose. '*Happy to stay?*' she mouthed to Gully.

'This business – what we deal with here – it's bigger than all of us. So what *do* we deal with?' A slow smile crept across his face. 'Beasties, monsters, prowling flesh-feasters, heart thieves, demons, whatever you called them in the past, the creatures of myth and nightmare, they're real and they're here. If you know any of the old Lore, you may have heard the name *dredretch*, the deathly scavengers.'

Ottilie had heard of dredretches. They were mythical underworld beasts, drawn to the surface by acts of terrible violence. Old Moss had told her that they stole hearts, and fed on death and human wickedness, but it was a myth. Mr Parch had always been very clear on that.

'The infestation began in the unoccupied west. The Laklands are overrun. When the scourge breached the Narroway, this land was sealed off and the threat contained. That's what we do here – we hunt dredretches. There is only one thing standing between the dredretches and the Usklers, and that is our Narroway Huntsmen.'

'Blimey,' muttered Branter Scoot.

'That is why you are here.' Captain Lyre paused dramatically. 'You will train to become Narroway Huntsmen.'

Ottilie noted his use of the word *will*. It was quite clear they would be offered no choice in this. But could it be true? Could these monsters be real? And these huntsmen, all young boys snatched from their homes … why? Why not a real army?

Tossing his cane into the air, Captain Lyre said, 'Obviously' – he caught it – 'there is a lot you don't know. There will be plenty of time to get into everything over the course of your training. For now, this is what you need to know. Fort Fiory, where we are now, is one of three stations in the Narroway, each named for one of the old gods. Fiory, after the black lord of the raptors. Arko, in the east, named for the silver mare. And Richter, in the west, named for the mother wolf. Every year one station hosts the fledgling trials; this year it's us, Fiory.'

Ottilie ground her teeth. She didn't like the sound of the word *trials*.

Captain Lyre opened his arms in a paternal, welcoming gesture. 'The trials will measure your strengths and weaknesses so that we can appoint you a guardian for your first year with us – your *fledgling* year.' He gestured to a group of uniformed boys, including Leo and Ned. 'Your guardian, a personal mentor of sorts, will come from the select elite …'

Ottilie felt her attention slipping away. This was irrelevant. She and Gully were leaving. Nothing Captain Lyre said could change that. Someone would figure out she was a girl before long, and she didn't think these secretive people would be pleased to discover they had an imposter in their midst. She couldn't risk being separated from Gully, not now she had found him again.

She pictured the two of them sneaking back the way they had come, through the forests, over the lake, beyond the mountains. A host of monsters prowled out of the shadowy corners of her mind, sullying the landscape and making their quest for freedom seem impossible.

'Now for the fun part,' said Captain Lyre, twirling his cane. 'It's not all work. That would be awfully dull. There are five tiers of huntsmen. You, fledglings, or fledges, are our first tier. You will gather an individual ranking over the course of the hunting year. The top-ranking huntsmen in the third tier and beyond become our select elite – the best of the best. You receive points for every dredretch you fell and at the end of each year one huntsman per tier is named champion. This is a great honour – the ultimate achievement. It is the title that every huntsman in the Narroway strives to attain.'

Ottilie found herself shaking her head. Hunting dredretches? She wasn't sure she could believe it. How was there was a stretch of land full of monsters hiding west of Longwood? How did no-one know about it? And – if it was true – how long would it be before the dredretches spilled out of the Narroway and into the Usklers?

It was too much. It was too ridiculous.

'Now, I'll be back in two shakes … discuss.' Captain Lyre crossed the room and disappeared out the door.

The stillness bristled with uncertain whispers. No-one seemed to want to talk loudly, and no-one seemed to have a whole lot to say. Ottilie felt as if she had just been hit over the head with a shovel.

'What do you think?' said Gully quietly.

Ottilie shook her head. She didn't want it to be true. 'His name's Captain *Liar*.'

'Well … spelt differently,' whispered Preddy.

Branter Scoot gazed at him in disbelief.

Preddy turned pink. 'He said …'

'It doesn't make any sense. How can all this be going on and no-one know about it?' said Ottilie.

'I would imagine some people know about it. The King's Company must,' said Preddy.

'He means all … everyone – ordinary people,' said Branter Scoot.

'The thing is, if it were actually true, they wouldn't be kidnapping kids and making us deal with it,' said Ottilie.

Branter Scoot nodded grimly, his narrowed eyes darting towards the door.

'But what if it is true?' said Gully. 'What if there really are monsters here?'

'I doubt it,' said Branter Scoot. 'Ott's right. They think they can fool us, convince us we're here in the service of the king. Make us want to stay by talking about honour and duty and protecting the Usklers. I tell you Captain Lyre would have to walk through that door with –'

The door at the back of the room swung open and Captain Lyre strode in, a birdcage clasped firmly in his hand.

11

Death Crows

Ottilie felt her blood drain from her skull to her toes. Her hair began to prickle and something felt very wrong in her chest. It was as if her lungs were filling slowly with water, drip by drip, and she could do nothing to stop it. Ill and confused, she tracked Captain Lyre with heavy eyes. He proceeded to the front of the room and held the birdcage aloft.

Inside the cage was a birdlike creature, made of feathers, shadows and scales. Ottilie tried to focus, but it was difficult to see it clearly. The bird looked like a crow, only larger. Dark vapour trailed from its shiny black wings. Where there should have been eyes, Ottilie saw only gaping sockets. Its talons were made of peeling scales, red as blood, and its narrow black beak was whittled to a needle-sharp point. The monstrous bird was eerily calm. It clung to the bottom of the cage with bloody claws, its beak poking through the gaps in the bars.

'Eddy Skovey, could you take care of that for me,' said Captain Lyre.

Ottilie watched as if from a dream as Ned took the bird from Captain Lyre and calmly left the room.

'It'll take a little while. Just breathe through it,' said Captain Lyre.

Feeling hideously nauseous and halfway to a faint, Ottilie looked around. The select elite seemed completely unaffected, but the captives looked – well, they looked like Freddie, withering away in the depths of winter.

'That, my dear fledges, was a dredretch, albeit a minuscule one. There are many different species, and they come a lot bigger and a lot fiercer than that, believe you me.'

Ottilie glanced at Gully. He looked positively corpse-like.

'*Death crows*. We call them jivvies. They're blind as bats but they can still do you a lot of damage. Now, you're probably all wondering why you feel like you're about to drop dead. That would be the presence of a dredretch. Get too close and they start literally drawing the life out of you. It's one of the things we will train you to deal with here. You'll notice none of our elite look half-melted like you lot. But until you're able to manage it, we have ways of helping.'

He held his hand up and pointed to a flat bronze ring around his thumb. Ottilie felt her fingers creep over to her own naked left hand, yearning for the protection, for the cure.

'Our experienced huntsmen don't wear them anymore – don't need them. You'll be getting yours back in a bit, but obviously I needed to show you what we're dealing with. These things are unnatural. Their very presence triggers our demise. If so much as one itsy jivvie crossed the border and made its way to Wikric Town, it could cost dozens of lives. More. So, as I said before … this is important work. The most important work there is – and we need *you* to do it.'

The room almost came back into focus. Even through the dredretch sickness, Ottilie knew he was about to answer a very important question.

'The thing about a dredretch is that it can only be felled by an innocent,' Captain Lyre said. 'That's why we have to recruit you young. Once you turn eighteen, any weapon you wield will be ineffectual.'

Ottilie was almost disappointed by the explanation. Was that really true? Was it logical? But perhaps dredretches, being some strange form of living death, defied logic. It also didn't explain why only boys were recruited, or why they had to be kidnapped. Why was everything done in secret? She glanced around to see if anyone else seemed sceptical, but most of them just looked concussed.

Ottilie's breathing had eased and she sensed her colour returning, but she felt no less disturbed. Was this why she had always hated Longwood – why it always felt so funny in there? Longwood bordered the Narroway, a home to monsters whose very presence made you sick.

No wonder.

***

Captain Lyre divided them into four training squads for the trials, based on their current sleeping arrangements. Thankfully this meant Ottilie and Gully were in the same group.

Their squad was led into a small chamber with a high ceiling. It was chilly and completely unadorned, but for several half-melted candles shoved onto the spikes zigzagging up the walls. The boys hovered awkwardly in the centre of the room. Ottilie glanced out the enormous window to her right. There was a spectacular view of dark green hills and a snow-capped peak beyond the high boundary walls.

The door slid open and they were greeted by two men; an enormous balding man with a tangled ginger beard, and another supremely tall fellow, broad-boned, but gangling, and lacking any appearance of muscle. He had a very crooked nose and neatly combed hair. There was something very wet about him.

'Hello, hello,' said the fellow with the crooked nose. He was a pompous sort with a false smile, and Ottilie felt immediately that she did not like him.

'My name is Tudor Voilies and this is Reuben Morse,' said the fellow, gesturing to the ginger giant. 'We are what we like to call *wranglers* here in the Narroway. Your instructors, essentially. We will manage your training for the five or so years you'll spend in the service of the Narroway Hunt. We organise and co-ordinate all guard shifts, watches, hunts and patrols …'

Ottilie chewed on her lip, feeling panicky. She didn't want to hear anything more about 'five years' or 'patrols'.

'… And if you're lucky enough to be placed with a Fiory guardian after the trials, Wrangler Morse and I will be two of your permanent instructors.' Wrangler Voilies clapped his superlatively clean hands together. 'Your physical training begins tomorrow. We will meet in this chamber at the seventh bell. Lateness will not be tolerated and attendance is mandatory. Do we have any questions?'

Ottilie had questions, plenty of them, but none that she dared to ask aloud.

Wrangler Voilies raised his eyebrows and gazed about the room. Not a single person raised their hand. Ottilie wasn't sure, but she thought he looked a bit pleased.

'Now, just a few more things to discuss, and then you can all go and have a rest – you look as though you need it,' he said, somewhat coldly.

'Lyre hit them with a jivvie,' said Wrangler Morse.

Wrangler Voilies chuckled in a haughty sort of way. 'Well, that would explain it! Good. Good that you know what awaits you out there.' He paused. 'Oh, and also, you will be facing jivvies in your trials.'

Ottilie's chest contracted. She wanted to lie down on the ground and close her eyes.

'Nope,' muttered Branter Scoot, his jaw clicking. 'No way. Not doing that.'

'You and a flock of *ten* jivvies,' Wrangler Voilies went on. 'You will try to take down as many as you can, and you will receive one point per jivvie felled. But here's the good part.' He held up his left hand. Wrapped around his pale squishy thumb was a bronze ring. 'I've got one ring here for each of you. Put it back on your thumb and do not remove it again. Not even when you sleep. These rings could save your life. They *will* save your life. So long as you wear one, the dredretches can't hurt you.'

'Unless they get hold of you,' said Wrangler Morse.

'Of course, yes, like any beast they will tear you to pieces, but so long as you wear your ring they won't be able to kill you just by lurking nearby – which should be a comfort to you all.'

Ottilie pictured herself lying on the ground with no legs, and a shadowy creature chomping loudly on something nearby. Feeling nauseated, she shook her head, expelling the thoughts.

Wrangler Morse stepped forwards, clutching a box in his large, hairy hands. One by one, he returned their rings. Ottilie slid hers on immediately. Just as before, it seemed to resize to fit her thumb perfectly. That same odd sensation flickered up her arm, and finally her stomach settled and her headache numbed to nothing.

'Are they spell'd, do you think?' muttered Gully.

'I didn't think spell'd objects were real, not now there are no witches. Mr Parch always said the faulty peddlers are just pretenders,' whispered Ottilie.

Wrangler Voilies clapped again. 'One more thing, lads. You are not the only occupants of Fort Fiory. There are of course the custodians, the interior types going by the name of sculkies. Like you, the girls are here to work. Different work, of course,' he smirked, 'in a position more suited to their natural abilities. They cook, clean, launder, garden, and generally serve the Hunt.'

So it was confirmed. The only other girls at Fort Fiory were servants. That hardly seemed fair. *Natural abilities* made it sound as if girls were born with the gift to serve and clean – but that didn't seem right. Freddie didn't know how to scrub a muddy potato, let alone their hollow – Ottilie and Gully had always split the chores equally. Who had decided only boys should hunt monsters? Why couldn't a girl? Ottilie decided there wasn't an answer. Of *course* a girl could hunt monsters.

Wrangler Morse cleared his throat. 'This is your home now, lads. It's good work we do here. Worthwhile. You don't know it now, but you're going to love it here. And the sooner you accept your part in all this, the better for you. Maybe you're already getting it. And if you're not, just wait until you see a few more of those monsters beyond that wall out there. They come much bigger and much uglier than jivvies.'

That was a horrifying thought. Ottilie found it hard to believe that there could be something worse than a jivvie.

'When you spot a full-grown scorver, a fire-breathing oxie, or – what's the biggest, do you think, Tudor?'

'Barrogaul,' said Wrangler Voilies, the corners of his mouth quirking upwards.

'That'd be the one,' Wrangler Morse frowned. 'Trust me, you spot yourself a barrogaul and you'll get it. You'll get why we're here. We hunt dredretches, monsters, evil in solid form. These things need to be contained for the good of everyone in the Usklers and beyond.'

Right then and there, Ottilie decided that for the rest of her life she would do whatever it took to avoid coming into contact with a barrogaul.

'You were chosen because you've got the right stuff in you,' said Wrangler Voilies. 'You're the only men for the job, and before long you'll start to take pride in that. You just wait and see.'

'Nope,' muttered Branter Scoot.

Ottilie caught his eye and nodded in agreement. She would *not* wait and see. She and Gully were leaving.

12

Training

Gully just couldn't come around to the idea of breakfast. Ottilie, on the other hand, embraced it wholeheartedly. The next morning, she gladly took care of his tray along with her own. It was better food than they had ever had access to. The bread at Fiory wasn't stale, and the beans weren't dried. For dinner, they were given root-vegetable stew, which was far more appetising than the common Swamp Hollows delicacy of mushroom broth with soggy river weeds.

Brushing the breakfast crumbs off her blanket, Ottilie turned to Gully. Pillow at his feet, Gully was lying on his bed staring at the ceiling. Soft morning light filtered in through the window, forming a barrier of floating dust between their corner and the rest of the room.

'Here's what I'm thinking,' said Branter Scoot. His voice was low and his eyes were shifty. 'I'm thinking we get out of here.'

Wary of eavesdroppers, Ottilie scanned the room. Some of the boys, like Gully, were lying on their beds, others were gathered in groups, and some even seemed cheerful. No-one was paying them any attention.

'Run away?' said Preddy, his eyeglasses magnifying his eyes to the size of apricots.

'Before they get too attached to the idea of us being here!'

'I think they're already attached to that idea, Scoot,' said Ottilie. 'They dragged some boys all the way from the Claw.' The Claw was the east-most tip of the Usklers.

'But maybe it's worth all that,' said Preddy. 'Maybe they're right and this is really important work.'

'You can't be serious!' said Branter Scoot, who was quickly becoming simply *Scoot*. 'Preddy, they kidnapped us! You can't go round snatching people and telling them to hunt monsters for you!'

'But it's for the king ...'

'First, I haven't seen the king anywhere. Have you? And second, the king's never done anything much for me. In fact, no-one in the Usklers cares two brakkernuts for a kid from the Wikric slum tunnels,' said Scoot. 'What about you Colters? How was life in the Swamp Hollows? You feel like you owe the king your loyal service?'

'I don't know,' said Gully, pushing himself up to sit with his arms wrapped around his knees.

Ottilie had become particularly observant of the way the boys around her moved. Some were stooping and clumsy with their limbs, others stood square and appeared to stretch and spread themselves, as if to take up as much space as possible. Preddy had impeccable posture, and seemed to move most similarly to the sculkies, whereas Scoot was the opposite, hunched and unpredictable with sharp, exaggerated movements.

Ottilie had grown so paranoid that she had begun to question her every gesture and posture, often altering her stance several times to find something that seemed naturally male – although she was beginning to suspect there was no such thing. The fact was, she needed to get out before anyone noticed she was different.

'We need to go home,' said Ottilie, careful to keep her voice quiet.

Gully nodded.

'I can't believe they took the both of you,' said Scoot. 'You're the only set of brothers here, far as I know.'

Ottilie's lungs seemed to deflate.

'Must run in the family,' said Gully quickly, catching her eye. 'Whatever it is they choose us for.'

'True,' said Preddy, readjusting his eyeglasses. 'It is surprising that there aren't more siblings here, if you think about it.'

'Maybe there are in different tiers,' said Ottilie. 'Gully and I shouldn't have been taken at the same time. He's younger than everyone …'

'Why is that?' said Scoot. 'Why'd they take you so young?'

'They must just take some people early if they think they're ready,' said Preddy. 'The earlier the better, by the sounds of it – if you can't hurt a dredretch after you turn eighteen.'

'Well, I'm not ready. I'm going home,' said Gully.

'Hear, hear,' muttered Scoot, scowling at the door. 'I'd go right now if I could figure out how to do it. But there are people everywhere, watching … even guarding the boundary walls. I saw them when we came in.'

'We should get down to the springs and clean up,' said Preddy, changing the subject, 'or we'll be late for our first training session.'

Gully looked sideways at Ottilie. She did her best to keep her expression blank. It was at this moment that she was in the worst danger. Preddy and Scoot headed for the door. Gully got up to follow.

'You coming, Ott?' said Scoot.

The muscles in her shoulders and neck bunched up. 'No, I'm going to stay and finish this.' She pointed to Gully's breakfast tray. 'I went late last night.'

'You did?'

'Couldn't sleep.'

It was true; Ottilie had sneaked out when all the boys were asleep, to scrub herself properly clean in the bath. How she was going to keep that up without arousing suspicion she did not know. It seemed that only the fledges used those particular springs. She'd heard they would get their own bedchamber after the trials, so perhaps the other tiers had private washrooms. She supposed it didn't matter. She wouldn't be sticking around long enough to find out.

'You sure eat a lot,' said Scoot.

'Just not used to having so much food thrown at me,' she said, forcing a smile. 'There wasn't much to go around back home.'

'Fair point,' said Scoot, eying the tray greedily. 'Toss us that apple, Ott.'

With a sharp breath of relief, Ottilie threw the shiny red apple across the room. Scoot caught it in his left hand and tore a chunk out of it. 'Fanks,' he said, lumps of apple flying out of his mouth.

Just after they left, two sculkies came in to clear the breakfast trays. Ottilie immediately recognised the dark-haired girl with the mysterious gaze. She was accompanied by a fair-haired friend that Ottilie hadn't noticed before. Neither girl paid Ottilie any attention until they had collected all the trays and were halfway out the door. Later, Ottilie would decide that she had imagined it, or at least exaggerated it in her mind – but as they passed through the doorway, she was sure the dark-haired sculkie whispered something about her, because a second later, her companion turned. She could have been looking through the window, but Ottilie was certain she was looking at her. A cat's smile stretched across the sculkie's face. Unnerved, Ottilie turned away.

>>————————————————————>

The bells tolled seven and there was no sign of wranglers Voilies or Morse. Instead, Leo and Ned were standing by the window in the high-ceilinged chamber. Leo was gesturing towards a dark shape in the distant sky. Ned nodded and muttered something with a smile.

The group stood in silence for a moment, unsure of what was going on.

'Morning all,' said Leo Darby, without looking at them. 'We're to take you down.'

They were led down several flights of stairs and out into the morning sun. They moved through archways of grey stone, across a clover-strewn field, past an orchard of trees bursting with speckled dustplums, and finally met the waiting wranglers by a vast pond near the boundary wall. A harmony of croaks beat out between the reeds and a lone red-feathered goose eyed them malevolently from across the glassy water.

'Good morning,' said Wrangler Voilies. 'So. Well. Good, you've met my boys here properly – Leonard Darby and Edwin Skovey. You are extremely fortunate to have these two working with this squad. They're both from Fiory, and select elite of course. And Leo has been the reigning champion of his tier for the two years he's been with us.'

Wrangler Voilies patted Leo on the back, a close-mouthed smile contorting his face. Leo looked so imperiously smug that Ottilie would not have been surprised if he ordered them all to kneel at his feet.

'To business,' said Voilies. 'The boys are going to take you for a run. Two laps around the inside of the boundary walls – you will hear this referred to as the inner shepherd perimeter. And please note, fledglings, that the lower grounds are out of bounds until after your trials. Now off you trot, and no walking!'

Ottilie had always liked to run, but she had never *gone running* in her life. It was not easy. Thankfully she was not the only one who struggled. Perched high on a hill, the Fiory grounds were not flat, and it was not an easy track to run. Here and there they passed groups of off-duty huntsmen, some of them heckling as the puffing fledglings struggled past.

The squad curled around a huge, somewhat overgrown vegetable patch tucked behind an apple grove, and a buzzing apiary with rows of bee gums and krippygrass hives. They circled another crystalline pond, beating with frog song, crossed a muddy creek, and stumbled through a stretch of wet wilderness with tightening chests and limbs growing heavier by the second.

Just when Ottilie thought her lungs were going to give out, she realised they'd lost someone. 'Where's Preddy?' she wheezed.

Scoot jerked his head backwards, half-grinning, half-grimacing in pain. Preddy was right at the back. His face was bright red everywhere but around his mouth, which was ringed with white. He looked like any breath could be his last. The truth was, Preddy looked exactly how Ottilie felt. There was a strange blood-like taste leaking up from her throat, and were she not caught in a pack she knew she would already be walking.

They finished their run at a bouncy march.

'Disappointing,' sniffed Wrangler Voilies. 'I'd expect better from a squad of sculkies.' He rested one neatly manicured hand on his rather flabby stomach. 'Fitness will always be a priority,' he said, breathing heavily as they trekked up a hill to a set of training yards. 'For your fledgling trials, reflex and accuracy will be our main focus during your training. After that, we will introduce you to a wider range of weaponry, and our three hunting orders: foot, mounted, and flight.'

'Flight?' whispered Ottilie, with an unexpected smile.

Beside her, Gully's eyes were stretched wide.

'But for now, we will be focusing on your trials. You'll need to use a bow, and a bit of skill with a cutlass, clubs and a slingshot could also be helpful.'

Ottilie felt a tingle of excitement. She and Gully had been play-fighting for years, pretending to defend the Swamp Hollows from devilish Laklanders and dodging invisible jets of flame from imaginary firedrakes. Now they were actually going to get to learn these skills.

They followed the wranglers into the training yards, gathering in one of three archery ranges. Above all, Ottilie had always wanted to learn how to shoot an arrow. They had seen she-oak longbows slung across the backs of fur-clad hunters around Market Town, and she and Gully had even tried to build their own from sticks and string.

When Wrangler Morse placed a short, curved bow in her hand, Ottilie almost squeaked with excitement. She glanced over at Gully and saw that he too, despite his determination to go home, was delighted by the prospect of learning to use a real bow.

But as it turned out, archery was not at all easy.

'Always remember, bow arm – elbow out. Don't let me see them pointing to the ground!' called Wrangler Voilies.

'Keep that shoulder down, Ott,' said Wrangler Morse, checking her form. 'And don't grip. Keep it supported in the pad of your hand. If you grip, you might twist the bow on release.'

'Right,' muttered Ottilie, trying hard to take it all in.

'Use the muscles across your back! Do not pull with the arm,' said Wrangler Voilies. 'And draw!'

Ottilie took a breath and tried her best to keep her arm in line with the arrow.

'Loose!'

Looking beyond the bow to the very centre of the target, Ottilie released her breath and the arrow at the same time. She was sure she had met her mark. Fists clenched and eyes blazing, she watched the arrow shave the edge of the wooden target and bounce off the wall beyond, falling to the ground like a useless twig.

Her face fell. She looked around. Almost everyone had missed their targets. Some had managed to hit the outer edges, but only one boy made it anywhere near the centre.

'Well done, Mr Preddy! Fine form,' said Wrangler Voilies.

'Shot before, have you?' said Wrangler Morse.

'Yes, a bit,' said Preddy.

'We don't get a lot with previous training,' said Wrangler Morse. 'You done any riding or swordplay?'

'I was never trained with a blade, but I've been riding since I could walk,' said Preddy.

'Good, good, excellent,' said Wrangler Voilies.

Ottilie noticed scowls on the faces of the other boys. Preddy was one of the very few in their group to have come from decidedly privileged circumstances. They weren't all from such lowly dwellings as the Wikric slum tunnels like Scoot, or the Swamp Hollows like her and Gully, but there were very few upper-crust sorts.

'All right. I would say *not too shabby* ... but I can't. For the most part, shabby, shabby, shabby,' said Wrangler Voilies. 'I see timidity! I see scattered focus! I see weak limbs and empty heads! Was there a mix-up? Did they send us girls by mistake?' He clicked his tongue and shook his head.

Leo chuckled, and Wrangler Voilies smirked. Ottilie couldn't believe what she was hearing. Beside her, Gully looked confused, and a little angry.

'Let's have a demonstration,' said Wrangler Morse. 'Boys?'

'Ned,' said Leo, with disinterest. 'It's no fun if the target's not moving.'

'All right, Eddy, you're up,' said Wrangler Morse.

Ned moved forwards. 'Can I borrow that for a minute?' he asked Gully.

Gully passed him the bow.

Ned smiled and in about ten seconds flat, he hit three separate targets almost square in the centre.

Ottilie's jaw dropped. She wondered if, with two years' training, she could be as good as Ned. But she shrugged off the thought. It didn't matter.

'Thank you, Mr Skovey, that's what we like to see,' said Wrangler Voilies. 'Let's give it another go, shall we, fledglings?'

'Don't worry, on my first try I broke the arrow in half,' said Ned, passing the bow back to Gully with a wink. 'Don't ask me how.'

Leo snorted. 'I remember that!'

'And what happened to yours, Leonard? Up over the wall, wasn't it?'

'Raw power,' said Leo.

'Elbows out, shoulders down. Square your feet, Mr Scoot,' called Wrangler Voilies. 'Aaand loose!'

Ottilie's arrow went up over the wall.

'Well, there's hope for this one,' said Leo, clapping her hard on the shoulder. 'Raw power,' he muttered out of the corner of his mouth.

Ottilie nearly flinched at his touch. She didn't like the others getting too close. It was probably irrational, but she had a strange fear that one of them would smell it on her, as if they might sniff out the difference and realise she didn't belong.

13

Skip the Secret Keeper

That night, their bedchamber was buzzing.

'How about when Leo Darby shot that ball they threw over the fence?' said a boy perched on a bed by the door.

'I could've done that, if they'd given me a go,' said his neighbour.

'You didn't even hit your target once!' said another boy from across the room.

'Still did better than you. You shoot like a girl!'

Ottilie cringed. There had been lots of that kind of talk. Wrangler Voilies was the worst. He mentioned the sculkies almost every time he was displeased with their form. It seemed absurd to Ottilie. So far, she was performing at the same level as the boys around her. She couldn't see a difference.

She lay on her bed, listening to them argue. The day had been long and hard, but there was no denying they'd had fun, and most of them were looking forward to tomorrow.

Ottilie wondered if *she* was looking forward to tomorrow. She couldn't be sure. The thing was, she didn't think it was possible for her to really have fun, not with Gully there. She felt responsible for him, and was quite sure he felt the same for her.

The babble and banter lasted well into the night. It wasn't until the muted night bells tolled twelve that Ottilie could be sure they were all asleep. She coughed quietly to check. Not a single boy stirred. Careful not to make another sound, she pulled on her slippers and crept from the room.

Ottilie liked bathing late at night. It was a peaceful in-between time. Nothing and no-one held claim over her at midnight and the moon was so much better at keeping secrets than the sun.

She slipped into the water. The pools were perennially warm, fed by hot springs below. It was wonderfully relaxing after such an exhausting day, and before long Ottilie began to drift off to sleep. Had she managed to keep her eyes open just a moment or two longer she would have heard footsteps in the corridor.

Even catching the sound of the door opening might have given her enough time to scurry into the shadows. But Ottilie's eyes were closed and her mind had sailed away. She didn't hear a thing, not even the surprised squeak that rang crisp and clear in the empty chamber.

What she did hear, however, was the cacophonous clatter of a metal bucket hitting the marble floor. Ottilie's eyes flew open. Every muscle hardened to stone, and her stomach lurched up into her ribcage.

'I'm so sorry!' It was a sculkie. She was standing dangerously close, only a few feet away. 'I didn't see you there!' The sculkie stooped to pick up the bucket. 'We clean late at night when it's empty. I thought you were all in bed.'

Ottilie froze. She didn't know what to do. After several terrible moments of silence she said, 'That's all right. Sorry. I couldn't sleep, so I ...'

'Not a problem,' said the girl. Around her middle, she wore a belt with different cleaning utensils dangling from rings. 'I'll leave you to hop out. I do need to get started as soon as possible if I want to get some sleep tonight.' But she didn't turn away. Instead, she narrowed her eyes and took a step towards the bath. 'I – sorry,' she began, her voice confident and clear. 'It's just ... you're not a boy.'

Ottilie felt her face drain of all colour. Why hadn't she covered herself up? What was wrong with her? She was caught – it was over! She couldn't think straight.

All she could hear was her own heart pounding in her ears. 'No,' she said finally.

The girl took another step forwards. Her hair was dark blonde and there was something rabbit-like about her face. Quite out of the blue, she cracked a wide, crooked grin.

'What?' said Ottilie.

'Well that's just – that's great,' the sculkie breathed, her eyes bright.

Ottilie hardly heard her. 'Please don't tell anyone,' she begged, tears flooding her eyes. 'I don't know what they'll do to me.'

'Of course I won't tell anyone!' the girl half-yelled, before smacking a hand over her own mouth and flicking her eyes towards the door. 'How did you get here?' she whispered. 'They can't have picked you. You cut all your hair off to look like a boy, so … what? You snuck in?' She spoke almost indecipherably fast.

'It's a long story,' said Ottilie, her heart still thumping.

'You have to tell it.'

'All right, but I might put some clothes on first if that's all right with you.' Ottilie dried herself off and forced her jittery limbs back into her nightclothes, trying very hard not to panic.

'I'm Isla Skipper, but everyone calls me Skip,' said the sculkie. She held out a hand for Ottilie to shake.

'Ott Colter,' said Ottilie, taking her curiously small, very calloused hand.

'Ott?' Skip grinned.

'Ottilie.' It felt strange to say.

'That's more like it.'

Skip flipped her bucket upside down and plonked herself down upon it, gazing up at Ottilie expectantly.

Ottilie perched on the edge of the bath and laid out the bare bones of the story.

Skip's eyes shone with excitement. 'I never would have guessed – that you're a girl. But, well, of course you are! I can't un-see it now.'

'As long as no-one else can,' said Ottilie, frowning. How could she have let herself be caught so soon!

'So which one is your brother? Where does he sleep?'

'Um, Gulliver – Gully, next to me, second from the window.'

'With the dark curly hair?' Skip looked her up and down. 'I like him,' she said. 'He's always very polite when we bring the trays. Always says thank you. I can usually count the thank yous on one hand – once they start feeling important they tend to get rude.'

'How long have you been here?' said Ottilie.

Skip screwed up her face, thinking. 'Four years?'

'Four years!' Ottilie couldn't believe it. 'How did you get here? Do they snatch girls too?' Was snatching girls to be servants worse than snatching boys to hunt monsters? Ottilie wasn't sure.

Skip scowled.

'Nah. I applied for the job. Speaking of, I'll have to get started.' She dipped her bucket in the bath to fill it, and began scrubbing at the tiles using soap that smelled like bramblywine and cloves.

But Ottilie wasn't ready to leave. She wanted to know more. 'Let me help,' she said.

Skip unhooked a narrow scrubbing brush from her belt and tossed it to Ottilie.

'Why did you want this job? Where are you from?' said Ottilie, working away on the mould between the tiles – not for the first time, she found herself marvelling at proper soap.

'Wikric,' said Skip. 'I was in a children's home, but I ran away when I was six or seven.'

'But … where did you go?'

'Where does anyone go? The slum tunnels, of course. I used to steal quite a bit. Got into some trouble and needed to get away, then I heard about this job where they take you far off and give you food and a safe place to sleep for as long as you want. They like taking kids off the streets – no-one to miss them.'

Of course poorer boys were easier to take. Ottilie found herself wondering why they had taken someone like Preddy.

Her elbow was cramping up. Sitting back on her feet, she gave it a rub. 'So you know all about this place then?' she said, her mind humming. 'Is it all true? Everything they tell us, about the dredretches?'

Skip's face clouded over. 'We're not allowed outside the boundary walls, but I've seen enough. It's definitely true.'

Ottilie's heart sank. She had maintained a scrap of hope that things were not quite as grim as Captain Lyre had made them seem.

Skip pulled a mop from a peg on the wall. 'There's no denying the work needs to be done,' she said. 'Only I don't see why it's only boys who get to do it. The only girls here are us custodians and some bone singers. I've seen enough to want a crack at a dredretch myself!'

'What's a bone singer?' It didn't sound like a good thing.

'There's a whole bunch of them. A woman called Whistler's in charge but we hardly see her. They deal with the dead dredretches. They're always talking about fighting for glory and honour in service of the Usklers –'

'The bone singers are?' said Ottilie, trying to keep up.

'No, the huntsmen, the wranglers, everyone ...' Skip filled the mop pail and plonked it down with some force. Water slopped out onto the floor, and Ottilie skipped sideways to avoid the splash. 'It's as if they think girls can't have honour,' Skip continued. 'The boys fight for honour and we creep around cleaning up after them. Give me a dredretch over a bucket and scrubber any day.'

'I don't know. I might choose the bucket,' Ottilie muttered. 'Why *is* it only boys?'

Skip laughed. 'I don't know how things are in the Swamp Hollows, but I doubt it's a whole lot different. Of *course* it's only boys. That's the way things go, isn't it? Girls aren't allowed to do anything. Rich girls sit, poor girls clean, and girls with nothing at all hide in the dark.'

It still didn't make sense to her. 'But *why*?'

'If I could have my way, things would be a whole lot different!' said Skip, swinging the mop into her right hand and holding it aloft like a spear. 'Maybe now you're here, it can be! You could change things, Ottilie.'

Ottilie cast her eyes down, veiling the guilt. She wouldn't be changing anything. She was leaving. 'What happens when they turn eighteen?' she said. 'They say you can only kill a dredretch while you're still an innocent.'

'Well, I don't know about all that. But the boys stay till they're eighteen, then they get sent off into the world. They're loaded up with gold, given important roles in the King's Company and sworn to eternal secrecy.'

'But *why* all the secrets?'

Skip tilted her head. 'I don't have a clue. From what I've gathered, and I do a fair bit of eavesdropping,' she grinned, 'no-one knows. Just the king and a very select few. It's all managed out of Wikric, by the Wikric lord. He barely even communicates with the king, because the king wants to stay away from it.'

Ottilie scrubbed the edge of the bath, thinking hard. 'Maybe they just don't want to cause a panic, so they have to snatch people in secret.'

Skip shrugged. 'So, what are you going to do? You know they're going to figure out you're a girl eventually.'

Ottilie felt the panic creeping back in. 'You promise you won't tell anyone?'

'Of course!'

'I don't plan on staying here long enough for them to find out, anyway.'

'What do you mean?'

'Me and Gully, and maybe some others, are getting out of here.'

Skip stopped mopping. 'Ottilie, that's insane. I don't think you understand what's out there. They have guards with you when they bring you through the Narroway for a reason, and it's not to keep you from escaping – it's to *protect* you from the dredretches.'

'But ...' How many dredretches could there really be? 'I didn't see anything out there.'

'That's because they brought your mob in during the rain. I don't know why, but the way I hear it, monsters don't like to go out in the rain. And they had a lot of huntsmen out the day they brought you in, to make sure none of those things came near you,' said Skip.

'I just want to get Gully home.' Ottilie found it was easier to think of it that way. She felt braver because she was looking after him.

'Does he actually want to go?' Skip raised her eyebrows. 'It's just, funnily enough, most of them don't actually want to leave, not after a while.'

'People keep saying that,' Ottilie snapped.

Skip sat beside her on the edge of the bath. 'Think about it. He probably wants to get you home before they find out you're a girl. And you want to get him home because he's your little brother and you don't want him fighting monsters.

'But everyone else, well, they choose the boys carefully. They pick lonely, hungry boys, the really reckless ones. They bring them here, tell them they were selected specially for the job. They offer them a family, food, three stations full of brothers, and girls to wait on them.

'They say their king needs them, and then, and this is the genius part, they make it *fun*. They teach them to hunt monsters, and they make it a game. The boys aren't just serving the kingdom and saving lives, they get to be winners – champions even.

'You can scrap the hungry and lonely part. Take any twelve-year-old, tell them that instead of growing up in the real world they can go to a mysterious forest and have adventures for the rest of their young lives. Well ... what would you have said?'

Ottilie stared down at her knees. 'I don't know. I was never very brave.'

'Ha!' Skip covered her toothy mouth and glanced at the door again.

'What?'

'Look at you with your hacked-off hair, having a bath at midnight. You're great. You and I are going to be friends.' She snorted. '*Not very brave* – you're obviously the best kind of brave!'

Ottilie had never thought of herself as *any* kind of brave.

'What do you think Gully would have said, if they'd asked him to come?'

Ottilie thought she knew the answer, but she didn't want to say it out loud. 'It doesn't matter. It doesn't make it right, what they did – kidnapping Gully, taking him away from his home.'

'No. It's not right. But it's complicated. You can't just reset things back to the way they were meant to be. You have to adapt.'

Ottilie frowned at her feet. 'And what they do here, it's really important?'

'That's what they say,' said Skip.

Ottilie didn't look up. *Important*. She didn't think well enough of these people – these *kidnappers* – to trust their idea of what was important.

✦ 14 ✦

Caution and Counsel

Ottilie thought long and hard about her first conversation with Skip. They'd had more since, of course. Skip volunteered to take the springs shift a few nights that week so she and Ottilie could continue their midnight friendship. It was such a comfort to have someone to talk to who knew her secret. She could never seem to get Gully completely alone, so talking to Skip was her only chance to speak without watching every word she said.

Ottilie found deception unexpectedly taxing. It was such a relief to let it all go and just be herself for an hour. She realised she had taken honesty for granted before. Why did anyone ever bother lying, or pretend to be someone they weren't? It was draining and unpleasant. Ottilie wanted to never have to tell lies again.

Keeping Skip's words in mind, she had been watching Gully. Skip was right. He was enjoying himself. And despite all the tiresome lying, Ottilie was beginning to enjoy herself as well – but that was precisely why they had to go.

➤————————————➤

'Shh, I can hear someone coming,' said Gully, shoving the lantern behind him to mask the light.

They froze, tilting their ears towards the approaching clicks and clacks of a sculkie's boots in the corridor beyond the springs. It was past midnight and they were supposed to be in bed. Preddy had dark rings like bruises beneath his eyeglasses. Scoot's olive skin looked almost green. Gully's limbs hung loose and heavy, and Ottilie, who was getting far less sleep than the rest of them, could barely keep her eyes open.

The wranglers had been working them to the bone in preparation for the fledgling trials, which were now only two weeks away. They spent their days running around Fiory's perimeter, flinging stones from slingshots, slicing the air with cutlasses and landing arrows ever closer to their targets.

Preddy's soft sneeze broke the silence. Ottilie's gaze was fixed on the door. The footsteps dulled as the sculkie moved further off.

Scoot let his shoulders drop from where they had scrunched up to his earlobes. 'Good thing Preddy sneezes like a girl,' he said.

Ottilie's mind raced. What did it mean to sneeze like a girl? Softly? Had she been sneezing like a girl? She looked to Gully for reassurance, but he was busy rolling his eyes.

'You say the stupidest stuff sometimes, Scoot,' he said.

They had gathered in the springs to avoid being overheard. It was Ottilie's idea. She knew the cleaning schedule so well, she was positive they would not be disturbed. Ottilie had chosen a night Skip wasn't rostered on. Skip didn't approve of her plans and Ottilie didn't want her attitude to influence the others, not before they were properly on board.

'Right, where were we?' said Scoot.

'I was saying one more time, are we sure we want to do this?' said Preddy.

'And I was saying one more time, shut up, Preddy!' said Scoot.

'It wasn't a choice, Preddy. That's the point,' said Ottilie. 'Whatever work they do here, we didn't choose to come.'

'What about your family? Aren't you worried they miss you?' said Gully.

Preddy turned slightly pink and adjusted his eyeglasses. 'My father has a lot of enemies. I'm pretty confident he'll have used my disappearance to his advantage. He's been waiting for an excuse to take action against a number of them for years now. And anyway, I'm the youngest of six. My absence won't have left much of a hole.'

'How can you say that? Of course it has,' said Ottilie. She gazed at him in the lamplight. There was a hollowness in his pale eyes that she had not noticed before.

Preddy shook his head. 'Look, I'm with you, all right. I'll come. I'm not going to stay here all by myself.'

'Noble words,' said Scoot, snorting.

'Let's not pretend running away in the night is noble,' said Preddy, brushing a speck of dirt off his trousers.

'Neither is kidnapping,' said Ottilie.

'Or letting the kidnappers win!' growled Scoot.

It was funny, Ottilie supposed, that Scoot was so determined to escape this place. Ottilie was quite sure Fort Fiory offered more comfort and security than his life in the slum tunnels had. But Scoot was a wild thing, used to making his own decisions, looking out for himself. He was twitching like a caged animal behind the Fiory walls and Ottilie knew that he, like she, could not move past the fact that they had not chosen to be there.

'We have to stop fighting,' said Gully. 'Are we doing it or not?'

'Yes. We are,' said Scoot.

Ottilie and Gully looked at Preddy.

He frowned, pushing his eyeglasses higher up the bridge of his nose. 'Yes.'

'Good. Then we need to start planning,' said Ottilie. 'We'll come back here tomorrow at the same time. I know someone who can help us.'

'Are you out of your tiny minds?' said Skip, gazing at them in disbelief. 'Ottil – Ott, didn't we already talk about this? It's impossible!'

'I know what you said,' Ottilie replied. 'But we don't have a choice.'

'This place is evil,' said Scoot. 'I'm not waiting around to get chomped on by a monster just because some lunatic with a nifty beard says the king wants me to hunt for him.'

Skip looked him up and down. 'What's your name again?'

'Branter Scoot.'

'You from the slum tunnels?'

'Why? Do I know you?'

'Doubt it. Just can pick it from your voice.'

They stared at each other for a moment, lost in old memories, until Skip blinked and scratched her nose. 'Look, here's the thing, if the dredretches aren't enough to scare you, and they should be, you should know what they do to rule-breakers around here,' she said.

Preddy paled.

'What do they do?' said Gully, seemingly undaunted.

'There's a story about a boy who tried to get out. He stole a sackful of silver from the vaults, released all the dredretches they keep locked up for training as a distraction, and tried to escape back to the Usklers. They caught him before he even made it to the boundary wall – and he was a third-tier huntsman who knew his way around.'

'So what did they do to him?' said Ottilie.

'Well, people died, see – when he let the dredretches out, it caught them off-guard and they lost two huntsmen. So they held a trial to decide whether he should be hanged or marooned in the Laklands. They decided on the Laklands. And trust me, hanging would have been kinder.'

'Did it actually happen? Or is it just a story?' said Ottilie, her voice shakier than she would have liked.

'I wasn't here, but it definitely happened, and that's not the only story. There was another boy, over west at Richter. He started skipping out on his wall watches and guard duty, someone got hurt, so they took off his ring and locked him in a cage next to a dredretch until he nearly died. They say it took weeks for his body to get better, and his head's never been quite right since.

And, there was another boy who got caught stealing food –'

'Well, we're not stealing anything … except weapons … and I guess food,' said Scoot, 'but we're not getting caught, and no-one's going to die because of us trying to escape. I want to get out of here before I get skewered by a death crow in the bleeding fledgling trials.'

'You realise going out there untrained and unsupervised is more dangerous than any situation they will ever put you in,' said Skip.

'At least it's our choice,' said Preddy, surprising them all.

'You'll get caught,' said Skip.

'Not if you help us,' said Ottilie.

'I'm not going to help you get yourselves killed. You don't even know anything about dredretches yet. You wouldn't last ten minutes out there on your own.'

'We're going to wait for rain, then we at least have a chance. We just need you to help us get out of the grounds. Skip, please,' said Ottilie, desperation pitching her voice a little too high. She cleared her throat and glanced at Preddy and Scoot. They hadn't seemed to notice.

Skip crossed her arms and sighed loudly. 'I can tell you where to go and when it'll be clear, but that's all, Ott. I don't want you to go.' She looked directly into

Ottilie's eyes, and Ottilie knew what she wasn't saying in front of the others. Skip thought Ottilie could change things. She thought that a girl hunting dredretches was the beginning of something exciting, something new, and maybe it could have been, but all Ottilie could think about was getting Gully out of the Narroway. She had come to take him home and that was exactly what she intended to do.

15

Hero

To Ottilie's increasing irritation, the days that followed were perfectly lovely. She didn't think she had ever seen such a string of bright, unblemished skies. Their plan to escape was sufficiently reckless; Ottilie wasn't stupid enough to attempt it on a clear night. Not only did dredretches apparently stay away on wet days, the cover of mist and cloud could only be helpful.

It had been five days since Skip had agreed to help. She told them exactly where to go, even reluctantly offering to snatch some food so that they need not go near any of the kitchens.

Their first task would be getting past the boundary walls, their second would be navigating the Narroway,

131

avoiding dredretches and detection, and their third would be sneaking through the border, back to the Usklers.

They had tossed around several plans involving stealing guard uniforms and commandeering food-supply carts, but the truth was, even with Scoot's expertise in sneaking and thievery, their lack of knowledge about the Narroway meant they were going to have to rely on chance and luck far more than planning ahead.

It had worked for Ottilie before. She had managed to sneak in, hadn't she? She had found Gully. If she could do that, then she could do this. She had to believe it would work. If she stopped believing, they might as well just settle in and continue counting down the days until the fledgling trials.

It didn't matter; until the blue skies yielded even a drop of rain, they were stuck. The upside was, the longer they remained, the more training they received, and knowing more about dredretches could only help.

Wrangler Voilies led them across a clover field. The bells tolled and a scattering of huntsmen strode out of the fort, heading purposefully in different directions; squad training, watch duty, guard shifts and hunts. Ottilie looked up at the tall boundary walls. She could see huntsmen pacing the parapets, and higher still, a wrangler in one of the sentry towers, gazing out into the endless forest to the north.

'We have an entire library of bestiaries here at Fiory, and at Richter and Arko too,' Wrangler Voilies was saying. 'You will be assigned weekly study tasks once your trials are complete. Just one of the reasons we require you to be able to read.'

They had undergone a literacy and numeracy test a week ago. Although they wouldn't be privy to their results until after the trials, Ottilie was sure she had done better than most. Certainly she had left many questions unanswered, but half of the fledges couldn't even read so she was already at an advantage, thanks to Old Moss and her refusal to sell *Our Walkable World*.

'The thing to remember, always, is that a dredretch is an unnatural beast. They are a plague upon humanity and serve no purpose to the living world. We are not their food source; they do not attack us out of necessity. It is merely their primary instinct to attempt to tear us apart, starting with the heart – a dredretch will always, *always* go for the heart.'

Prompted by his words, a long-lost memory stumbled across Ottilie's mind.

'If you do something wicked, the dredretches will come. They'll sneak up behind and snatch your heart to put in their pies,' whispered Old Moss, baring her blackened teeth.

'Pies?' a much smaller Ottilie had squeaked.

Old Moss nodded grimly. 'Pies.'

'To our knowledge,' Wrangler Voilies continued, 'dredretches don't eat or drink, nor do they excrete waste, unless you consider a general oozing and dribbling of toxic mucus and other forms of goo to be excreting waste.'

Ottilie screwed up her nose and Scoot pretended to vomit beside her. Having just completed their morning run, they were heading up the hill to the training yards. Ottilie was still very red in the face and Preddy was noisily struggling to catch his breath.

Igor Thrike, one of the select elite assigned to assist them that morning, thumped Preddy so forcefully on the back that he stumbled forwards, tripping over his own foot.

There were sniggers from all sides. Gully pulled Preddy to his feet and Ottilie glared at Igor Thrike. She could hear Scoot cracking his knuckles beside her and sensed him glaring too. Igor Thrike simply smirked and walked ahead.

The most unpleasant of all the select elite assigned to their group, Igor was a tall, narrow boy, at least fourteen years of age, with dark hair and a hollow, harshly angled face. He seemed to shift between two expressions: haughty and threatening. Ottilie disliked both equally, and she wasn't the only one. Leo Darby had been holding himself stiffly since Igor's arrival that morning, and Ottilie could have sworn that every time Igor spoke it was followed by the subtle click of Leo's clenched jaw.

'The sickening effect of a dredretch's presence is a uniquely human weakness,' said Wrangler Voilies from up ahead. 'And it is only humans that they actively pursue.

'Other animals are not affected by the sickness, but they do sense their unnaturalness and are generally repelled – just as well, as a dredretch will attack a natural beast when provoked.

'There are still other beasts living in the Narroway, although far fewer than there were before the dredretch scourge. The shepherds that help safeguard these grounds are dusky wild dogs, native to these lands. You will have seen them prowling the inner and outer perimeters. You may also come across our leopard shepherd. Hero, as she is affectionately known, is a grey coastal leopard who sought refuge from the dredretch-infested land and joined our shepherd pack.'

Ottilie's ears pricked. The leopard shepherd; Skip had told them about her. Getting past the leopard shepherd was a key part of their escape plan.

'But back to dredretches,' Voilies continued. 'However unnatural, they do have hearts that pump blood, or something similar, and brains that function at varying levels depending on the species. If you manage to pierce the heart or the brain of any dredretch they will perish almost instantly.

'However, it's not that simple. Dredretches have defences like no natural animal. In certain species, the barrogaul for example, a shell-like cage, as strong as iron, encases the heart. Nothing, no weapon, can puncture it. But every creature has its weakness. How do you fell a barrogaul, boys?'

'The eye,' said Igor and Leo at the same time.

Igor's lips thinned.

They had reached the fence around the training yards. Chuckling, Wrangler Voilies turned to face them. 'Precisely! There's always a way. You will find that most dredretches can heal a flesh wound almost instantly, but an arrow through the eye and into the brain causes irreparable damage. Leo, tell us, what is the primary weakness that all species of dredretch share?'

Ottilie was sure he was going to say rain.

Leo's eyes flicked to Igor, and a smug smile lit his freckled face as he answered, 'Salt slows the healing process of any wound.'

'Indeed,' said Wrangler Voilies. 'Salt. Dredretches can't abide it. That doesn't mean you throw handfuls of rock salt at them, although that may sting, and in a pinch you can use a slingshot to do something similar – we have a more effective method. There is a particular type of salt that won't rust a blade, found in the southern salt springs. We use it to make our weapons poisonous to dredretches.

'Forged in salt flame, any wound from a salt blade will not heal as it should, weakening the dredretch until you are able to deliver the fatal blow. But do not forget the rule of innocence. All of this – a regular blade, a salt blade, any weapon – if the blow is delivered by a non-innocent, any fully-grown man, it will not so much as scratch the skin.'

Ottilie frowned. Of everything he had said, she found this detail the most difficult to accept. It was beyond reason that the age of the hunter could somehow protect a dredretch from injury. It didn't make sense. She looked around. Did anyone else notice this? But the wranglers were practically branding them as *chosen ones*. Perhaps they didn't care to question it.

'The point of all this is that every dredretch is different, and some are much easier to fell than others. Lucky for you, jivvies are relatively simple. Their skulls are paper thin; one good blow to the head would squash the brain and fell a jivvie with no blood spilled and no salt needed. The same goes for the ribs and the heart. That said, a nick from a salt blade will do the same in time. Salt can paralyse certain smaller dredretch kinds, and one arrow, anywhere on the body, is a death sentence to a jivvie. That's why, in our scoring system, jivvies are only worth one point and a barrogaul is worth one hundred.

'But. Mark my words, fledglings: do not underestimate them. Jivvies are difficult targets. And at this point, not a single one of you would have a chance against one, let alone a flock. So, let's see if we can improve upon yesterday.' He unlatched the gate and ushered them into the training yards.

By mid-afternoon, miraculously, the sunlight faltered and dark clouds rolled in from the south. They hung low, obscuring the peaks beyond the fort. It was going to rain. This was it. Tonight was the night. Ottilie was overwhelmed with apprehension. Their plan was ridiculous – hardly a plan at all. What had they been thinking? It would never work!

Ottilie couldn't focus, couldn't think. Subtle tremors quaked from her thumbs to her elbows. She missed every shot she attempted, and earned herself a mortifying scolding from Wrangler Voilies when she nearly pierced Igor Thrike's ear with an arrow, and stumbled backwards into a weedy fledge called Dimitri Vosvolder, jabbing him in the gut with the tip of her bow.

When she missed her next shot, hitting Scoot's target rather than her own, Wrangler Voilies bellowed, 'That's it Colter, weapon away. A lap of the shepherd perimeter. Now!'

Scoot let out a loud bark of laughter.

Red-faced and riled up, Wrangler Voilies rounded on Scoot and snapped, '*Three* laps for you, Mr Scoot!'

They marched towards the yard gate. Leo nudged Ottilie as she passed. He was very obviously trying not to smile. 'A little to the left next time,' he whispered, tilting his head in Igor's direction.

Ottilie swallowed her laugh, fearing it would get her into more trouble. She and Scoot broke into a jog, leaving the training yards far behind.

'Are we really doing this tonight?' said Ottilie, gesturing to the darkening sky. She was actually glad to have been sent on a punishment run. The exercise was already calming her nerves.

'If it rains,' said Scoot, deliberately crushing a patch of whiskerweed underfoot.

There was no chance that it wouldn't rain. Thunder rumbled somewhere far off, and a few moments later a fork of lightning lit the sky.

'Witch,' said Scoot.

'What?' Ottilie was distracted, trying to avoid the whiskerweed. She knew her boots were thick enough, but avoiding those needle-sharp spines was an old habit.

'When lightning strikes the ground, means there's a witch buried alive below. There's a song about it,' said Scoot.

'That's not what the lightning song's about ... is it?'

'*Wail, whine, dinnertime*,' he recited.

'What's that got to do with witches?'

'Because witches used to eat their babies.'

'What? No they didn't!'

Scoot shrugged. 'Just what I heard.'

They passed into Floodwood, a damp stretch of forest in the eastern part of the grounds. The world grew very dark and Ottilie felt oddly tense. She shivered, the hairs on the back of her neck raised.

Through fish-scale leaves she could see swollen clouds, black as soot, and something up ahead – a shape between the thin, winding trunks. A person? Ottilie slowed. It was a figure in a hooded cloak, she was sure of it.

'Scoo–' Something rustled by her ear. Ottilie's head snapped to the right. 'Did you hear that?' she hissed, tripping to a halt. She felt light-headed.

'Probably just a shepherd,' said Scoot, stopping beside her.

Gooseflesh spread up her arms, but Ottilie wasn't the tiniest bit cold. Her breath caught in her chest. Out of the corner of her eye she could see a cluster of shiny black legs creeping around the trunk of a viper-spine tree.

It was as if she was having the memory of a headache. She couldn't quite feel it, but she was somehow reliving it. She glanced down at the bronze ring on her thumb.

Scoot cursed and stumbled backwards. 'That is the biggest bleeding spider I've ever seen in my life!'

Trying to stay calm, Ottilie backed away on unsteady legs. 'Scoot,' she breathed, 'I don't think that's a normal spider.'

The shiny eight-legged thing scuttled around the serpentine trunk, prying its hairy front legs off a blotch of lichen and raising its sharp, orange-tipped pincers to the air. It was enormous, twice the size of her hand, but it wasn't the size that bothered her.

'Has it … I think it's got … it's got wings!'

The spider unfurled two translucent wings, something like a cross between a moth's and a bat's wings.

'Yep, wings. And friends!' Scoot released a high-pitched squeak, stumbling backwards again as four more gigantic flying spiders scuttled out from behind the tree.

Heart flipping and falling about like a dying bee, Ottilie crouched down and picked up the two biggest sticks she could reach. She tossed one to Scoot, but he didn't catch it. Scoot blinked and gazed down at the stick, looking as if he were about to be sick.

One of the spiders fluttered its wings, peeling its horrible hairy legs off the bark to hover in thin air.

'I think we need to run,' Ottilie whispered.

Scoot grabbed the stick, and together they bolted. They came off the path and forced their way through the bracken, dodging tussocks of sword grass and slipping on moss-covered logs.

The world was dark. Ottilie could barely see where she was going and all she could hear was the bizarre buzzing and clicking from the monstrous spiders zooming just behind their skulls. It was a horrible sound. Every click seemed to prick at her eardrums; every buzz made her teeth hurt.

Ottilie couldn't stand it anymore; finally, she turned around. There was a spider an inch from her face, its eight legs moving as if it were scuttling through the air. Yelping in surprise, Ottilie tripped sideways, knocking Scoot off his feet.

The pair of them tumbled to the ground. The spider landed on her thigh. The tips of its needle-sharp legs sunk into her flesh as if her muscles were butter. The spider raised its poisonous pincers into the air, ready to bite. Ottilie struck out with the stick, just missing the spider as it withdrew, but hitting her own leg so hard that she cried out in pain.

Blood seeped through eight holes in her trousers but she was well enough to clamber to her feet. Forcing her breath to dive deeper, Ottilie pulled Scoot up beside her.

Another spider shot at her face. Scoot grunted and nearly knocked it out of the air with his stick, missing by half an inch. They were surrounded. Back to back, Ottilie and Scoot raised their sticks and faced the nightmarish swarm.

Ottilie was sure this was going to be the end of her. Her pulse pounded deafeningly in her ears and all she kept thinking was, *They go for the heart*. She took a deep breath, gripping the stick so hard her fingers cramped.

There was a moment of stillness.

A shape leapt out from the shadows; an enormous white feline, covered ear to claw in dark spots. Mid-leap, it caught a spider in its jaws, shook its head and flung it away in a shower of black shiny shards.

Hero, thought Ottilie.

Hero sounded out a series of guttural, grunt-like roars. The leopard's call was answered immediately by a distant howl, followed by another and another. Ottilie shivered, but it was a good shiver. The howling somehow fortified her, replenishing her courage, returning her hope.

In an instant they were surrounded by a pack of snarling dusky wild dogs, their bright amber eyes fixed on the spiders hovering above. The spiders seemed unfazed. Thirty-two legs still danced horribly in the air, and their jarring noise still crawled over her skin, pinching, pricking and scraping as it hummed.

Without warning, the remaining spiders shot at Scoot. Hero leapt again, knocking Scoot sideways, taking one spider in her jaws and striking another out of the air with her paw. It was caught by a shepherd, crushed between its teeth and tossed aside into the dark.

'Get down!' someone yelled from behind.

Ottilie and Scoot threw themselves to the ground.

An arrow shot overhead. It pierced a spider squarely between the pincers. Impaled, and dripping with dark tar-like goo, the spider plummeted down, landing with a crunch by Ottilie's arm.

She didn't recognise the huntsman. He was off-duty, in a daywear uniform, and with the exception of a bow, he wasn't armed. The huntsman seemed to think the danger had passed. He took a step towards them – then suddenly lurched forwards.

'*They'll sneak up behind …*'

It happened in an instant. Mid-fall, his eyes widened and he cried out in pain. Ottilie stepped towards him, hand outstretched, searching for some way to help. In the blink of an eye his shirt tore open over his heart and eight hairy black legs emerged, followed by the great shiny body of the fifth flying spider.

The monster crawled out of the huntsman's chest as if it were creeping out of a hole in a tree. Ottilie's gasp finally escaped her lips as the huntsman hit the ground with a horrible thump.

Scoot got shakily to his feet. There wasn't time to scream or cry or vomit. The spider was still lingering in the dark, waiting to strike again. It flew at Ottilie. She dove out of the way, scraping her already injured leg against the sharp remains of one of the dead spiders. The shepherds were growling, hackles raised. Hero was bent low, poised to leap.

Ottilie could hear more people approaching. The spider had disappeared, but she knew better than to think herself safe. She sensed motion behind Scoot.

'Scoot, move!' she bellowed.

Scoot threw himself back onto the ground. A dagger flew out of nowhere, colliding with the spider in the exact spot where Scoot had been standing. It was not enough to pierce the shiny black armour, but one of its thin wings was crushed by the blow.

It was Leo – he had thrown the dagger. Igor was just ahead of him. The spider writhed and wriggled in the air, losing height. Igor lashed out, slicing it clean in half with a cutlass.

Leo and Igor looked down at the fallen huntsman, lying in a twisted lump upon the ground.

'It's Chris Crow,' said Igor, utterly calm.

Leo didn't respond.

'Idiot,' said Igor, rolling his eyes. 'Imagine getting taken by a yicker. I can't believe I only get two points for felling a dredretch that just took out a fourth-tier huntsman. Pathetic.'

For just that moment Ottilie's head cleared, the numbing clouds of shock pulled back, and she was able to feel true revulsion. It wasn't only Igor's indifference that disgusted her, or his cruel attitude. It was that *thing*, that dredretch, that foul, unnatural monster that had brutally, senselessly slaughtered the brave boy who had just saved their lives. She didn't think she had ever felt anything so much like hatred in her life.

Leo looked like he was about to punch Igor, but before he could, a group of huntsmen and wranglers appeared. Jaw clenched, Leo moved over to the fallen huntsman and gently rolled him into a more dignified position, resting his hand over the gaping hole as if that might somehow mend the damage.

Despite his harsh words, Igor had turned pale. He was looking anywhere but at the fallen huntsman. Ottilie, on the other hand, couldn't look away. Beside her, Scoot lurched onto all fours and vomited. Less than a minute later, Ottilie did the same.

16

A Change of Heart

It was an ancient Uskler belief that if a person was laid on a funeral pyre without their heart, they could not pass on as they should. The sleeper wouldn't come for their soul, and they would be pulled down to the underworld to exist eternally among the dark creatures that dwelt there.

Mr Parch said it wasn't true. He said it was simply a story, and that no human being could pass down to the underworld. A person couldn't descend those stairs unless they had spent their entire life doing truly evil things, and never felt the least bit sorry, so that by the time they died, their heart was so malformed it could no longer be recognised as human.

Whether it was believed or not, people still acknowledged the tradition, and if someone passed away without their heart intact, great pains were taken to recover and restore it. Such was the case for the heart of Christopher Crow.

'This was a tragic accident,' said Captain Lyre, his candlelit face a mask of grim calm.

The fledges were gathered in the largest lounge in their corridor. It was a stark room, with a single square hearth and a shabby tapestry depicting a witch hunt. The yickers had attacked only hours before and Captain Lyre had called an assembly to offer some explanation.

Ottilie was uneasy. For the first time, she felt it might be wrong to leave the Narroway. But how could she stay? Just sitting in this lounge was making her nervous. She was getting far more attention than she liked. What with the bruising and bandages there was no hiding the fact that she and Scoot had been the two fledges involved.

They had been treated for their cuts and scrapes in the infirmary. The young assisting physicians, or patchies as they were called, dabbed leatherwood honey on the puncture wounds on Ottilie's lower thigh. Sitting quietly, Ottilie overheard them muttering that the huntsmen were still trying to track down the scraps of Christopher Crow's heart so that he might be burned with as much of it as possible the following day.

The conversation had been so disturbing that Ottilie had barely felt anxious as they cut her already torn trousers, splitting them halfway up her thigh. Only just in time did she think to slump and let her hands rest in the space between her legs, so that the patchies would not notice anything suspicious about her body.

'It is very important that you understand this sort of thing does not happen here in the Narroway, not within our three stations' walls,' said Captain Lyre. 'Yickers cannot fly higher than the boundary walls. They were constructed at a height specifically calculated to keep the smaller flying dredretches out. And nothing larger will ever make it past our guards undetected.'

Larger? Ottilie squeezed her eyes closed. She had come into contact with two types of dredretches now; jivvies and yickers. Both were horrifying and, by all accounts, small. The thought that there were bigger monsters out there, lurking beyond the boundary walls, should have frightened her, but a peculiar emotion was stifling the fear – a mix of outrage and fury. Ottilie was angry at the dredretches, furious that they existed.

'These yickers came through a fracture at the base of the wall that should have been discovered and mended long before now,' Captain Lyre continued, 'and were it not for the disturbance of the coming storm, our bone singers would have sensed the dredretch presence immediately.

'This was a rare mishap that has resulted in tragedy. Christopher was an excellent huntsman and he gave his life for a noble cause. This is a very dangerous job, I won't deny it, but you were chosen for your exceptional potential and we train you very well. It is horribly unfortunate that this occurred so early in your time with us, but perhaps it has helped you to understand how important it is that we continue our fight against the dredretches in the hope of not only keeping the Usklers safe from this scourge, but one day eradicating these monsters all together.'

'He's worried we've been spooked,' said Preddy, after Captain Lyre had left.

'We? You didn't have those things flying at your face. It's me and Ott that's been spooked,' said Scoot.

They were huddled in a corner of the lounge. Ottilie chose a stiff, orange-cushioned armchair facing away from the rest of the room. She was sick and tired of the staring, and worried that if so many of them kept looking, one of them might somehow figure out she was a girl.

'Wish they'd all go to bed,' hissed Scoot, glaring at a group nearby.

'*We* should really go to bed,' said Preddy, brushing his fair hair out of his eyes and covering a yawn.

Prompted by Preddy, Gully yawned loudly – not bothering to cover his mouth. Ottilie gazed at him. In that moment he seemed very young, and it was nearly enough to make her keep her mouth shut – but not quite.

'The thing is,' said Ottilie, 'He's right.'

'Who is?' said Gully, blinking sleepily.

'Captain Lyre. It actually sort of *has* helped me understand.'

'What are you saying, Ott?' said Scoot, his jaw twitching.

'We're too stubborn, you and me,' said Ottilie, looking Scoot directly in the eye. 'We were so angry about being brought here in the first place, we couldn't see the bigger picture.'

'You can't be saying you've changed your mind!' he hissed. 'You can't want to stick around here after seeing that ranky thing crawl out of his ribs?'

'I've got to say, I'm not so keen on going out there untrained, and I didn't even see it happen,' said Preddy. 'And what is *ranky?*'

'That's part of it,' said Ottilie. 'We were crazy to think we could handle ourselves out there alone. Skip said so, I just didn't want to listen.'

Scoot stuck his jaw out, glaring. He looked as if he were about to bite her head off, but he didn't speak.

'But that's not the main point,' said Ottilie. 'If it was just that, then I'd say let's stay and let them train us, then make a break for it when we think we've got a fighting chance.'

'But you're not saying that?' said Gully, watching her closely.

'No. Seeing those things, seeing what it did to him … for no reason … it just … it's not right.' Ottilie was convincing herself as she spoke. She didn't want to feel this way, but she did. She was speaking a truth from deep down – something she could no longer ignore. 'I think, even though the pickings and everything are so wrong … I think the work needs doing, and I want to help.'

'You want to stay here and hunt those things?' said Scoot. 'You're bonkers, Colter.'

It was mad. She knew it was mad, but something had changed in her that day. Her priorities had shifted. Ottilie couldn't think about the fact that she was unwelcome. She couldn't think about going home, or even taking Gully home. She wanted to learn to defend herself, to be strong, and to beat back these monsters that had no place in her world.

'We'd have to travel through the Narroway to escape … so we'd be facing them either way,' said Preddy, warming to the idea. 'At least this way we're choosing to hunt them, instead of them hunting us.'

'And we're hunting them to keep people safe, instead of fighting them off to save our own skins,' said Gully, picking at a loose thread in his cushion.

'So you agree then?' said Scoot to Gully.

'Think so,' said Gully, looking up.

'Skip said to me, you can't just reset things to the way they should have been – sometimes you have to adapt,' said Ottilie. 'We were upset because they didn't give us a choice to come here, but we can make it our choice to stay. I know we could have escaped … I really believe we could have after a few months of training.'

'Course we could have!' said Scoot.

'And knowing that means it's our choice to stay or go, really. So I'm making the decision right now that I want to hunt dredretches.'

'Me too,' said Gully.

Preddy nodded.

They all looked at Scoot.

'Oh all right,' he grumbled. 'But if I end up having my heart pecked out by a bloody jivvie in a week and a half you're going to be really sorry you ever made that rousing speech, Ott Colter.'

Later that night, when Preddy and Scoot were snoring, Gully crept onto Ottilie's bed. A sliver of moonlight framed the window shutters, offering a shred of visibility in the blackness.

'Can't you just tell them?' he whispered. 'Now that we're staying …' his tone was eager. 'Why don't you just tell them you're a girl.'

Ottilie grimaced. 'Because I can't. They'd make me leave ... or worse.' She felt the covers move as Gully scrunched them between his fists.

'How do you know?' His whisper was whiny with impatience.

'Because I do ... because ... you've heard them, they don't think girls can hunt, or should be allowed to, or both. And don't forget, they didn't pick me in the first place. It's not just that I'm a girl. I was never meant to be here.'

'But you're the same as the rest of us in training. You're better at shooting than me!' He moved to slap the mattress, but Ottilie grabbed his shoulders.

'Gully, we can't talk about this here – not again. Someone could hear,' she hissed. 'No-one can know, not even Preddy or Scoot. The more people that know, the more likely it is that someone – any of us – could slip up. Do you understand?'

'No,' he said sullenly. 'I don't.'

'Are you all right with what I said? That we're staying ... do you want to?'

Gully fidgeted, and didn't answer. 'Do you think Freddie's noticed? Do you think she cares?' he said.

Out of habit, Ottilie glanced around the room before taking his hand in hers. 'Of course she does.'

His shoulders slumped. Ottilie knew he didn't believe her. She wasn't sure she believed herself.

'I do want to stay,' he said eventually. 'I like learning this stuff … I want to be good at it. I want to be a huntsman.'

'Me too,' said Ottilie. It was the first time she had properly admitted it to herself. She wanted to be one of them. She wanted it more than anything.

⬦ 17 ⬦

Stage Fright

Ottilie couldn't believe how quickly the days flew by. Suddenly there were only four days until the trials. Four days left to train. Four days until she would be locked in an arena with an entire flock of what Captain Lyre had called death crows.

How she fared against these monsters would determine her guardian pairing and her permanent station. There was only a one-in-three chance that Ottilie and Gully would remain together. Ottilie knew it, but there was nothing she could do about it, so for now, for the sake of giving herself the best chance of surviving the trials, she buried the thought.

As if things weren't bad enough, Wrangler Morse announced that the trials would run over four days – one day for each squad. Their squad was last and they would be confined to their corridor until the final day to prevent them from copying the earlier fledges' tactics.

'So, that means three long days of waiting, but lots of time to ready your head,' said Wrangler Morse, hitching an unconvincing smile onto his red-bearded face. He cleared his throat loudly. 'Right, let's get to work.'

He had replaced their usual targets with jivvie-sized grain bags that hung from a rope. They were grey, to match the wall, which made them much harder to see, let alone hit, and on a breezy day they shifted a little, creating an introductory moving target. Ottilie's aim had improved considerably, and despite the increase in difficulty she almost always nicked the edge at least, with the majority of her shots creeping towards the centre.

Wrangler Voilies informed them that, despite the fact they had been shifted back three times, they were still standing pitifully close to their targets. Ottilie didn't care. Every time her arrow hit the bag, her confidence grew. She was determined to be good at this – to be good at anything. She longed to be as good as Preddy, who was retrieving his arrow from the centre of his bag.

'Don't look so smug, Preddy. Just try to beat me with a cutlass!' said Gully.

Gully was a natural with a blade, and although the bow would be more effective during the trials, Ottilie had seen how a cutlass could be used against a flying dredretch. She was terrible with her cutlass. Her wrists were stiff, elbows awkward, fingers clumsy, and she was showing very little sign of improvement. Her only comfort was that Preddy was worse.

'My father always said it was vulgar to move close to make the kill. He didn't like spears either,' said Preddy.

'You're vulgar,' said Scoot, grouchily collecting his arrow from the grain bag three rows over from his own.

'All right! Quiet!' called Wrangler Voilies. 'Well, generally I am pleased. Most of you are improving at a reasonable pace, with a few notable exceptions.' His gaze fell upon Scoot.

'I'm good at the cutlass,' muttered Scoot. 'Gulliver can't shoot either!'

'What was that, Mr Scoot?'

'Nothing,' said Scoot.

'I can shoot better than you can,' whispered Gully.

'Obviously, in the trials your targets will be much more difficult to hit, as they will not only be moving, but most likely plummeting towards your eyeballs.'

Ottilie blinked.

'So, onto moving targets. Bacon here is going to throw these balls into the air. Do not shoot him. Do you understand me?'

Bacon was one of the three select elite helping with their training that day. He wore a Fiory uniform, with a bronze pin in the shape of a horse. Ottilie wondered what the pins were for. Leo's was a raptor, Ned's a wolf,

158

Bacon's a horse ... she had noticed them before, but couldn't recall anyone explaining their purpose.

'Shooting Bacon is an extremely undesirable outcome,' continued Wrangler Voilies. 'If you shoot him I will be very displeased.'

Ottilie grinned and Scoot snorted loudly.

'Mr Scoot.'

'Sorry Voilies – Wrangler Voilies – sir.'

'Form a line and let's begin.'

Preddy, of course, hit the falling ball with ease. Scoot missed by a mile, as did Gully. When Ottilie stepped up to the mark she was confident that she would at least come close. But as she stood there, all eyes upon her, her heart started to thump hard and fast. She felt the colour rising in her cheeks. Her focus shifted. Her vision blurred. The pressure of everyone watching was too much, and the image of a great hairy black spider crawling out of Christopher Crow's chest flickered before her eyes.

Bacon threw the ball into the air, and Ottilie braced, waiting to catch it on the fall. Trying to concentrate on the shot, and not on her glowing face and racing heart, she bit her lip. Three ... two ... one ...

She missed – by a lot. Somehow she had misjudged the speed of the fall. Her arrow was too late and by the time it shot over Bacon's head the ball had almost reached the ground.

'Disappointing, Mr Colter,' said Wrangler Voilies.

'You'll get her next time, Ott,' said Wrangler Morse, ruffling her hair. 'Good aim. Just the timing.'

Ottilie did not *get her next time*. In fact, she didn't hit the ball once. It was not only disheartening – it was terrifying. What was she going to do in the trials? If stage fright was her problem, she was doomed. Wrangler Voilies had told them that they would have an audience, and a large one at that. The fledgling trials were attended by not only the select elite and the Fiory wranglers, but the cardinal conductor from each station, all three Fiory directors, and any Fiory huntsmen not on duty. There would be hundreds of eyes upon her and, as she'd just learnt, an audience was crippling. What would she do if she couldn't shoot? At least Gully could use his cutlass, and Scoot was great with a slingshot. If she couldn't stop the jivvies with her bow she would be torn to pieces.

'I'll be watching too,' said Skip, later that night.

'What! The sculkies come?'

'Oh sure, a lot of the custodians do. Some of us will be there waiting on the conductors and directors, and they usually let the rest watch from the back. Fiory hasn't hosted the trials in two years. I'll be watching!'

Ottilie flopped down on the blue tiles edging the bath, and buried her face in her hands.

'You'll be fine. You're obviously good under pressure.'

'I'm not! That's the problem!' Ottilie's shrill voice rang high and sharp in the cavernous springs. She flinched and glanced at the door.

'I mean real pressure. A flock of real live jivvies will snap you out of it, you'll see.'

'It better,' said Ottilie, gnawing at her fingernails. 'Otherwise I'm dead.'

'No more talk of leaving then?'

Ottilie shook her head. It was true. Getting home wasn't her goal anymore. When she pictured the Swamp Hollows, she saw it crawling with dredretches, and herself, untrained, powerless to stop them. She wanted to learn how to defend herself, how to keep them from hurting people.

Of course this meant she would have to keep pretending to be a boy. It was becoming a second skin. She didn't have to think about it too much. It was just there – but her anxiety about being uncovered never fully went away.

Ottilie still caught the dark-haired sculkie and her friend giving her odd looks, but she got the sense that this was relatively normal behaviour for them. Even so, she was sure they glanced in her direction far too often, and Ottilie had taken to avoiding them when she could manage it.

'Good,' said Skip, tugging Ottilie away from her thoughts. 'I never wanted you to go. And not just because you'd be dead beyond that wall without a bit more training.'

'Thanks, Skip.'

'It's nice having a friend here, Ottilie Colter. I'd be awfully sad if you got eaten.'

'I might get eaten in a week anyway.'

'Of course you won't,' said Skip, but Ottilie was sure she detected a hint of uncertainty in her tone. How many of these huntsmen had Skip seen get hurt? Captain Lyre said what had happened to Christopher Crow was rare. Was that true? Or was he just lying to keep them feeling secure?

'You haven't seen me out there,' said Ottilie. 'I can't focus, and if I'm not worrying about myself then I'm worrying about Gully!'

'Oh, I wouldn't worry about Gully. He's younger, isn't he? Only just eleven? They only ever take them that young if they think they're going to be exceptional.'

'I thought they chose boys because they were lonely, or had no proper families?'

'They do still pick a certain personality type; fearless, adventurous, athletic, that sort of thing. Reckless, mostly,' said Skip. 'You know that smug ginger?'

'Leo Darby?'

'They took him from a filthy rich family over on All Kings' Hill, just snatched him off the street. There were probably plenty of people out looking for him, but they can afford to do that once in a while, as long as it's not too often.'

'Why did they want him so much?'

'Same reasons they must have wanted Gully. Darby was the same age too. He was the only one that young I ever saw come in, until your brother. And it paid off, I suppose. He's a champion two years running, and last year, when he was a second tier, he actually scored higher than the champion of the third tier. All the wranglers love him, you must have noticed.'

'What about the one that's always with Leo? Ned, or, what is it, Eddy – Edwin Skovey?'

Skip shook her head. 'Don't know much about him. They're good friends, the two of them, but people talk about Leo Darby all the time, that's why I know so much. You'll know more than me soon enough,' she said. 'You better get paired with a Fiory – I don't want you moving stations! Plus you're going to need me around. We'll have to cut your hair soon. You should probably keep it as short as possible, else they might start noticing your girly nose. Actually,' Skip narrowed her eyes and grabbed a chunk of Ottilie's hair, 'we should really cut it now. What did your friend Bill hack this off with, a sharp rock?'

Ottilie laughed. 'No, a knife, and it was dark.'

'That's exactly what it looks like. It looks awful! Lucky they know you're from the Swamp Hollows, otherwise you'd have a bit of explaining to do. Tell you what, I'll bring scissors next time and we'll cut it nice and neat for the trials.'

Ottilie stomach lurched. The last thing she wanted to think about were the fledgling trials.

18

The Fledgling Trials

'Big day, boys!'

Captain Lyre was back. Tapping his cane on the door, he whistled a lively tune until they roused.

'Up, up, up! It's my second-favourite day of the year – for the fourth day in a row … I want you dressed and breakfasted before that bell tolls.'

'What is he doing here?' grumbled Gully, as Captain Lyre continued to whistle down the corridor.

'It's his second-favourite day of the year,' mumbled Ottilie with her face pressed into her pillow, 'for the fourth day in a – agh!' Something soft hit the back of her head. She swatted her arm at the air but didn't roll over. 'I know that was you, Scoot,' she mumbled.

Scoot cackled.

They had gone a bit stir-crazy after three days confined to their corridor, watching the other squads head off for their trials and never come back.

'Just practicing my aim, Ott.'

'Practice on Preddy!'

Another something hit Ottilie's head. She rolled over, grabbed the knotted pair of underpants that she hoped were clean, and threw them across the room. They hit Scoot square in the face. Gully and Preddy laughed loudly and Scoot hurtled across the room, tackling Ottilie off the bed and onto the floor.

'Get off me, you mongrel!' she laughed, momentarily forgetting it was a dangerous position to be in. Sense quickly caught up with her. Passing it off as part of the game, Ottilie shoved him away. She was just about to try to tie him up with a pair of trousers when there was a soft knock at the door. Their breakfast had arrived.

Skip was first in, carrying three trays at once, with one on her head so she could open the door. She made straight for the back of the room.

'Thanks,' said Gully, as she placed a tray at the end of his bed.

Ottilie smiled secretly to herself and Skip shot her the tiniest of winks.

'Thank you,' said Ottilie.

'My pleasure,' said Skip. 'Good luck today.'

Heat spread across Ottilie's chest, creeping up her neck. This was it. The wait was over. It was trial day.

The fledges were shown in while the stands were still empty. Their arena was an enclosed amphitheatre. Ottilie noted the thin-barred cage encircling the stands, to protect the spectators from the dredretches. She'd heard this space was sometimes used for training with captive dredretches, and she assumed that in those instances, the wranglers sat safely behind the cage.

'Here,' said Captain Lyre, 'is where the jivvies will be released.'

There were two black marble blocks a bit taller than Ottilie's knees, one towards the south and the other towards the north. Ottilie noted the animal carvings that covered the entire surface of both blocks. She had seen similar carvings on many of the Fiory doors and wondered if they were depictions of the old gods. Considering she kept coming across the same image of an ordinary-looking duck, she wasn't entirely sure about that.

'These both open to the burrows below,' said Captain Lyre. 'The jivvies will be released from one of them, but you won't know which one.'

Ottilie had a closer look. She noted the subtle split down the middle of each block. They were doors; two dense, very heavy doors.

She swallowed.

'We're going to draw numbers out of this pail to determine your trialling order. And don't be nervous if you get number one! Believe me, better one than twenty-one. Your score will be determined by the bone singers and will appear on that board over there immediately after your trial.' He pointed to a square panel of white marble above three throne-like chairs.

Ottilie was confused. Skip had said the bone singers dealt with felled dredretches. Why were they in charge of scoring?

'There will be no argument about your scores. The bone singers know a thing or two about dead dredretches and you will be scored in the same manner that every huntsman is scored throughout the course of the year. All right, line up now, and one at a time draw your number from the pail.'

Of her friends, Preddy was first in line. He drew number fourteen. Next was Scoot. Twelve. Then came Gully. Four. Ottilie slipped her sweaty hand into the pail. She didn't know what she wanted. Somewhere towards the beginning she supposed, to get it over and done with. Her fingers closed around a small, smooth cube and, holding her breath, she drew it out.

Twenty.

'At least you're not last,' whispered Gully.

'No, second to last is much better,' said Ottilie.

It was going to be a very long day.

There was no way of knowing how much time had passed. The usual bells were silenced, so as not to distract a fledge during his trial. Ottilie's only method of keeping time was watching the waiting room empty little by little as the fledges moved out to face their fates.

The muffled whistling and applause seemed very far away and Ottilie grew tired and tense with boredom. It was only when the room had emptied to four people that the boredom lifted, leaving anxiety to govern her mind. Gully was long gone, as were Preddy and Scoot. There was no way to know how they had done. The noise from the amphitheatre sounded much the same for each fledge.

By the time she was left with only two boys, Ottilie began to panic. She focused on her breathing.

In and out.

In and out.

In and out.

It didn't seem to help. It also didn't help that one of the boys, the weedy Dimitri Vosvolder, kept staring at her. He had a pinched face with large front teeth. His pouty mouth quirked up at the sides as he watched her struggle to stay calm. She felt a flicker of rage spark beneath her nerves and turned her back to him. She was already shaking, and she knew it was only going to get worse if she let herself feel angry.

Only minutes later, Ottilie watched with eyes the size of dustplums as Dimitri Vosvolder was led from the room by a huntsman. This was it. She was next. She clung to her bow with slippery palms and stood, unmoving, by the door. Time flew. It felt like less than a minute before the huntsman returned to lead her into the arena.

'Ready?' he said.

Ottilie nodded, jaw clenched. Her teeth ground together as the pair of them marched down the passageway to a small metal door. The huntsman knocked once and a single knock sounded in return from the other side. The huntsman lifted the iron latch and Ottilie passed through.

The weary crowd clapped politely as she stepped out into the arena. Ottilie was too anxious to single anyone out, but she did note the six or so huntsmen standing with bows at the ready around the edges of the arena. They were behind the cage with the spectators. Were they there to protect the crowd if a jivvie got loose?

Wrangler Voilies had said the jivvies would be released at the sound of the gong, but she didn't know how long she would have before that. Ottilie fingered the bronze ring on her thumb. Suppose it fell off and she was left unprotected? She closed her eyes and shook her head to clear it.

Ottilie could feel hundreds of eyes upon her. Face reddening, she thought fast. She would move into the centre so as not to get cornered. She ordered her shaky feet to walk and, after a breath or two, they did.

She remembered Wrangler Morse's words from a training session a bit over a week ago: 'Jivvies are blind. They rely on sound and movement to navigate, so you'll be at an advantage. The crowd will confuse them.'

She would limit her movements. Once that gong sounded, Ottilie would not move. At least she could trust her body to freeze. Quickly she nocked an arrow. Her palm was sweaty but it did not slide on the grip. 'You're fine,' she whispered.

The gong sounded. The block to her left split down the centre and slid apart with a scrape, leaving a wide gap between the two halves. There was a terrible whooshing and a chorus of high-ringing *caws* as a swirling black cloud of jivvies swooped up into the arena.

The crowd made a great deal of noise. Ottilie wondered for a moment if it was true excitement or if they were just trying to help by distracting the jivvies. If the latter was the case, it was working. The flock of jivvies flew in a circle around the edge of the cage, quickly discerning their surroundings.

She had to act fast, before they had a chance to fully know the space, but there were too many! The moment she aimed for one, the rest would be upon her.

Ottilie made a snap decision.

She stood frozen. She barely breathed. Just as the jivvies circled back to face her, Ottilie lowered her bow, lifted her fingers to her lips, and released an ear-splitting whistle.

The jivvies screeched in response, the entire flock rolling to face her. Ottilie froze, letting them focus. Just as the flock dived, Ottilie spun on the spot, took two long running strides and in one scrambling leap threw herself behind one of the big black blocks. She curled herself into the smallest ball she could manage and listened to the sick crunch of little bones meeting solid marble.

One jivvie missed the trap and shot right past. Ottilie clambered up to stand upon the block. She was just about to aim for the bird when she caught sight of another survivor. An injured jivvie bounced off the marble and spiralled into the air. The other jivvie circled back and raced towards her. Ottilie ducked. It missed her by a breath. Hot air ruffled her hair as it shot overhead. The injured jivvie was regaining its control – still unsteady in the air, it flew towards her, its wing beat uneven. Ottilie took aim and fired. Her arrow caught it squarely in the breast and it fell to the ground with a thump.

Ottilie spun to face the other jivvie and, just as she turned, it was knocked out of the air half an inch from her nose. One of the huntsmen had shot it down – mere seconds before it could pierce her skull.

Ottilie froze, panting and shocked. Tears welled in her eyes. That thing had nearly had her. One second later and it would have skewered her face. It took a moment for her mind to settle and her tears to withdraw.

She gazed around and saw that three of the six huntsmen had opened doors around the arena, ready to shoot that last jivvie down. So that was why they were there – not to protect the crowd, but to step in to save a fledge in danger. She couldn't be sure which of them had done the deed, but she was grateful beyond belief.

The sounds of the amphitheatre slowly filtered back in. The crowd was on its feet; people were going wild. How they were so excited after watching eighty-five other fledges over four days she did not know.

Ottilie looked down, avoiding all the eyes upon her, and that was when she noticed the bones. She gazed at the pile of felled dredretches. It was as if their flesh had melted away. A dark, sticky substance clung to their bones like bloody tar. Withered feathers stuck out here and there, and dark vapour spiralled from the mess like black spirits breaking free.

It was impossible to be sorry for her part in their death. These things weren't animals; they weren't living creatures of soft flesh and red blood. They were malice solidified, death in bestial form. Even with the bronze ring protecting her, Ottilie could sense it. She could smell it. The vapour trailing from their bent feathers and sticky bones conjured sense-memories of pain and fear. What were these unnatural beasts? What evil had invited them into the living world?

An image of a hooded figure swam to the forefront of her mind. What memory was this? Something from a nightmare? She couldn't remember. Feeling sick, Ottilie tore her eyes away from the bones. Unsure of what to do next, she turned towards the throne-like chairs. Upon them sat three elderly men; the cardinal conductors of the Narroway Hunt. Above their heads was the white marble scoreboard; scratched into the surface, as if carved by a ghost, there appeared a thick, midnight-blue number nine.

A huntsman appeared beside her and directed her to the edge of the arena. Her legs were shaking but she resisted the urge to grab his arm for support. He opened a door and nudged her through. Ottilie climbed a steep staircase and joined her fellow fledges in the stands. She received many congratulations and pats on the back but was still too shaken to distinguish individuals. She sat down on the bench and stared straight ahead.

Somebody gripped her arm from behind. She turned. It was Gully, and he was grinning from ear to ear.

'You got the most!' he said.

'What?'

'I went fourth. I've seen almost everyone. No-one's getting *nines*. You got the most!'

19

Guardians

'I can't believe they gave you a nine!' said Scoot. 'You only actually hit one.'

Ottilie couldn't believe it either. No-one else had got a nine. They were finally allowed to talk to the other fledges and word spread fast that little Ott Colter from the Swamp Hollows had outscored everyone by at least four points.

'Ha! Jealous, Scoot?' said Gully.

'No. I'm very happy with my three, thank you very much. Just wish I'd dived behind that block instead of facing them like a man. Then I'd have a ten,' said Scoot.

'I suppose he's just cleverer than you, Scoot,' said Preddy.

A drowsy grin spread across Ottilie's face as she sat back and let them argue. All she could feel was relief and utter exhaustion; the anxiety leading up to her trial had really taken its toll.

'Shut up, Preddy. Nice *two*, by the way,' snapped Scoot.

'Five,' said Preddy.

'No, Gulliver got five,' said Scoot.

'I got four,' said Gully, flashing four fingers.

'Don't worry, plenty of people got less than three,' said Preddy earnestly.

'That wasn't why I – shut up, Preddy.'

Ottilie had heard all about Scoot's trial. He had actually done very well – using a slingshot to scatter the jivvies, then knocking them back one by one with his club.

The fledges had been led out of the stands and back into the waiting room. Beyond the windows, the sky was dark and an ocean of starlit cloud whirled above the treetops.

'How long do you suppose it will take them to decide? Do you think they'll tell us about our guardians tonight?' said Ottilie.

'It sounded like they want to partner us up as soon as possible,' said Preddy.

'Is it just based on our scores?' said Scoot.

'Don't know,' said Gully.

'I guess we'll see,' said Ottilie. For the first time, she was feeling excited about being assigned a guardian – someone to focus on teaching only her.

There was a loud knock at the door, then Captain Lyre flung it open.

'Well done boys! Solid efforts all round. What a show! Now, I'm sure you're about ready to drop –'

Ottilie yawned loudly. She had quickly learned that bodily functions like coughing, sneezing, and yawning drew less attention if their full power was unleashed. Scoot was constantly mocking Preddy for his discreet sneezes, and scoffing at the way he covered his mouth when he yawned. Ottilie had never been taught to cover her mouth anyway, but she was making an effort to amplify the volume.

'– so it's off to bed with you. We'll have your meals sent up immediately, and I want you all to get a good night's sleep. Big day tomorrow. My third-favourite day!'

'What do you suppose his first-favourite day is?' muttered Gully.

'We need to get our select elite back to their stations as soon as we can,' said Captain Lyre. 'We've been holding them captive for a month now, and Richter and Arko want their boys back. So, we're going to be up all night deliberating, and tomorrow at noon we'll let you know your pairings,' Captain Lyre continued. 'Which means that for some of you, this will be your last night at Fort Fiory.'

Ottilie frowned. She had been trying hard not to think about the fact that she and Gully might be sent to different stations. What could she do about it? Even if she changed her mind about making a run for it, she knew there was no chance of surviving while they were so ill-equipped to deal with the dredretches.

Ottilie trudged up to the bedchamber in a weary daze. Gully was quiet and she knew he was wondering if he was about to be separated from his sister yet again.

The next day, they gathered in the Moon Court, a circular courtyard at the heart of Fort Fiory. Sitting upon three thrones were the most important men in the Narroway, the cardinal conductors of each station – Fiory, Arko and Richter. Ottilie also saw several wranglers sitting behind Captain Lyre and his fellow Fiory directors.

Sculkies lined the walls, their hair braided specially for the occasion. The select elite sat at the front of the curving rows of huntsmen, and Ottilie noted the difference in the colours they wore – green and grey for Arko, and green and brown for Richter. Those in the centre wore green and black, identical to the other Fiory huntsmen filling the courtyard.

The bells tolled twelve and without so much as a word from the front, the courtyard fell silent. Ottilie expected the Fiory cardinal conductor to speak, but it was Captain Lyre who leapt to his feet.

'Welcome all to this most marvellous of occasions.' Cane clicking on the stone paving, he came to stand beside the thrones. 'My dear fledges. For many of you this will be goodbye from us here at Fiory. You will have a new adventure to embark upon, a new fort to explore, and new friends to make. I know you're all anxious to find out, and we do have a lot of names to get through, so I'll hop right to it.' He whipped a long scroll of parchment from behind his back. 'I am going to move alphabetically according to the surname of the guardian. When I announce your pairing please come forward to meet your guardian and receive your station uniform. Let us begin.' He tapped his cane and a line of sculkies stepped away from the wall, holding piles of folded uniforms.

'Banjo Adler of Arko, with fledge Petri Horn.'

Petri Horn moved forwards and shook Banjo Adler's hand. He received his folded green-and-grey uniform from a sculkie and took his seat at the fledgling table.

'Bayo Amadory of Fiory, with fledge Branter Scoot.'

Ottilie's stomach flipped. Scoot prowled over on his bandy legs and shook Bayo Amadory's hand.

So Scoot was staying at Fiory. He and Skip were both at Fiory. As Captain Lyre flew through the names, moving from B to C to D, Ottilie wondered if it was it too much to hope that she, Gully, and Preddy could also stay.

'Vincent Dane of Richter, with fledge Holden Hervey.'

Holden Hervey took his seat.

'Leonard Darby of Fiory, with fledge Ott Colter.'

Ottilie felt like she had lost the feeling in her face. She was staying at Fiory. She would be with Skip and Scoot. Gully gave her a little nudge. Ottilie stumbled forwards. She looked up at Leo Darby and shook his rough hand. Her mind was too muddled to make much sense of his reaction to the pairing.

In a daze, she took the uniform presented to her by the dark-haired sculkie with the strange, bright eyes. For the briefest moment, the girl's finger brushed Ottilie's hand and an image flashed in her mind of serpentine trunks, orange-tipped pincers, and a shadow, like a hooded figure in the dark.

Ottilie blinked and it was gone. She shook her head and hurried over to a seat at the fledgling table. It wasn't the first time she had found herself remembering that horrible day. And now really wasn't the time to dwell on it.

Captain Lyre moved further down the alphabet, but neither Gully nor Preddy were called. The suspense was unbearable. What was she going to do if Gully was sent away? She had come here for him, come to get him.

He couldn't leave Fiory, not before they'd even had a chance to figure out some sort of plan for the future. What was she doing here, being paired with an elite, pretending to be a boy? This was mad. She was mad. Dark clouds of panic were closing in, only to be cleared by the name, 'Noel Preddy.'

Ottilie snapped out of it.

Captain Lyre had called for Preddy. She looked up. Who had he been paired with? Where was he going? She didn't recognise the huntsman who shook his hand but she could see his uniform was green and brown.

Richter.

Ottilie's breath caught in her throat. Preddy settled into a seat beside her and Scoot. None of them spoke. Scoot glared at the green-and-brown uniform in Preddy's hands. Ottilie couldn't dwell on it. She was too busy worrying the same thing would happen to Gully.

'Porter Quoll of Richter, with fledge Andre Rhodes.'

There were only a handful of fledges left. Ottilie couldn't take it much longer.

'Bertram Rittaker of Arko, with fledge Murphy Graves.'

She crossed her fingers under the table.

'Rudolph Sacker of Fiory, with fledge Klaus Crowder.'

Gully looked nervous. Ottilie wanted to catch his eye but he didn't look over to her.

'Bacon Skitter of Fiory, with fledge Rodney Wolfe.'

'Did you know his first name was Bacon?' said Scoot. Ottilie didn't respond.

'I thought it was his family name. Whose first name is Bacon? Who calls their son Bacon?'

Ottilie was staring so hard at the side of Gully's head, she wondered if he could feel it.

'Edwin Skovey of Fiory, with fledge Gulliver Colter.'

Ottilie's face broke into a wide grin. She could have laughed out loud.

Scoot actually did. 'Yes!' he said.

Ottilie didn't speak. She was so relieved she could have cried. Miraculously, she didn't; instead, she gripped Gully's arm in excitement and glanced apologetically at Preddy.

'Igor Thrike of Fiory, with fledge Dimitri Vosvolder.'

Captain Lyre went on and on, but Ottilie didn't hear another name after that. Nothing could top that moment for her – the moment Gully had been paired with Ned. Not the music played by the strange figures in blue hats and robes, or the fizzing flagons of apple cider that sculkies offered on trays, or the mountains of fruit and cakes that followed.

As the festivities wore on, several Fiory huntsmen trickled out of the courtyard. Ottilie supposed they were called to hunt.

'Don't get used to this.' It was Leo.

'To what?' said Ottilie.

'All this.' He grinned and gestured to the courtyard. 'Now the hard work really begins. You're mine tomorrow, see you at dawn.' He thumped her on the arm and Ottilie was too slow to cover her flinch. Leo made a face, like a mix of mirth and disgust, and strode away without another word.

'What do you suppose he meant by that?' said Preddy.

Ottilie shrugged, but she felt uneasy. She had been so relieved to be staying at Fiory that she hadn't really considered her pairing. Truth be told, she wasn't overly excited at the prospect of working with Leo. He was smug and superior, and had so far seemed more interested in showing off than being a good teacher.

'I'm afraid the time has come to say goodbye,' said Captain Lyre, marching into the centre of the courtyard. 'Those of you heading to Fort Arko and Fort Richter, please find your guardian and follow their instructions, because we're finished with you here.' He saluted theatrically. 'Safe journey, boys, be seeing you out there!'

There was much scuffling and shuffling as the fledges crossed the courtyard to join their new stations.

Preddy turned to them. 'I suppose this is goodbye.'

Ottilie wanted to hug him. She rocked forwards on her feet, but panicked before she could complete the gesture. Rocking back, she hitched a smile onto her face and said, 'We'll see you soon, I bet.'

'Definitely,' said Gully.

Scoot didn't speak. He clenched his jaw so tightly that just looking at him made Ottilie's teeth hurt. Then he lunged forwards and wrapped his arms around Preddy in a forceful hug.

Preddy grinned. 'Be seeing you, Scoot.'

Scoot released him and glared over at the Richter group. Ottilie felt silly that she had thought boys couldn't hug, and considered trying to sneak one in now, but there was no time. Preddy turned his back on them and they watched as he trotted over to join the Richter huntsmen. Noel Preddy was the first friend Ottilie had made in the Narroway. She didn't want him to go.

Captain Lyre made his way towards them with a fresh jaunt in his stride. 'As for you, my fine Fiory fledglings, time for a little relocation of your own! Please follow Wrangler Voilies here to your new sleeping quarters and he'll give you an idea of things to come.'

Wrangler Voilies led them to the east wing, where he brought them to a wide corridor.

'This is your new home,' he said, with a sweeping gesture.

Ottilie felt herself smile. A new home. She was surprised to find that she liked the sound of that.

'These staircases,' Wrangler Voilies pointed to two spiral staircases at each end of the corridor, 'lead to the elites' towers. So your guardians are close by. You will be occupying these rooms along here. Take a closer look and you will find your name on a door. You have private wash facilities in your rooms –'

Ottilie swallowed a sigh of relief.

'– and you will share the third-floor dining room with your guardians.

'Now, as to your schedule, you will accompany your guardian on any and all hunts, patrols, wall watches and guard shifts that do not coincide with our group training sessions. We like to throw you in the deep water here at Fiory. Tomorrow is going to be an orientation day of sorts. Your guardians will take charge, and you will get a sense of what life is like as a Narroway huntsman.'

Scoot elbowed Ottilie in the ribs and she grinned. They really were huntsmen now.

'There are a few surprises in store for you, but I'll leave it to your guardians to talk those through. Their job is to introduce you to the work; my job is to refine your technique. That's all from me tonight. Explore, get acquainted with your new surroundings. Dinner is at the seventh bell. Good luck tomorrow.'

Wrangler Voilies marched back down the corridor. The moment he disappeared from sight, the silence boiled over into spirited babble and the fledges began hurrying back and forth, looking for their name on a door.

11. Ott Colter

Ottilie found her name down the far end, by the stair to the elites' tower. The letters were inscribed on a copper plaque attached to the dark green door. Scoot's room was right next to hers and Gully's was further towards the middle. She felt curiously nervous lifting the latch. The moment felt somehow significant.

Her bedchamber was cosy and warm, with a low, curved ceiling and pale walls that were rounded into arched alcoves. The window shutters were painted light green and a small desk was pressed into the corner. An empty bookcase sat by the bed, which was wide enough to fit three Ottilies in a row. At the end of the bed was a big pine chest, packed with folded green-and-black uniforms.

There were two small, arched doors within the room. Ottilie opened the first and found a wide cupboard packed with all manner of salt-forged weaponry. She shut that door quickly. Now wasn't the time to be thinking about that. The other door opened into a small washroom with a bath and a bell for ringing for hot water. Another job for the sculkies, she supposed. Ottilie wondered what Skip's sleeping quarters were like, but she couldn't dwell on that for long. The excitement of having her own room for the first time in her life was too much to be suppressed by guilt.

Ottilie shut the door to the washroom, spun on the spot and leapt onto the bed. She rolled around for a bit, relishing all the space. Ottilie wondered how it would be, sleeping alone in this big room.

There was a knock on the door.

'Come in!'

Gully sprang into the room and flopped onto the bed, kicking her to the side and stretching out like a starfish.

Ottilie hit him in the face with a pillow just as Scoot appeared in the doorway.

'How big are these beds, Scoot!' said Gully, sitting up with an expression of dazed bliss on his face.

'And how soft!' said Ottilie.

'Are they?' said Scoot.

'Haven't you tried yours out?' said Gully.

'No. Should I? They're not that big, are they?'

'Are you being serious?' said Gully.

'Ha! No, I was just being Preddy.'

Gully laughed maniacally, rolling from one end of Ottilie's bed to the other, this time knocking her onto the floor.

'I'm going to kill you, Gully!' she said, her scowling brow peeking up over the edge of the bed.

'Couldn't if you tried!' he cackled.

'Don't forget who got the nine,' she said, scrambling to her feet.

'I guess that's why you got Leo Darby, isn't it,' said Gully, pausing mid-roll.

'Everyone says he's the best, don't they? Plus he's a champion. I bet that's why Ott got him. The best fledge with the best elite.'

'Hold up right there! Ott got the best score – doesn't make him the best fledge,' said Scoot. 'Sorry, Ott.'

Ottilie shrugged.

'Pretty big difference between a nine and a three, Scoot,' said Gully.

'Yeah, well. We'll just see, won't we, once the games really begin,' said Scoot, chucking a pillow at Ottilie.

Ottilie caught it before it hit her head. Hugging the pillow to her chest, she glanced over at the shuttered window. Caught up in the competition, Scoot's attitude towards the Narroway Hunt had utterly reversed. It was amazing what a difference a few weeks could make.

'I wonder what tomorrow will be like,' said Ottilie.

'When they say we're with our guardians tomorrow, do you think that means we're actually going out there … outside the boundary walls?' said Gully with a glint in his eye.

'Course it does,' said Scoot. 'We've spent weeks cooped up training in this place. Course we're going out.'

'But we don't know anything,' said Ottilie. 'We've just been training for the trials. We don't know anything about the different kinds of dredretches, or how to deal with them. What about all … the rest of it all?'

'That's why they're taking us out, I think. So we can learn all the rest of it out there,' said Scoot.

'Voilies did say *deep water*,' said Ottilie.

'He also said *surprises*,' said Gully.

Ottilie felt her jaw lock. Wasn't the existence of dredretches enough? She wasn't sure how many more surprises she could take.

20

Maestro the Wingerslink

Ottilie splashed her face and pulled on her uniform in the light of the early-morning moon. The fledges had been fitted weeks ago, their measurements recorded so that a uniform of the correct size would be ready when they were finally assigned to their permanent station. At the time Ottilie had thought she and Gully would be leaving long before that day would come. Now that it had, she wished she had paid a little more attention when Wrangler Voilies talked them through strapping on all their weapons and protective leatherwear. There were buckles and straps all over the place. It would have been terribly confusing at any hour, but before dawn it was downright impossible.

There were two sharp thumps on her door. 'Dining room, ten minutes!' barked Leo, without opening the door. 'And dress warm.' He didn't wait for her response.

Ottilie's heart rate increased. She would not panic. There would be far more difficult and terrifying things to face today than getting dressed. She could do this.

Ottilie wasn't sure why Leo had told her to rug up. Summer was only weeks away, and although it was eternally frosty in the mornings, the late spring days were generally warm enough. But he must have had his reasons, so Ottilie layered up with the lightest wintery pieces she could find in the uniform chest, choosing the sheepskin jerkin, tucking a green scarf into her shirt, and grabbing a pair of black wool-lined gloves.

Finally, when everything was locked in place, Ottilie stood before the looking glass. She had never had a looking glass before. She had seen her reflection plenty of times in water and shiny objects – not that there were many shiny objects to be found around the Swamp Hollows. But before he'd had to sell it, Mr Parch owned a hand glass in which little five-year-old Ottilie had examined her face very closely.

Little five-year-old Ottilie was well and truly gone. The figure standing in front of the looking glass was not Ottilie but a 'brother' of Gully. Different shades of skin and hair, ever so slightly taller, but every bit as small. She wondered if it was true that the Swamp Hollows had stunted their growth. But no, Peter Mervintasker had always been tall and he'd lived in caves for as long as Ottilie had.

She glanced at her green-and-black uniform. It was better than any of the clothes she had ever owned. The shiny new boots reached up to her knees, protecting her shins, and for the first time in her life they actually fit her feet. Beneath the black sheepskin jerkin a leather-covered breastplate locked her heart away.

Ottilie looked herself up and down. It was surprising how ordinary her short hair seemed. This was the first time she had really seen it, but it didn't seem particularly unusual. Nor did the uniform, the boots, the knives and bow and quiver across her back, the cutlass at her hip – she was becoming the part she had been playing. The game was less exhausting now. Ott was her name. It was no longer an unwanted nickname from a noxious fool. It was the name her friends called her, even Gully. They were never alone anymore, so Gully never got the chance to use Ottilie, but Ott fit so well she wondered if he would ever switch back.

Time was up.

Ottilie took a deep breath and headed for the dining room. Breakfast was still being laid out when she arrived. Leo's unusual gingery hair and upright posture made him immediately distinguishable in any space. He was standing by a long table laden with mountains of apples, pears and dustplums, jars of assorted tree nuts, stacks of warm brown bread, and pots full of hardboiled eggs.

Leo was talking to the dark-haired sculkie. Ottilie's chest tightened at the sight of her, but she shook it off. This girl was nothing to be afraid of. If no-one else had noticed Ottilie was different, why would she have figured it out?

Even so, Ottilie became very aware of the way she was walking. She noticed that Leo's arms hung further out to the side than hers did. Was it something to do with his muscles? Or was he just stiff that way? As she approached, Ottilie subtly tested shifting hers a little out to the side. It felt strange, and she was fairly certain it looked strange, so she quickly dropped them.

'You took your time. Come on, grab a plate,' said Leo.

Ottilie snatched a plate off the stack and began piling it up with food.

'Maeve, meet my fledge. This is Ott Colter. Ott Colter – Maeve Moth.'

'Hello,' said Ottilie.

'Pleased to meet you,' said Maeve, in a low, confident voice.

For the first time, Ottilie allowed herself to hold the girl's gaze. Maeve Moth had soft, round features, but there was a quality about her eyes that hardened her face, and there was something else about her, an air that somehow aged her. Ottilie couldn't guess how old she might be. She was odd – it wasn't in her expression, or even in her voice, there was just something about Maeve Moth that Ottilie couldn't understand, an unknowability that put her on edge.

Her fair-haired friend wafted past. 'Montie's watching,' she whispered in a singsong voice, ignoring Ottilie completely.

Maeve smiled almost maliciously and turned away. A middle-aged woman with a pink-and-gold scarf tied around her head was staring pointedly at them from the other side of the room. There was something different about one half of her face, but distance and dim light made her features difficult to discern. Ottilie caught her eye, but quickly looked down. It was probably just the paranoia Maeve Moth inspired, but she felt there was a touch too much interest in the woman's gaze.

'Right,' said Leo, leading Ottilie to a table. 'I'm not rostered on until seventh bell and you're lucky because it's a patrol today, no active hunting, so we'll only get dredretches we happen across on the patrol route. You get much better numbers on a hunt – when you can look for dredretch trails and go wherever you like.' A rather sullen expression took hold of his face. 'All us guardians are just patrolling for the next three days to give you fledges time to adjust. Good for you, not so great for me. That's a whole three days' worth of points down the drain, unless we get really lucky.' He sighed. 'But, it's necessary. There's a couple of things you're going to have to get used to.'

'What kind of things?' said Ottilie.

'Eat up and I'll show you. Your trial was interesting. Honestly, I thought your brother was better.'

Ottilie had heard about Gully's trial. Like Ottilie, he had stayed still to avoid detection. He then threw his club to the ground in one direction and his slingshot in the other. The flock divided to investigate the sounds, and Gully attacked one group, taking them by surprise. He cut three down with his cutlass before the other group even noticed what was happening. When they swung and advanced upon him, he took one last jivvie before he had to be rescued by the huntsmen around the edge of the arena.

'But,' Leo continued, 'I can appreciate a good score. That's why they gave you to me, you know – your high score.'

'Right.' Ottilie couldn't help but feel a little proud.

He grinned. 'So you're winning already. That's good for you. Doesn't much matter for me. Your points don't affect mine, but your performance will. We're supposedly a team now. I'm almost literally going to be carrying you on my back for the whole year, so I need you to keep up, understand?'

She nodded. An entire year ... she was going to be spending a lot of time alone with Leo. It was dangerous.

He was in the best position to find her out. She would have to be extra careful around him.

'If you don't keep up, or if you get in the way, we're going to have a problem.'

'I will – I mean I won't.' She took a breath. 'I won't get in the way.'

'Good. Come on.'

Ottilie hadn't finished her breakfast but she thought it best not to argue. Sneaking a handful of brakkernuts into her pocket, Ottilie had a sudden vision of Bill crouched in front of her in the tunnels. Bill thought she was coming back. Was he expecting to see her again? He had probably forgotten her by now. The thought prompted a familiar ache, a feeling she usually associated with Freddie. Ottilie pushed it down and followed Leo out of the dining room and into the grounds.

The inky skies had paled to grey and a glimmer of gold-washed pink hovered over the trees to the east. A thin mist blurred their surroundings, and it took her longer than it should have to realise where they were going.

'We're going to the lower grounds?' she said.

Leo just nodded.

The lower grounds had been completely off-limits to the fledges until now. Tucked away beneath an overhanging cliff, it was impossible to glimpse what was down there from above.

Amber eyes glinted behind the veil of mist as they crossed the only place where the inner shepherd perimeter cut away from the Fiory boundary wall. Even the shepherds didn't go near the lower grounds. As they passed through, low rumblings and growls undercut the morning birdsong. Ottilie was alarmed. The shepherds hadn't growled at her since she'd got in the way of one when she first arrived.

'They can smell it on me,' said Leo. 'They'll growl at you a lot from now on. You'll get used to it.'

Ottilie had no idea what he was talking about.

They came to a short fence by the edge of the cliff. Leo opened the gate and led Ottilie through. 'Here. Sit.' He directed her to a pile of large rocks near the edge.

The world was growing lighter by the minute and she noticed a patch of blue rock poppies at her feet, snaking around towards the edge of the cliff. Leo sat down opposite her.

'So, hunting orders. They leave it to us to explain, maybe because we've been in your shoes. Plus they don't like you knowing too much until you're paired with a guardian, in case you start getting your hopes up about a particular order. You get what you're given. But don't worry, you got me, and my order's the best.'

'Order?' said Ottilie.

'There are three hunting orders: foot, mounted and flight. Footmen, obviously, hunt on their own two feet. The mounts ride horses and the flyers fly.

'Fledges spend a year hunting with their guardian, in whatever order they belong to. At the end of your fledge year you'll have another trial and they'll place you permanently in one of the three. Most end up in the same as their guardian, but a few of them turn out to be more suited to a different style. Ned, who you've met, spent his fledge year with a mount but ended up getting placed with the footmen. They'll train you as a group in all three styles later this year so you'll get a taste of each.'

'Which order are you?'

Leo pointed to the bronze pin on his chest in the shape of a raptor. 'The pins are for orders. Raptor for flyers, mare for mounts, wolf for footmen.'

Ottilie's mind was in a muddle. It was too much information so early in the morning. 'But it's not only flyers at Fiory?'

Leo laughed. 'You seemed smarter in your trial. No. There's a mix at each station. Our uniform colours show our station, our pins show our order. There are huntsmen with raptor pins in every station.'

Ottilie shook her head. Of course, she'd just realised that Ned lived at Fiory and he always wore a wolf pin because he was a footman. 'Right, got it.'

'So like I said, my order's the best.' Leo grinned. 'We get to fly.'

Ottilie's stomach swooped. 'Fly?'

'Ever heard of a wingerslink?'

She shook her head.

'Nah, you wouldn't have, they're not from the Usklers. We ship them in from far south Triptiquery specially for the Hunt.'

'What is –'

'They're winged felines. Picture Hero, but thicker, heavier. And bigger – bigger than a really big horse.'

She narrowed her eyes. He was having her on.

'You don't believe me? Doesn't matter, you'll see soon enough.'

She pointed beyond the cliff edge. 'So down there –'

'That would be the wingerslink sanctuary. The plain old horse stables are over on the other side of the grounds. Horses and wingerslinks don't mix well. Actually, wingerslinks don't mix well with anything. The shepherds really don't like them, hence the growling when a flyer walks by. Though Hero doesn't mind so much, now that I think about it.

'Anyway, that's why the sanctuary is so far down, and the shepherd perimeter cuts through back there rather than following the full stretch of the boundary wall. It also helps that fledges don't get a glimpse of the wingerslinks when they first arrive. They like you to focus on the trials. Giant flying beasts can be pretty distracting.'

'And you have a wingerslink?' she asked, her breath short.

'I ride one in particular.'

'Will I?'

'Ha! Absolutely not. You'll be riding with me. There's room enough for two so long as you don't start weighing me down. Come on.'

He led her to a steep stairway that zigzagged down the face of the cliff. Thankfully the mist was clearing and Ottilie could see at least four or five steps ahead as she followed Leo into the lower grounds.

'They key is confidence,' said Leo from below. 'You're all in the same position. Some of those fledges will never have seen a horse before, let alone ridden one, and they won't be sitting on the back of their guardian's horse either, they'll have their own. Don't know if you've ever ridden a horse, but riding for the first time isn't easy. And the ones paired with footmen, well, some dredretches look pretty big from down there, takes a lot of tricky footwork and a lot of nerve. You want to be handy with a cutlass, and spears too. Don't tell your brother I said that – hate for it to get back to Ned.'

An image of Gully holding a spear up to a monster the size of a bear flashed in her mind. She blinked it away. It was no good thinking about that now.

'You got the best end of the deal by far. If you're going to face a monster, might as well be riding a monster. I'm not saying it's easy. It's hard, hard as riding a horse if the horse had fangs and could buck you off fifty feet from the ground. But like I said, it's about nerve. It was never that tough for me, but from what I saw, you're going to have to work hard.'

They came to a stretch of flat ground. They were still quite high up, nowhere near the base of the hill, and the Fiory boundary wall lay ahead. Wide green fields covered most of the space. Ottilie could see a set of training yards and a collection of pointy pale stone buildings curving around the edge of a field. That, she supposed, was the wingerslink sanctuary.

Leo pushed open the sanctuary doors and he and Ottilie stepped inside. Deep growls sounded from all around, and bright eyes blinked from shadowed corners. To her right Ottilie spotted a dark mass snoozing in a sunbeam. Leo was right. It was an enormous chestnut-brown feline with two vast, sleek-feathered wings curled around its sleeping body like a cocoon. The wingerslink rolled onto its back and stretched its front legs over its head, showing its golden belly to the sun. The sight of it took her breath away.

The sanctuary was huge. After many twists and turns, past many a dark pen rumbling with throaty hums, Leo stopped and said, 'Here's my partner in crime. Maestro, say hello.'

A dark shape lunged from the shadows. Halting a whisker from the gate, the great beast let out an ear-splitting roar. The combination of shock and the wave of hot breath rushing out from behind sword-like fangs was enough to knock Ottilie off her feet.

She stumbled back, just managing to keep her footing. She also managed not to scream, but it was a close call.

Leo laughed, reaching over the gate to pat the wingerslink's smooth head. 'Sorry Ott, that's how he says hello.'

Ottilie was shaking all over.

Maestro was silvery grey and utterly, ferociously beautiful. He had huge, ice-blue eyes with a blotted golden ring around the pupil, enormous padded paws with claws like curved daggers, a heavy, dark grey tail that looked strong enough to crack stone, and two glorious feathered white wings with inky-tipped ends.

'Hello Maestro,' said Ottilie, moving towards the pen.

'Best keep your distance for a bit.'

'Right.' Ottilie took a huge step back.

'I meant don't pat him.'

'I wasn't going to. You think I was going to stick my hand in there?'

Leo laughed. 'You looked like you might.'

'I thought you decided I'm clever but not very brave.'

'Actually, I think I decided you're stupider than you seem and not very brave.'

Ottilie could have kicked him, but she was distracted by the tolling of the bells.

'Better get to it,' said Leo. 'We need to be out there in half an hour.' He lifted the latch on the gate. 'Come on Maestro, time to get acquainted.'

They passed through the swinging doors at the back of Maestro's pen. There was no latch – it was clear that these wingerslinks could come and go as they pleased. Ottilie supposed she should find that comforting. They were obviously very well trained, or at least exceedingly loyal to their flyers.

Leo and Ottilie climbed down a wooden ladder to the field below. Ottilie had to duck as Maestro leapt over her head to land smoothly on the grass, flattening vast patches of wildflowers under his enormous paws. She and Maestro followed Leo across the field and into a fenced practice yard, both eyeing each other suspiciously behind his back. Leo tightened the double saddle and a disgruntled rumbling sounded deep within Maestro's chest.

'You'll get used to it,' said Leo, scratching his mount's rounded ears.

Ottilie could see several other pairs moving out into the practice yard. She was happy to note that all the other fledges looked rather white, some even a little green. She wasn't the only one who was nervous.

'All right,' Leo turned to Ottilie. 'It's all in the legs. That's how you let him know where you want him to go. Obviously I'll take care of that for now – we need to get you used to being up there first. Plus, I doubt he'd listen to you even if you tried. For today, I'm going to strap your legs in.' He pointed to two buckled straps. 'But leg straps are usually just a precaution – if you're injured and can't grip with your legs, you can strap them in. Once you get the hang of it, you use the stirrups.' He pointed to two slots in the leather saddle. 'If you're doing it right, you'll barely need the stirrups, they're there mostly for if he rolls or tilts, but you want to keep your feet loose enough to jump off if need be.'

Ottilie nodded. Her limbs were uneasy and her stomach churned, its contents scrambled by dread and delight. Leo whistled and Maestro lowered himself right down to the ground.

'Come on. Up,' he barked.

Ottilie gripped the saddle and clambered onto Maestro's back, trying hard to ignore his protesting murmurs and growls.

'You can do the uppers,' said Leo, buckling a strap around her left ankle. Ottilie found two more straps and buckled her legs in just below her knees.

It was an unnerving concept, lashing herself to a flying monster's back, but as the prospect of flying with nothing but her leg muscles to secure her was worse, Ottilie did her best to quash her concerns. Once she was strapped in, Leo leapt up into the saddle in front and settled his feet into the stirrups.

Ottilie couldn't be sure exactly what Leo did with his legs, but without even transitioning to standing Maestro leapt up into the air. The ascent was a jerky, uncomfortable experience. His great white wings beat up and down, and with them his entire body rose and fell. Ottilie gripped the saddle so hard her fingers cramped.

They rose higher and higher, nearly levelling with the clifftop. Leo seemed to be waiting for something. They circled the lower grounds until the bells sounded. Someone raised a blue flag at the lower boundary gate and Leo nudged Maestro forwards and out over the wall.

They were no longer tucked safely behind high walls, guarded by shepherds and surrounded by armed huntsmen. They were out in the unprotected Narroway. But for Leo, Ottilie was alone with the dredretches. For the first time she felt very thankful that she had been paired with a champion for a guardian, and even more thankful that he was a flyer. She couldn't bear to think of Gully down below, wandering the forest on foot. She hoped Ned knew what he was doing.

The ride smoothed as Maestro turned his back on the mountains and soared out over the trees to the north. She knew now why Leo had told her to dress warmly. As the cold air lashed her face she felt very grateful for all the wool she'd wrapped around her body.

'Don't get lazy. Grip with your legs as if you didn't have the straps,' said Leo, and without warning he turned

Maestro so sharply that Ottilie was flung sideways and completely unseated but for the lower half of her legs.

'See, lazy! If you were using the stirrups you'd be hanging from a tree right now.'

Shaken and queasy, Ottilie concentrated on her legs. She didn't have much time to correct her grip. Leo leaned forwards and Maestro shot almost directly upwards. Flattening his wings to his side, he rolled over in the air three times in a row before spreading his wings and steadying to a glide.

'Better,' said Leo.

Ottilie felt giddy – in the best way possible. She was smiling. Mad as it seemed, she did feel safe up here, all strapped in. It was exhilarating.

The feeling didn't last. A dark shape was approaching from the east. The glare of the sun made it difficult to distinguish, but Ottilie was quite sure it wasn't another wingerslink.

'It's my lucky day,' said Leo, reaching for his bow.

What was it? Dredretches – it had to be. What kind? Jivvies? Yickers? Ottilie didn't know any other kinds! Swallowing hard, she reached for her bow.

'You got your ring on, Ott?'

'Yes.'

'Good. They're flares. They'll have sensed us by now. They'll come to us – they can't resist. Flares are really poisonous, so you might feel a bit sick when they come close, but don't panic. Trust the ring. You'll be fine. They travel in threes, so you can try for one. They're quick. You have to anticipate their movements. They tend to move in spirals, it's their giveaway.'

'Right.'

'And always go for the heart – they'll go for yours.'

Heart pounding in her ears, Ottilie gripped her bow hard. The flares were moving closer. They looked like black lizards the size of small crocodiles. They had thin, batlike wings and long, dark fangs that jutted out of their closed mouths. As they spiralled through the air, tiny fizzing sparks sprung from their crusty black scales. Coming into range, they shrieked in a chorus of shrill whistles, almost too high to catch.

Ottilie's head felt a little light and beads of sweat appeared on her nose. She glanced down at the ring on her thumb. Before she could even look up, Leo took out one flare with an arrow.

As the arrow hit, the flare gave a screech so unpleasant Ottilie almost covered her ears with her hands. The other two, excited by the death of the third, sped up their flight, spiralling so quickly around Maestro that Ottilie could barely see them.

A flare dived at Maestro's neck.

Maestro bared his teeth. Ottilie took aim and missed by a mile, but Leo struck it through the top of its head with a long hunting knife. With an ear-splitting shriek it plummeted towards the ground. Flesh coming apart in the sky, the flare dissolved into a collection of sticky scales and bones.

The third flare came for Maestro's side. Ottilie moved to kick it out of the way but, inhibited by the straps, she was no use. Leo turned Maestro sharply, avoiding the attack.

Maestro tensed and roared, sending shivers down Ottilie's spine. The flare was frantic now. It moved so fast it was no more than a black blur against the blue sky. Ottilie had no chance of hitting it. Leo seemed to be thinking the same thing. He circled Maestro, pulled him up to hover, and leapt off the saddle. Holding on to Ottilie's straps, Leo flung out his leg and kicked the spiralling blur off-kilter.

The flare spun off-course and slowed to right itself in the air. But before it had the chance to speed up, Leo pulled himself back into the saddle and shot an arrow through its heart.

It was over, and Ottilie had never felt more useless.

21

Rankings

'Well, you didn't get in my way. So you did good,' said Leo, unbuckling the strap around her ankle.

It was late afternoon. The sun was low in the sky, and the wind that had picked up an hour ago had frozen Ottilie's fingers and toes to icicles. Despite her frozen exterior, her back, chest and legs were caked in sweat. Her skin itched where her uniform stuck to her, glued down by sweat, and she was sure she must be showing a wet patch on her green trousers from clinging to the hot leather saddle for hours on end.

'Why did they keep going for Maestro? I thought dredretches didn't care about normal animals,' said Ottilie, trying to distract herself from the discomfort.

'They were under attack and they took Maestro for the biggest threat. It happens a lot as a flyer. Once you advance they go for the wingerslink first – it can work in your favour, but obviously you need to protect the wingerslink at all costs. If he falls, you fall.'

Ottilie tumbled down Maestro's side.

'You need to work on your aim, and you're not gripping hard enough with your legs. If you don't try harder I'm going to make you go up without the straps.'

Ottilie didn't respond. Her legs were so stiff and shaky she needed to focus all of her concentration on staying upright. How could he possibly say she had not been gripping with her legs? Her legs were one shake away from coming apart at the joints. They must have been doing *something* all day.

'Tomorrow I want to give you a go at guiding him. The sooner you start that, the better, because he's not going to listen to you for a while. When's your next training session?'

'Tomorrow morning.'

'Tell the wrangler I want you practising with knives. They're really useful when dredretches get up close, but you never go for them. You won't always be able to angle the bow for close-range shots, especially with two people in the saddle. You need knives in your arsenal.'

Ottilie nodded, her eyelids heavy.

'And you need to work on your stamina,' he said, looking her up and down with a disgusted expression. 'Wake up.' Leo whipped out his freckly arm and splashed her face with water from Maestro's drinking trough.

'Agh!' Wiping her eyes, she considered splashing him back. It didn't seem like a good idea.

Leo patted Maestro's wide, smooth head, muttering something to him that Ottilie couldn't catch. Maestro curled around, rubbing his nose against Leo's shoulder.

'Here, come with me. This'll wake you up,' he said, pulling the pen gate shut. 'I do this most days after I go out. Gives me a sense of accomplishment.'

How Ottilie made it all the way back up the steps into the main grounds she would never understand. Her leg muscles were beyond exhausted and her arms and back didn't feel great either. Everything felt heavy, shaky and tight, and she had a horrible feeling she would be in a great deal more pain in the morning. When she finally stepped onto the rock poppies at the cliff edge, it felt like more of an achievement than felling those nine jivvies in her trial.

Ottilie followed Leo across the grounds, through a set of arches with raptor statues bursting from the stone, and into a small pentagonal courtyard. Eyes drooping, Ottilie gazed around. Scratched across the surrounding walls were hundreds of names and numbers, filled in with midnight blue paint.

'We get the scores from all the stations so we can see where we're at. There's me, third tier,' said Leo.

Ottilie looked up. At the very top of ninety-two names, the line read:

1. Leonard Darby 5437

Igor Thrike was below him in second place, down by more than a hundred points.

'So are today's points there? What did you get, fifteen?' said Ottilie.

Leo had taken out a flock of jivvies not long after the flares, and there had also been five yickers below the treetops, which Ottilie had felt particular pleasure in assisting to dispatch by pinning one to a tree with an arrow.

'No. Seven each for the flares, one each for the jivvies, and eight for the yickers. So forty. That's pretty good for a patrol day, considering we stuck to the quiet areas.' He gestured to the right. 'The fledges' points are over there. Looks like you need to watch your back.'

Ottilie looked over at the fledges' rankings. Leo was right. It was a thrill, seeing her name at the very top. Ottilie had managed to fell one jivvie and one yicker, so her score was sitting at twelve. Scoot had crept up to six, and Gully was sitting in second place at eleven. She ran her eyes down the list, looking for Preddy. She spotted him a third of the way down. He was still on the five points from his trial. She supposed he hadn't taken to the field yet, having only left for Richter the day before.

'How does the scoring work?' said Ottilie. 'How do they know?'

'I don't know the ins and outs of it, but the bone singers know every time a dredretch dies. They can sense the death and how it happened, so they know who the points belong to.'

'But who writes it up there?'

Leo shrugged. 'It just appears. It's some trick.'

'Like a spell?'

'I guess.'

'But they can't be witches?'

Leo laughed. 'No, of course they're not witches. There aren't any witches anymore. The bone singers just do the odd trick, like a mystic or a timekeeper. Who knows. Doesn't matter to us. As long as they don't miss any of my points, I don't care what they do.'

That seemed to be a common attitude in the Narroway: no-one questioned anything. As long as they had their brotherhood, their monsters, and the pursuit of glory, they didn't seem to care about the details.

'Ha! Looks like Ned let your brother take all his points. He's fallen down to seventh!'

'I was teaching. That was what we were supposed to be doing,' said Ned, approaching from between the raptor statues. Gully was just behind him. He was filthy.

A leaf was sticking out of his hair and he looked about ready to drop.

'I taught,' said Leo, grinning.

'You got fifty points, did you even let him take a shot?'

'Forty, and yes, plenty. He just kept missing. Didn't you, Ott?'

'That is true,' said Ottilie, shrugging.

'We got a trick of flares and a bunch of yickers and jivvies. What did you get?' said Leo.

Ottilie assumed *trick* was the name for three flares grouped together.

'It was quiet, didn't come across much. I took a lone lycoat and Gully got a scorver.'

'You let the fledgling have a scorver? Soft, Ned.'

'You two should get some rest,' said Ned. 'Good work today, Gully.'

'Thanks,' said Gully.

'Ott, work on your aim,' said Leo.

Ottilie scowled. She and Gully trudged inside. After checking to see no-one was around, Ottilie gently brushed the leaf out of his hair. 'How'd you go?'

Gully grinned. 'Great. Did you get to fly? Ned told me about the wingerslinks. I saw one, up through the trees. Couldn't see who was riding it, though.'

'Yep. I flew.' She still couldn't quite believe it herself.

His eyes widened. 'Wow.'

'Gully, what's a scorver?'

'Really big thing with spines down its back.'

'And you took one down?' She couldn't picture it. She didn't want to picture it.

He grinned. 'All by myself.'

She narrowed her eyes. 'No you didn't.'

'Well … Ned knocked it down first, then he gave me the shot.'

'How is Ned? Do you like him?'

'He's great. Do you like yours?'

Ottilie frowned. 'I don't know. Not very much.'

'Least he's good.' Gully yawned loudly, his throat croaking in the same way Ottilie's did when she yawned – which she did, a couple of seconds later.

It had been a very long day, but it would take more than sweaty legs and stiff muscles to make Ottilie skip a meal by choice. The sleepy pair lugged their limbs up the stairs and tramped into the dining room. Scoot was already there, and they ate their dinner to the tune of Scoot bragging about topping Preddy's unmoved score by one point.

'I'm coming for you two tomorrow,' he said, pointing a carrot at them across the table.

'Gwait,' said Ottilie, her mouth full of mashed potato.

'Good luck,' said Gully.

'Oh I don't need luck, Gulliver Colter,' said Scoot, gesticulating wildly. 'You'll see.' He sent the carrot flying across the room. 'Oops.'

22

The Withering Wood

The final weeks of spring were the most exhausting and exhilarating of Ottilie's life. She had never known there could be a good kind of tired. A kind of tired that didn't come from hours of gathering kindling, picking fruit and half-carrying Freddie away from Gurt's hollow. A kind of tired that didn't come from hunger, or cold, or sleeping on the floor. This was the kind of tired that came from long days, working hard, eating well and sleeping soundly in a warm and comfortable bed.

Ottilie wasn't in charge anymore. She felt so much younger than she ever had before. This made no sense, considering what they were doing, but Ottilie found that she wasn't so worried – not the way she had been.

Freddie had been lost to them for so many years that Ottilie had taken over her mother's worrying. She had worried about Gully all day long. It was crippling.

It wouldn't go away completely; Ottilie would always worry about him. That was what came of having an adventurous brother. But having all these people here – all these adults organising things, making sure they were fed, looking out for them – meant she could finally worry like a sister, not a parent. The Hunt was invested in their huntsmen. They looked after them properly. Ottilie had never been healthier, and she had never felt so free.

But not everyone felt the same.

'I feel like a slave!' moaned Scoot, flopping down on Ottilie's bed and miming some strange action with his hands – it looked like he was pretending to tear off his head.

'Scoot, you're getting mud all over the place! Get off my bed,' said Ottilie, shoving him off with her foot.

Scoot hit the floor with a thump. 'That's what happens when you're stuck on your own two feet all day. If I got to snooze on the back of a wingerslink I'd be shiny and clean too.'

The door slid open and Gully tramped in, leaving a trail of mud behind him.

'I'd like to see you have a go on a wingerslink, Scoot,' said Ottilie. 'Leo says they're a good judge of character. Maestro would eat you the moment he saw you.'

Gully jumped onto her bed, landing flat on his back. Ottilie sighed. There was mud everywhere – mud, twigs, slimy leaves and splatters of miscellaneous dredretch gloop. She was used to mud. Growing up on the edge of a swamp was a mucky existence. A filth-free bed was all she asked, but she wouldn't say anything more about it, not with Scoot in the room. Admitting to care about cleanliness, she had learned, was fairly uncommon among these boys, and Ottilie could not afford to stand out from the crowd. Preddy wouldn't have rolled on her bed. He would have settled carefully on a chair, or hovered awkwardly in the centre of the room so as not to sully the furniture. Just for a moment, her whole body felt heavy. She wished Preddy had stayed with them.

'Are you finished for today?' she asked.

Gully grinned, his eyes half-closed. 'All done. And tomorrow's my day off.'

Tomorrow should have been Ottilie's day off too, but she was terribly behind on her last four study tasks. She would have to spend the entire day with her nose in a dredretch bestiary.

'Did you see Preddy's moved up? He's third now,' said Scoot, narrowing his eyes.

'I saw that,' said Gully. 'I wonder what order he's with.'

'Mounts, probably,' said Scoot. 'Voilies practically drooled on him when he said he could ride a horse.'

'He got thirty points yesterday,' said Gully. 'Must have been a good day.'

'A good day for Leo is a hundred and fifty points,' said Ottilie, feeling a little proud. 'If he's on a hunt. Fifty if he's on a patrol.'

'I've never got thirty points in one day,' said Gully, who had overtaken Ottilie in the rankings a week ago. 'I'm still beating Preddy, though.'

Scoot groaned loudly. 'Ugh, you're coming second, Gully, aren't you!'

Gully grinned. 'Murphy Graves from Arko is still winning,' he said.

'Well, not for long!' said Scoot.

'You keep saying that, but when I checked you were seventeenth,' said Ottilie.

'Yeah well,' said Scoot, '… not for long.'

When the bells chimed, signalling half an hour until dinner was served, Scoot and Gully hurried back to their own bedchambers to wash and change into their daywear uniforms.

Ottilie snuck in some reading before dinner. Her most overdue study task was a series of relatively simple questions about jivvies. She had almost finished the relevant chapters; some of the information would have been very helpful three weeks ago during the fledgling trials. For instance, she now knew that the only scent jivvies could sense was freshly spilled human blood. That single sense was so heightened they could smell it ten miles away, and the scent drove them mad. They would work themselves into such a frenzy that they sometimes killed each other in pursuit. This, the bestiary said, was one of the very few circumstances in which a dredretch would turn on one of its own kind.

By the time the seventh bell rang, Ottilie was starving. She hastened down to the dining room to find Gully sitting at a table with Ned. Her plate nearly overflowing, she practically skipped across the room and slid into a chair opposite Gully.

'Hello,' she said quickly, before tearing into a cob of corn like Hero ripping meat from the bone.

'Evening Ott,' said Ned. 'Good work with those stingers this morning. Gully and I saw from the hill.'

'Thanks,' said Ottilie, chomping down on six or seven green beans at once.

Leo had shown Ottilie the best way to fell stingers with a cutlass. Like horrible green flying eels, stingers moved through the air as if it were water. Covered in needle-sharp barbs, they had an excruciating sting, and would often try to wrap themselves around a limb or an exposed neck, attempting to incapacitate the huntsman and giving the stinger the opportunity to go for the heart. Like yickers, they were low flyers, unable to fly higher than the boundary walls.

They tended to stick to the wetlands and Ottilie and Leo happened across the swarm in a marshy field of krippygrass. Leo had noted that, like many of the groups of dredretches they encountered, they were greater in number than the previous year – a fact Ottilie found deeply disturbing.

As if summoned by her thoughts, Leo appeared in the doorway. He was still in his hunting gear, though their shift had ended hours ago. What had he been doing – training? He was fanatical. Didn't he ever rest?

'Why are we sitting with the fledges, Ned?' said Leo with an exasperated sigh.

'You can sit wherever you want, Leonard,' said Ned. 'Look, there's a spot over there by Igor Thrike.'

Leo looked distastefully at Igor and plonked himself down next to Ottilie. 'You know he's second now, don't you, Ott?' he said, swiping a carrot from her plate and pointing it at Gully.

'Yes. I know,' said Ottilie, resisting the urge to say that if he'd stop hogging all the shots she might have a better chance of keeping up.

'I don't know what things are like in the Swamp Hollows,' said Leo, chomping loudly into her carrot, 'but where I'm from the older brother usually wins. How does it feel being beaten by your little brother?'

'Maybe Gully's just got a superior guardian showing him the ropes,' said Ned, a twinkle in his dark eyes.

'Ha! We both know that's not the case, Ned.'

Ned speared a potato with his fork and grinned.

'Look, in all seriousness, Ott,' said Leo, 'you can let your little brother beat you if you want, it's no skin off my nose. But if you let Igor Thrike's fledge overtake you, I'll feed you to a giffersnak.'

Ottilie didn't know what a giffersnak was, but she had a horrible feeling Leo was deadly serious, and made a mental note to keep an eye on Dimitri Vosvolder's scores from then on.

Maeve Moth moved to the table next to theirs and began clearing empty plates, and Ottilie caught Maeve looking at her more than once. She found it very unsettling. Maeve seemed too interested in her, as if she knew Ottilie was out of place. Just when she was beginning to feel comfortable, Ottilie was reminded that she did not belong.

'Why don't any of those girls hunt?' said Gully, gesturing at Maeve.

Ottilie choked loudly on a bit of carrot.

'Ha! You're not serious?' said Leo.

Ottilie was still choking. Leo thumped her on the back and she spat out a large orange chunk. She was very red in the face, and hoped they would attribute that to the choking, rather than the topic of conversation.

'I am,' said Gully. 'Why? No-one's said anything about it that makes sense.'

Ottilie stiffened. How many people had he asked?

'Girls can't hunt. They're too soft. They're not clever enough and they'd be too scared –'

'You don't really think that, Leo,' said Ned, glancing at Maeve, who was quite obviously listening to their conversation.

'I do –'

'All these custodians are here because they applied for that job,' Ned interrupted. 'They don't pick girls for the Hunt because it's not the sort of work they let girls do in the Usklers, or anywhere that I know about. It's the way things have always been, but –'

'Why are we talking about this?' demanded Leo.

Ottilie felt herself shrink in her chair.

'I was just wondering,' said Gully, innocently.

Under the table Ottilie kicked him in the shin.

>>————————————→

Just as she feared, Ottilie's entire day off was consumed by her last three study tasks. She knew if she could just focus a little better on what she was doing, she might have done them in half the time. But she was distracted. Their conversation over dinner the night before had reminded her how unwelcome she was in Fort Fiory, and how dangerous it was to stay. She couldn't help but worry that she had chosen the wrong path. Now, the day was gone, her back ached, her vision was going fuzzy, and she felt stubbornly, irrepressibly grumpy.

It was this sullen mood that triggered an odd thought. There was something funny about what she had been reading. She couldn't be sure, but Ottilie didn't think she had come across a single mention of the fact that only a child, an innocent, could kill a dredretch.

She had seen the shepherds kill those yickers. Were animals discounted from the rule? Or were they simply considered innocent at any age? Shrugging inwardly, she shook it off. It couldn't be a lie. What would be the point? Why would the king order children to be sent to do the work of a proper soldier?

As if seeking the answer to her questions, Ottilie flipped through the pages of the volume in front of her.

'What … ?' she muttered.

The page she had landed on, page 472, was blackened in the centre. It almost looked burnt, but there was a smoothness to the damage, like spilled candlewax. Ottilie ran her fingers over it, which sent an unpleasant tingle up her arm. Dredretch. Dredretch blood, or some other foul fluid, had burned a hole in the page – perhaps it was a smear from the previous reader's sleeve.

She flicked back through the pages to find the chapter title. *Wyler Venom: A Slow Death*. Of course it was precisely the chapter she needed to read. Ottilie sighed and snapped the book closed. She would have to get a different copy from the library.

Ottilie descended a narrow stone staircase. She had never had access to books before, apart from *Our Walkable World* of course, which she had read ten times over, maybe more. They were such rare and expensive things. It was bizarre to see piles of them gathering dust on the shelves.

The library itself brought to mind an abandoned beehive. Made up of arched tunnels lined with identical volumes, the space was difficult to navigate and it wasn't long until Ottilie was completely lost.

The air seemed to thicken around her, and Ottilie felt the colour rising in her cheeks. She was sure she could hear her own heart beating in the silence – a silence that was broken by a high-pitched sneeze.

Ottilie jumped and stumbled backwards into the stacks. 'Who's there?' she demanded.

No-one answered.

She gathered herself, pulled a lantern from the hook behind her, and held it aloft to light the darkest reaches of the aisle. Sitting on the floor was a girl with a blue handkerchief pressed to her face and a look of alarm in her wide, dark eyes.

'Hello,' said Ottilie.

The girl sighed in relief, the blue cloth fluttering with her breath. 'Hello,' she mumbled from behind it.

'Sorry,' she lowered the handkerchief, revealing a long nose, 'the dust makes me sneeze.'

'Um, no problem … I'm Ott.' It was all she could of think to say.

'Alba.'

'Nice to meet you. Do you look after the library?'

Alba shook her head, her two braids swaying with the movement. 'I'm from the kitchens. I just like it down here.'

Ottilie noted the tower of books between Alba's outstretched legs.

'I'm not really supposed to be here. My mother will be mad.'

'Your mum lives here too?' Ottilie was surprised. It was the first she had heard of a real family in Fort Fiory.

'She's one of the cooks. Are you looking for something? I know this place back to front.'

'I'm trying to find – actually …' Here was someone she could ask! If Alba knew the library well, she might have come across something about the rule of innocence. 'Do you know, I've noticed something strange –'

'The age of the books?' Alba's voice pitched higher and faster. This was clearly something she had been eager to discuss for a while.

'No, what about it?'

'None of the books are more than thirty years old. There are a couple discussing the old legends about dredretches, but the rest, all the books you boys study — no more than three decades old. I don't know why, but I think that's strange.'

Ottilie supposed it was strange. 'We can't have been hunting dredretches very long, then.'

'No. That's what I thought,' said Alba eagerly.

'Have you read a lot of these books, Alba?'

'Almost all, I think. There really aren't very many.'

'Have you ever read about the rule of innocence?'

'I —'

'ALBA KIT!'

Alba scrambled to her feet. Knocking the pile of books to the ground, she tripped over one with a particularly fat spine. Ottilie managed to grab her just before she fell on her face.

Alba straightened up. 'I'm here, Mum,' she said, too quietly for her mother to hear.

It didn't seem to matter — in mere seconds Alba's mother appeared at the end of the aisle. Ottilie recognised her. It was the woman with the strange face she had seen in the dining room before her first patrol.

'Alba, I gave you one hour to read. It's been three and a half! I'm up to my ears in dishes — who is this?'

'I'm Ott,' she blurted, her face reddening.

'Ott? You're a huntsman?'

'I ... yes.'

Ottilie wondered for a moment if Alba's mother was worried about her daughter being alone with a huntsman in the dimly lit stacks. The woman moved towards them and Ottilie saw her eyes narrow and then soften to wide, dark pools like her daughter's.

'It's nice to meet you Ott, I'm Montie.'

Montie Kit wore a brightly coloured scarf wrapped around what Ottilie assumed was a shaved head. Creeping down from beneath the scarf was a vicious burn. The scarring spread across half her face, pulling her left eye and the edge of her mouth downward. Her long nose, and the right side of her face, were untouched. Ottilie's eyes flicked up and down. She tried not to stare.

'Come on Alba, kitchen – now. Ott, you should head up to dinner. They'll be clearing it soon.'

'I can't. I've got a study task to finish.'

'Come with us then. I'll give you something you can take back to your room.'

'I – thank you.' Ottilie felt strange, as if she had just been hugged. 'I just have to find a book.'

Montie sighed and said, 'Tell Alba the title. She'll sniff it out faster than you or I could manage.' Her face was unmoved, but even in the dim lantern light Ottilie could read the smile in her uneven eyes.

>>————————————→

The next day, their dawn patrol took them further west than Ottilie had ever gone. Flyers were often assigned patrol regions furthest from the station because they had the quickest mode of transport. Leo said he was glad they'd been given that route, because he wanted to show her something important. He wouldn't tell her what it was, but she gathered from the grim set of his jaw that it was nothing good. What *good* was there in this place – this strange place overrun by dredretches, where even books didn't have the answers to all her questions? For the first time since she'd decided to stay, Ottilie was seriously considering changing her mind.

But as they swept along with the breeze, Ottilie's thoughts digressed. She wondered how many dredretches were lying in wait, and how many points they might earn before their shift was through. 'Is the scoring really fair?' said Ottilie.

'What do you mean?'

'With the different orders. Surely one order is better than the others?'

'Flyers are the best, Ott. I told you that,' he said, his tone unapologetically smug.

'That's not what I mean.' She smiled all the same. Flyers *were* the best. 'I mean better with numbers – scoring points. We can cover so much more ground than the footmen, so can mounts, and we've got Maestro to help when dredretches attack.'

Maestro tilted and soared to the north. Leo and Ottilie braced and leaned with the movement.

Once Maestro slowed, Leo answered, 'It works out. Flyers can get into the Red Canyon, where no-one else can, but we're pretty useless in dense forest. And sure, we come up here and hunt all the winged types, but footmen and mounts can still shoot them down from below. That's the thing about a dredretch, they attack wherever you are. A flying dredretch is just as likely to go for a footman on the ground as a flyer in the air. Plus, footmen can go after all the smaller kinds hiding in the scrub and mounts can give chase through the trees, which we can't, unless they're wide enough apart.'

'So none of the orders usually have more champions?'

'Nah. It's usually a mix of the three. Here, look, this is what I wanted to show you.' Leo pointed to dark patch of forest over to the east.

Ottilie squinted in the sunlight. They headed in closer, circling the blackened trees.

'Was there a fire?' said Ottilie.

'No. Here, look closer.' Leo nudged Maestro down towards the drooping inky branches.

He was right. They weren't burned, or dead, they were … it was difficult to say what they were. It was as if someone had poured hot tar over a massive patch of forest. Like the page in the book she'd been studying, everything was blackened. The tree branches sagged as if weighed down by something invisible, and although the branches still had leaves, they were sparse and black, or sickly green.

'What ... ?'

'We call it the Withering Wood.'

'I'd call it melting,' said Ottilie. 'It looks like everything's melting.' She sniffed the air. 'Smells like it too.' The air around the trees was oddly warm and smelled unnatural, a similar smell to the dredretch flesh that had become so familiar, like rotting brambleberries mixed with burnt bread and old boots. 'Why is it like that?'

'We don't know, but it's spreading. Even since I've been here I think it's got bigger. It's obviously something to do with the dredretches. They're poisonous, and they're driving all the native animals out and killing the land.'

'What can we do about it?'

'Hunt dredretches,' said Leo simply.

Something moved down below. A rustle and snap was followed by an ear-splitting squawk that made Ottilie's head spin. The squawker shot up through the oozing, blackened trees, spiralling into the sky and unfurling a pair of dark red, scaly wings.

It looked like an owl that had been burned in a fire. Its empty eye sockets dribbled dark fluid and smoke seemed to seep from beneath the red scales between its sparse black feathers. It opened its wide beak and squawked again. Ottilie had to clench her fist to keep from crying out, so painful was the sound.

Leo shook his head as if to clear it, grabbed his bow, and shot an arrow directly into the dredretch's gaping mouth.

'Squail,' he said, as it plummeted back down into the Withering Wood. 'They're slow, easy targets, but don't ever let them screech for longer than a minute. It can knock you out cold.'

Maestro soared west and they continued on their patrol route, but Ottilie looked back, gazing at the poisoned patch of forest below. What would happen if it spread all the way through the Narroway? Was this the future of the Usklers – this festering, deadened land?

Captain Lyre said the threat was contained, that the dredretches had never made it past the border. But what if that withering sickness spread? If it took over the Narroway, surely the Hunt would have to leave, and then what? Would they keep backing away? Keep making new borders further and further east? Longwood would be the first to go, along with the Swamp Hollows. Mr Parch, Old Moss, Freddie, Bill, Peter Mervintasker, even Gurt … what would become of them all?

Ottilie remembered Christopher Crow. She saw his body resting on bundles of pale moongrass, and the soft feathers Captain Lyre had scattered across the funeral pyre. She couldn't think about leaving. Leo had said it. There was one thing she could do to help.

She could hunt dredretches.

23

The Red Canyon

The last days of spring sailed by. Every dawn crept backwards in time, waking the early birds earlier still, and before she could believe it, nearly a month of summer had already passed and Ottilie turned thirteen. She couldn't be sure which day was the anniversary of her birth, but Old Moss and Mr Parch had always celebrated her birthday in the first month of summer.

Gully remembered. Ottilie had come back from a morning hunt on the twenty-second day of summer to find an enormous bright yellow flower that smelled of muddy metal sitting in a jar by her window. She didn't know where he had managed to find a sunnytree in the

Narroway. The sight of it made her feel younger and older at the same time.

Skip noticed it the next day as she collected Ottilie's bed linen for washing. 'You're probably going to have to hide that,' she said.

It was raining heavily and, much to his irritation, Leo's hunt had been cancelled, leaving Ottilie with the morning off.

'Why?' said Ottilie.

'Boys don't usually get given flowers. Unless they're dying. Or someone wants to marry them.'

'I think that's stupid. Everyone likes flowers.'

Skip shrugged. 'You can say I gave it to you if you want. I can pretend I want to marry you.' She fluttered her eyelashes and flashed a crooked grin.

Ottilie snorted.

'What are you doing in here?' said a voice from the doorway.

It was Maeve Moth. She stood with her arms crossed and an utterly indecipherable expression on her face.

'Getting the linens, Moth. What are you doing in here?' said Skip.

'Getting the linens,' said Maeve, her voice icy.

'I don't think it really needs the both of us.'

'I thought I was doing the odds and you were doing the evens. Last I checked, eleven is an odd. This is room eleven?' She looked at Ottilie.

'Uh. Yes, this is room eleven,' said Ottilie.

'I was doing the evens, but I got them all, so I thought I'd help you catch up,' said Skip cheerily.

'You've been in here a long time,' said Maeve. Her eyes fell on the jar by the window. 'Nice flower.'

Ottilie flinched inwardly.

'I better get back to work.' With that, Maeve Moth slipped from the room.

'Witch,' muttered Skip.

'What?' said Ottilie, alarmed.

'Maeve Moth. Complete witch.' She glanced at Ottilie and laughed. 'Not a real witch, Ottilie! She's just rotten, can't stand her. She doesn't like me much either, as I'm sure you could tell.'

'She looks at me strangely … and too much,' said Ottilie.

Skip shrugged. 'I wouldn't worry about it. That's just what she's like – staring around with those witchy eyes, thinking evil thoughts. She's cracked.'

That was a relief. At least Skip had experienced it too.

'She knows Leonard,' said Ottilie. She had taken to calling Leo *Leonard* behind his back. It was something she had picked up from Ned, who called him Leonard whenever he was being particularly insufferable.

'She *wishes* she knew Leo Darby. Everyone gets silly about the champions – even the wranglers go weak at the knees,' said Skip, rolling her eyes. Ottilie knew what she was talking about. Wrangler Voilies looked like he was fighting the urge to bow whenever Leo entered a room.

'How's it going with him anyway?' said Skip.

Ottilie shrugged. 'He teaches me a lot. And he's keeping me high in the rankings. I'm fourth at the moment. Gully's first, Preddy's third, and a boy from Arko's second. He doesn't think I've noticed, but I can tell he wants me to win so he can brag that it was all down to him.' Ottilie didn't want to admit that she was also a little disappointed by her ranking.

'How many hunts have you been on now?'

'I've lost count. I actually like patrolling better because we have more time to practise flying. Maestro's used to me now, but he still doesn't listen to me. Leo has to help almost every time. I don't understand what I'm doing differently to him.'

'I've never ridden a wingerslink, but I've been on a horse,' Skip said, 'and they know when you're inexperienced. They sense it.'

'When have you been on a horse?' Although she'd never been there, Ottilie couldn't imagine there were a great many horses wandering the Wikric slum tunnels.

'The horse mistress here took a liking to me and gave me some lessons. She lets me ride a bit on my days off. It's not technically allowed but the stablehands keep their mouths shut, and most of them are girls so it doesn't look too out of the ordinary if I'm seen riding around.'

'There's a horse *mistress*?'

Skip nodded. 'Ramona Ritgrivvian.'

'But that's not a custodian position, is it? Wouldn't the horse mistress be a wrangler?'

'Ramona's the only female wrangler at Fiory.' Skip scowled and shook her head. 'Ramona's magic with the horses, you'll see. They'll be teaching you to ride soon.'

Ottilie flopped down on the bare bed. The fledges were to start their group riding and flying lessons in autumn. For now, they were focusing on learning to resist the dredretch sickness. This skill was called warding, and they had begun their lessons a few weeks ago.

'I should go before Moth gets more suspicious.' Skip rolled her eyes. 'We need to cut your hair soon. It's looking too long again. Whenever it gets long enough to curl, you start looking like a girl.'

'Gully's hair curls.'

'But Gully is a boy.'

'So am I, as far as they know.'

Ottilie knew things were going to get more difficult in the coming years, but for the moment no-one was questioning her. The thought of what might happen if she was found out was too distressing to bear, so Ottilie shoved it away, pretending it wasn't real.

Even so, sometimes she wondered about her friends. Right now she was treated the same as her peers, but how would it be if they knew the truth? Would Scoot treat her differently? Would Leo? Leo treated everyone like they were beneath him – how different could it be? In the end she knew it didn't matter. If the Hunt found out, she would be punished and sent away – or worse.

The Fiory fledges spent three separate hours a week doing nothing at all. Wrangler Morse was their warding instructor, and the aim of the exercise was to render their bronze rings redundant. They sat cross-legged on the floor, closed their eyes, and tried to muster their thoughts.

It was not easy. Ottilie was terrible at it on an average day, but even more so with rain hammering against the window shutters. There was a candle on the ground in front of her. She was supposed to be focusing on the light through her eyelids, but her mind kept slipping away. She was thinking about her last hunt. Leo had taken her down into the Red Canyon caves to hunt a wyler. He had tracked it from the hills behind Fort Fiory, showing Ottilie the trail of faint prints in the mud.

Wylers were horned, fox-like dredretches that were smart and notoriously difficult to track. Lucky for Leo and Ottilie it had been raining a lot of late, and mud caught the footprints of light-treading beasts in a way that dry dirt didn't.

Wylers were one of the most dangerous dredretches in the Narroway because they were so tricky. They fit into spaces that they shouldn't have fit, and despite their fiery coats they often slipped about unseen. They were particularly vicious attackers that could sense the huntsmen's protective rings. If a wyler got up close enough, one of the first things it would do was tear off a young huntsman's thumb to remove the ring. This wasn't a problem for the more experienced huntsmen, who didn't need them or wear them, but for a fledge, or a second-tier, losing the ring in a fight with a wyler spelled certain death.

Ottilie and Leo had moved to the ground to focus on land-based dredretches. They had been tracking an oxie, following a trail of scorch marks and scratches along the Uskler pines, when Leo pointed out a faint print in the mud. It didn't look like a print to Ottilie, just wet textured soil, but Leo was certain it was a wyler.

It took them an hour to track it down, following its trail all the way to the Red Canyon. They called it so because the river at the base of the deep ravine appeared red from above. Close up, though, the river rocks were splashed with mosses and waterweed coloured blue, red, amber and gold – all the colours of a flame.

Ottilie did her best to guide Maestro into the cave Leo pointed out, but the wingerslink ignored her, and instead an impatient yet smug Leo took over. Maestro wove through the damp tunnels and caves only to find the wyler had eluded them. Finally they found themselves back outside on a rocky ledge high above the fiery river. That was where Ottilie caught sight of the wyler for the first time. Its orange fur was tufty and uneven, its jet-black legs were tipped with razor-sharp claws, and its twisted horns tapered to black, curved points. It stood on a ledge up ahead, staring at them with eyes that burned red in the twilight. It was then that Ottilie realised they hadn't caught up; the wyler had just allowed itself to be found. The thought sent a shiver down her spine.

'Thirty points,' muttered Leo.

'What?'

'You get bonus points for a wyler.'

'It's making my head hurt.'

'They can do that. Just try to ignore it.'

'Will it come to us?'

Leo shook his head. 'No. It knows we'll go to it.'

'Can't we just shoot it from here?'

'Sure, give that a try.'

Ottilie drew an arrow and fired at top speed, hoping to catch the wyler off-guard. It seemed that the dredretch didn't even move, but the arrow cleared it by inches.

Ottilie was sure it should have hit. She drew another, but Leo pushed her bow down.

'Waste of arrows, it'll just move again.'

'I didn't see it move the first time.'

'It was quick.'

'So what then?'

'Knife at close range, while it's distracted.'

Maestro kicked off from the ground and hurtled towards the wyler.

'Knife, Ott!'

'Me?'

'Yes, you! Knife! When I say.'

Leo pulled Maestro around. The wingerslink let out a roar like thunder, landed in front of the wyler, and swatted at the dredretch with enough force to tumble a hut. The wyler skipped out of the way, almost too quick to see. Baring its rotting teeth at Ottilie, it pounced at her leg.

'Now!'

Ottilie lunged forwards, piercing the wyler in the side with her knife. Black dredretch blood spurted out of the wound, splattering her face. The bloodthirsty wyler shrieked with rage, rolling away and stumbling to its feet. She had missed the heart.

'Even with a salt blade it can heal fast. Shoot – now!' said Leo.

Ottilie's eyesight blurred as she squinted through the dredretch blood dripping from her brow. She raised her bow.

'Don't miss,' Leo growled.

She loosed the arrow. Through narrowed, blood-impeded vision, she watched it strike the wyler directly in the heart. The dredretch rolled over and toppled off the edge of the canyon with a piercing yowl. Flesh melting away, the bones plunged into the darkness and disappeared from sight.

'Good shot!' said Leo. 'You've been practising.'

Despite the fact it was the first compliment she had received from him, Ottilie didn't respond. She was busy trying to wipe the dredretch blood out of her eyes without vomiting or permanently blinding herself.

'That'll be a nice trip for the shovelies,' said Leo.

'Shovelies?' she said, squinting.

'They go out and bury the bones.'

'I thought the bone singers dealt with the bones.'

'No. The bone singers seek the bones, then sprinkle things on them and sing about it – the shovelies bury them.'

'So who are the shovelies then? Girls, like the custodians?'

'Ha! No girls are brave enough to come out here.'

Ottilie clenched her jaw tight.

'Well, some of the bone singers are girls, but we guard them – we'll have to do singer duty soon, I haven't in a while. No, shovelies are failed huntsmen, mostly.'

'What?' Ottilie had never heard of a huntsman failing. She wasn't aware it was an option.

'Sometimes they make a mistake with the pickings. They can't hack it as huntsmen so they join the shovelies. That way they're still contributing to the cause. Someone has to deal with the bones.'

He nudged Maestro back into the air.

What was failing, exactly? Was there a standard they all had to meet? Did they have to achieve a certain number of points per year? Ottilie imagined coming to the end of her fledgling year, having slipped to the bottom of the rankings. She pictured Leo's look of disgust as Captain Lyre announced she was simply not good enough to be a huntsman, and would have to join the shovelies.

Anxiety gripped her like a serpent coiling around her ribcage, squeezing her lungs. Was she good enough? Leo had talked her through every moment with the wyler. She had hardly done any of it herself.

'Why did you give me those points? I thought you were going to take it,' said Ottilie, bracing as they ascended.

'You could use them.'

Ottilie flinched at the words, but decided not share her doubt with him. More than likely his response would only deepen her concern.

'I'm well ahead,' he added. 'Thirty points hardly makes a difference to me.'

But Ottilie could tell he hated missing out on the points. It didn't matter in the end; Leo was in top form for the rest of his shift and by the end of it he had collected nearly two hundred points. He would never have admitted it, but Ottilie knew he was going hard to make up for losing the wyler bonus. Sharing was not one of Leo's virtues.

Sensing the warm light of the candle through closed eyes, Ottilie smiled. Leo was irate about the rain. Rain to him meant a wasted day. His shift was cancelled and he had a mandatory day off the next day. That was two whole days of zero points.

A bell tinkled from the front of the room. Ottilie's eyes snapped open.

'Slowly become aware of your surroundings,' said Wrangler Morse in his rough, deep voice. He was perched on a pillow at the front of the room, holding a tiny bell in his enormous hand. 'Ott Colter, I did not tell you to open your eyes.'

Ottilie snapped her eyes shut.

'All right. When you're ready, you can open your eyes.'

Ottilie opened her eyes again immediately. Doing nothing should have been easy, but Ottilie had never been worse at anything in her life. She looked across at Scoot. He looked pouty and disgruntled. At least she wasn't the only one struggling.

Gully seemed refreshed. A sloth's smile spread across his face as he strolled towards the door. How was it possible that fidgety little Gully was better at this than she was?

'Ott.'

Leo was standing right outside the door, holding a bundle of weapons. Ottilie almost walked into him.

'Finally. Come on.' He shoved the weapons at her and marched ahead.

Diving to catch a dislodged dagger, Ottilie adjusted the bundle in her arms and hurried after him. 'What are you doing here?' she said.

'Bone singers say the rain's about to stop. I volunteered for a night patrol.'

Ottilie rolled her eyes. 'Of course you did. I haven't eaten yet.'

He turned and tucked a single red apple into the crook of her elbow.

'Thanks.' She scowled.

— 24 —

The Barrogaul

Ottilie and Leo marched through the wet grass to the lower grounds. The sun had already set and twilight was folding in.

'How are you going with the warding lessons?' said Leo, pulling open the sanctuary doors.

'Awful.'

He turned. 'Why?'

'I can't concentrate in there.'

'You need to try harder. It's important. I stopped wearing my ring by the end of my fledge year. You don't want to be the last one to master it.'

'But how is sitting around staring at candles supposed to help?'

'Because once you win governance of your mind, you can start to strengthen your mental defences. It's all in your head, what dredretches do to you.'

'But I thought it was real. They can kill us by –'

'That's not what I mean. The dredretch sickness *is* real. But there's no physical injury. They just suck the life out of you.'

'What's that got to do with my head?'

'Because with nothing actually wrong physically, your body can't surrender your life without the consent of your brain.'

Ottilie scowled. Part of her hated that Leo was so well-educated. It wasn't fair. 'What do you mean?'

'Just imagine that dredretches suck your life out of your ears. Then imagine covering your ears with your hands so it can't get out. That's what you're learning.'

'I'm learning to cover my ears?'

'Yes.'

'Can't I just wear earmuffs?' she grumbled.

Leo snorted.

'And you were good at it – sitting still and doing nothing?' Ottilie found that very hard to believe.

'I'm good at everything, Ott.'

'And you wanted to be the first to stop wearing your ring,' she said, trying not to smile. 'Were you?'

Leo kicked a loose stone across the floor. 'No, that was Ned.'

'By?'

'Three weeks.'

She stifled a laugh.

'He's never beaten me at anything since, though.'

Ottilie couldn't keep it in. She let out a cough of laughter, disturbing a sleeping wingerslink. The great flying beast leapt up and slammed itself against its pen, roaring in protest at being woken. Ottilie yelped and bounded away.

Leo, grinning from ear to ear, shoved her back towards the pen.

'Agh! Leonard!'

'Call me Leonard again and I'll throw you in there with it!'

'Come on, Maestro's waiting,' said Ottilie, trying to muster a scrap of dignity.

Maestro was in a particularly friendly mood that night. He let Ottilie saddle him without complaint and even rested his velvety nose against her shoulder as she tied two vials of glow sticks to his saddle. His mood altered slightly when he leapt out into the damp night air, though. The weather hadn't entirely cleared – wafts of misty rain drifted from the sky, and Maestro wasn't happy about it.

'You should go in front tonight,' said Leo.

'What? Why?' He had never let her lead before.

'Because he's more likely to listen to you if you're up front, and I want you to have another go at guiding him.'

Ottilie climbed up into the front saddle. Leo buckled her legs in and pulled himself up behind her.

'You should really have a go without the straps,' said Leo. 'Not tonight; I want you to focus on guiding tonight. But I might book one of the yards for a training session in between hunts and you can have a go low to the ground. Don't want to waste hunting time on it. Come on, up, then hold him back until they raise the flag.'

Maestro had never taken flight at Ottilie's command and she didn't see why it was going to be any different this time. Squeezing her legs, she nudged him to take off. She was pre-emptively preparing for a second attempt when Maestro took her by surprise, leaping up into the grey veiled sky.

Leo didn't congratulate her. 'Hold him back,' he barked.

Ottilie released her leg grip, tilted her feet down and pressed in slightly with her toes. Maestro hovered in the sky, black-tipped wings beating up and down, his silvery body rising and falling in place.

A wrangler at the well-lit wall raised a blue flag to signal he had noted their departure. Ottilie squeezed her legs and leaned forwards and Maestro took off at top speed.

It was a miracle. He was listening to her. They soared over the boundary walls and out into the night. Maestro adhered to at least half of her commands and Ottilie and Leo racked up so many points she wondered if she might have jumped up even higher in the rankings.

She took a flare on her own, and four jivvies, which were worth two points at night due to their dark colouring. Leo even let her fell an oxie. Considering there were two of them, there really was no excuse not to let her have one.

Ottilie had spotted them. The red-hot cracks in their antlers shone like rivers of lava in the dark. The oxies were the size of large bulls and fairly slow. They were worth fifteen points for their size, despite being easy targets for flyers – even more so at night. It took a simple dive from Maestro and three quick arrows to dispatch them – one arrow for Leo and two for Ottilie, because she missed the heart the first time.

They weren't supposed to divert from their assigned path, but when Leo heard a strange rumbling from well beyond their patrol route, it seemed he couldn't resist.

'Take him down,' said Leo.

Ottilie flew Maestro down into a basin of krippygrass. The moment they landed, Leo jumped off and started unbuckling Ottilie's leg straps.

'What are you doing?'

'Barrogaul. Hundred points. No. I think night doubles apply. Two hundred points. We're swapping spots.'

Ottilie remembered the name barrogaul, but she couldn't be sure why. Anything worth two hundred points could not be good.

Legs free, she hopped into the back saddle. Leo strapped her in and leapt up into the front. Maestro took off in an instant. Ottilie clung to the saddle with one hand and her bow with the other, readying herself for chaos.

It was worse than she could have ever imagined. The barrogaul stood in a clearing high on a hill. It was twice the size of a full-grown bear. Its shiny black fur slid over a hump on its back. Its mouth was so wide it stretched up and back towards its rounded ears, and two huge, sabre-like fangs curled from its jaws. It stood on four thick, muscular legs, claws curling into the mud as it braced and roared at the moon.

Ottilie watched in horror as, with its wide, bloody eyes latched onto their position, the barrogaul unfurled two enormous scaly wings and rose, beat by beat, into the sky.

For a moment they hovered there, the wingerslink and the barrogaul. Neither moved.

'Just hold on,' said Leo. 'Don't do anything.'

The barrogaul rumbled like thunder and Maestro roared in response. Ottilie shivered. She could feel their cries deep in her bones. The barrogaul plunged forwards. Maestro rolled, dodging the barrogaul's fangs. Leo fired three arrows. The barrogaul dipped and swung, but one arrow caught it in the leg. It didn't seem to feel a thing. It advanced again, Maestro dodged, and Leo caught it with two more arrows. On his third advance Maestro lashed out with his claws, striking the barrogaul across the face. The wounds healed immediately, but the barrogaul rumbled with rage and dived at Maestro. They latched onto one another and spiralled through the air.

Leo, somehow able to move in the fray, plunged his dagger into the barrogaul's front leg and the monster released Maestro, falling a few feet before righting itself. Leo drew an arrow, ready to strike in its moment of weakness, but he was distracted at the last second by a flock of jivvies. He swore, taking two down.

'Ott, deal with them!'

Ottilie, dizzy and anxious, fired at the jivvies. She didn't hit a single one.

They were coming for Leo. His uniform was torn at the thigh. The barrogaul had caught him during the tussle and the jivvies could smell his blood. They swarmed around him. He took three more. Ottilie missed again.

'Ott!'

The barrogaul advanced. Leo shot it in the face, but the arrow bounced off its thick skull. He was aiming for its eyes. Of course, she remembered now. Leo and Igor

Thrike had answered that question in a training session before the trials. The only way to kill a barrogaul was through the eye. No wonder it was worth a hundred points.

A searing pain tore across Ottilie's arm. One of the jivvies had ripped into the flesh above her elbow. Leo swung around and shot it in the wing, knocking it out of the sky.

'Ott, deal with them or I'll shoot you next!' he bellowed, taking aim at the barrogaul's shining red eye.

There was a moment of calm. It was as if she, Leo and the four remaining jivvies knew what was about to happen.

Leo released the arrow, but at that exact moment a jivvie shot towards Ottilie. Without thinking, she dodged, throwing her body to the side and knocking Leo off-centre. His arrow flew far to the left, and from somewhere above another arrow plunged, striking the barrogaul square in the eye.

The massive dredretch plummeted into the dark. Leo swore loudly. There was laughter from above as Leo and Ottilie shot down the last four jivvies still swarming around their bloody wounds.

'Better luck next time, Darby!'

The speaker was riding a russet wingerslink. Ottilie couldn't quite make him out in the dark, but she had a horrible feeling that she recognised the voice. Leo was shaking with rage. That was clue enough; it was Igor Thrike.

'Where's your fledge, Thrike?' spat Leo.

'Tucked up in bed where he belongs.' Ottilie could hear the smirk in his voice. The guardians weren't meant to go on hunts or patrols without their fledges, unless the fledge was in a scheduled training session with a wrangler. 'You must be mad – trying to get a barro with your fledge on board.'

'I take my job seriously.' Leo almost growled his words.

'So do I, Darby. That's a barrogaul I just downed. Nice work with the jivvies though. What's that, eight points? Oh no, wait, night doubles, so – sixteen? Very nice.'

'That barro was injured. You wouldn't have got the eye if I hadn't slowed it first!'

'Yes. Thanks for that. I'll mention it in my victory speech. Looks like you both got a bit chewed up. You should probably go and get patched up before you attract every jivvie in the Narroway.'

Leo made a sound somewhere between a retch and a growl. Ottilie's heart was heavy in her chest. It was all her fault. Maestro circled and they soared towards home. When they landed, Leo didn't speak. Ottilie didn't know what to say. She felt wretched. They left Maestro in the field to cool off, climbed the cliff stairway in silence, and marched for the rankings.

Leo didn't so much as look at Ottilie, but she could feel his fury and she knew where he was laying the blame. They stood side by side and gazed up at the third-tier wall.

Leo was in second place.

Ottilie had heard about Leo's scores. No-one came near them, not after a month or so at the beginning of each year, not once the game was properly underway.

'Once a year,' muttered Leo.

'What?' she mumbled.

'Barrogauls. They're rare. We get one once a year. If that.'

'Leo, I'm really sor–'

'Go to the infirmary.'

'I'm –'

'Infirmary, Ott!'

With a lump in her throat Ottilie turned and hurried away, leaving Leo standing alone in the courtyard.

The infirmary was at the base of the west tower. Ottilie hated going there. Whenever she needed patching up, there was always a chance that she might be required to remove her clothes. She had avoided it so far, but with every trip she was reminded that this fear of discovery would never leave her. She would never be free.

The fastest route was around the outside of the building. If only she had chosen the longer way, through the corridors, everything would have been fine – but she hadn't. Ottilie slipped across the gardens at the west wall and walked headlong into a group of men.

'Ott, what are you doing out here?' said Wrangler Morse.

'Infirmary,' she muttered, showing him her torn arm.

He frowned with concern. 'What got you?'

Ottilie barely heard him. She was looking at the other men. There were four of them and they all looked horribly familiar. They walked freely, but each was blindfolded with an orange scarf. Even with their faces half-covered, Ottilie knew who they were. It was the four pickers from her journey. What were they doing in the Narroway?

'Ott? Nothing too poisonous?' said Wrangler Morse.

'Oh no, just a jivvie. I just need a bandage.'

Ottilie passed, but a few steps on something made her look back. She turned her head and caught the swamp picker doing the same. His blindfold had slipped just enough to free half of his left eye. He looked right at her. Ottilie froze. She didn't breathe. She didn't blink.

He knew her.

Even in the dark with her short hair, Mr Sloch knew her. She could see it in his body, his forehead, in the narrowing of his eye. Mr Sloch knew she was Ottilie Colter. He knew she was a girl, and he knew she was not supposed to be there.

25

Leo's Choice

Ottilie paced the length of her room so many times it was a surprise she didn't wear holes in her boots. She had not bathed. She had not changed. She had not had her arm tended to. Innumerable uneventful hours drifted by. Her clothes were heavy with dried sweat and her skin itched beneath them. Crusted blood fixed her shirt to her arm. Whether the wound still hurt, she couldn't quite be sure. There wasn't room in her brain to think about trivial things like jivvie gashes. Finally she ceased her pacing and sat by the window, staring out at the sky, waiting for something, anything, to happen.

The footsteps were nearly soundless in the hall, but she still sensed someone's approach. Her door was not locked. What was the point? Someone lifted the latch and a thin figure slithered inside – Mr Sloch, the swamp picker.

He looked her up and down, noting the bow and quiver tossed on the bed and the dagger strapped to her waist. He did not approach.

'What exactly do you think you're doing here, little Ottilie Colter of the Swamp Hollows?' His raspy voice was sharp with unspoken threats.

'How did you recognise me?' said Ottilie.

Mr Sloch laughed quietly. 'I watched you and your brother for months, you little runt. Knew you the moment I saw you – didn't even need two eyes.'

Her stomach lurched. 'Why were you watching us?'

'Wasn't watching *you*, was I? Was watching him. He was on the list.'

The list. The list the keeper had made – signing Gully's life over to the Narroway Hunt.

'What are you doing here?' she hissed.

He scratched his ragged goatee. 'I asked you first.'

'I came to take my brother home.'

'Did you now? How did that work out for you?'

'Why are you here?'

His small, bloodshot eyes narrowed. 'Here for a disciplinary meeting. Took them a while to track us down.' He smirked. 'Then they dragged us all the way out here to make us sick and scare us with noises in the dark – blindfolded us so we can't see what's going on here, but of course we know. I've known for years. I always thought they were selling the boys as slaves – I suppose they are, in a way. They locked us up in a room below. Ha! Like I can't get out of a locked room. It's my job to get in and out of locked rooms!'

'Why do you need a disciplinary meeting?'

'That would be on account of a late delivery and a misplaced list.'

Ottilie felt a flicker of pride. She had played them. She and Bill had outsmarted those slimy pickers and now they'd been hauled in for punishment. They deserved it. 'What do you want from me?' She squared her shoulders. 'Why are you in here?'

'Because, Ottilie Colter, you wretched little lass, if they find out that a girl from the Brakkerswamp followed me, found her way in here and took to masquerading as a boy, they'll cut off my legs and make me eat them.'

He moved towards her. Ottilie's hand came to rest on the hilt of her dagger.

'They been training you up, have they?' He snorted. 'They wouldn't have if they'd known. What do you think they'll do to you if they find out?' He looked directly in her eyes. 'Bad things, to be sure.'

He lunged forwards and grabbed her shirt, gripping so tight it bent her neck back. She struggled, but didn't draw the dagger. This was a man, not a monster. She wouldn't cut him. Not unless she had to.

'What do you want?' she spat.

'You listen close, you sneaking little weasel. If you open your stinking, swamp-licking mouth and tell anyone your secret I will hunt you down, boil your bones, and sell your skin as a rug.'

Ottilie wriggled out of his grip and shoved him away. 'Of course I'm not going to tell anyone, you lunatic!'

He looked her up and down, breathing hard. 'It's good luck your little body is so boyish.'

Ottilie drew her dagger and pointed it at his stretched, lumpy throat. 'Stop looking at me like that.'

'You just mind what I've said, Ottilie Colter.'

Mr Sloch turned, headed for the door, and froze. It was ajar – he hadn't shut it properly. He took a step towards it, but before he could reach it, it swung open – and Leo stood in the doorway.

Ottilie's breath grew very short. She felt her hand shake on the hilt of the dagger. What had he heard? What would he do to her?

Leo took hold of Mr Sloch, who was several feet taller than he was, and threw him bodily out the door, slamming it shut behind him. Ottilie stared, panic locking her limbs in place. Judging by his expression, Leo had heard something, maybe the whole exchange. Either way, it was crystal clear – he knew.

'Is it true?' he said, his voice shaking with rage. He looked like he wanted to punch something. 'Who are you?'

'Ott Colter.'

'Ott Colter,' he repeated with a snarl. 'You're not though, are you?'

'Gully's my brother. I'm from the Swamp Hollows.'

'But you're not *his* brother.'

Ottilie froze. She didn't know what to do. Could she keep lying? After what Leo had heard, it seemed mad to continue. Her lies could so easily be proven false.

'No,' she said quietly. 'I'm his sister.'

Leo's face flushed scarlet. He looked on the verge of exploding.

'My name is Ottilie Colter.'

'You stupid little *girl*!' He picked up her bow and threw it against the wall. It fell to the ground with a clattering scrape.

Ottilie felt her eyes flash. 'I'm your age,' she said steadily.

'What?' said Leo, angrier still.

'You called me a stupid little girl. I'm your age.'

He glared at her. 'What are you doing here?'

'I followed the pickers after Gully got taken. I stole the list and pretended to be a boy. I just wanted to get him back.'

'And then what? You liked it here so you just thought you'd stay?'

'I didn't have much of a choice. I didn't know what I was getting into.'

'You're damn right you didn't! Who do you think you are, coming here? Learning to hunt, training with me!'

Rage churned like hot lava in her stomach. 'Why shouldn't I?' she demanded. 'Why shouldn't a girl hunt monsters?'

'I'm not even going to answer that! And it doesn't matter anyway. You lied, Ott – Ottilie!'

'I lied? These people kidnap children! They snatch them from their homes! They kidnapped you and you forgave them. Don't pretend it's the lie that bothers you. It's because I'm a girl.'

'Of course it's because you're a girl!' he snarled. 'I should have known, you pathetic, useless, *weak* little witch.'

Fury seemed to muffle her hearing. As if from a distance, she heard herself growl, 'I'm not! I'm not any of those things!'

'Ha! Your performance tonight proves me right on all counts!'

'It does not!'

Leo began pacing. Ottilie took several sharp breaths, determined to calm herself. She realised he was limping and glanced at the wound on his thigh. Dark patches of blood were seeping through his trousers.

'What are you going to do?' she said quietly.

He didn't answer.

'Leo?'

He glared at her from across the room. 'What do you think I'm going to do, you stupid girl?'

'Don't tell them.' Her voice was low and quiet. She would not plead. She refused to plead.

'Of course I'm going to tell them.'

'If you do, they might take me away from Gully.'

'They might do worse than that.'

She knew it was true, and the thought made her unsteady on her feet. 'Don't tell them. You're just mad because I ruined your hunt and Igor Thrike's beating you. If you tell them, you'll regret it!'

For a moment Leo looked as if he was going to laugh, or possibly hit her. She could almost see the thoughts ticking over in his mind. Mentioning Igor Thrike had definitely been a mistake.

'I won't regret it,' he growled. 'You can count on that.'

He stormed from the room, slamming the door behind him.

Ottilie stared at the door. Thoughts drifting away, she wondered why he had come to see her – maybe to berate her about the barrogaul, maybe to apologise for being short with her, maybe to check on her wounded arm. Now she would never know. She felt lost and oddly empty.

There was movement in the corridor. Ottilie whipped around. Who was it? Mr Sloch, again? Leo? The latch lifted with a scrape. Ottilie gripped her dagger with a shaking hand.

'Ottilie?'

Ottilie's breath caught in her throat. She almost sobbed. 'Skip?'

Skip slid into the room, closing the door soundlessly behind her. Ottilie didn't even have time to ask why she had come. The moment Skip's eyes met hers, she dissolved into tears.

Skip guided Ottilie to the bed, where she collapsed in a heap of sweaty clothes and tears. Skip stroked her hair and patted her back, calmly waiting for the sobs to subside.

After several heaving breaths, Ottilie found her voice. 'What are you doing here?'

'I saw Leo in the corridor. He came out of here looking like he'd just committed murder. I waited until he was gone and then came to see what happened.'

Ottilie took a shuddering breath and told her the story. When she finished, Skip looked grave.

'What do you think they'll do to me?' she whispered.

Skip shook her head. 'Do you think he'll tell?'

Ottilie nodded.

'You could run. You could handle yourself out there now.'

Skip was right, but one thing hadn't changed: Gully. 'I won't leave Gully here alone.'

'They were bound to find out sooner or later. You wouldn't have lasted another year still passing for a boy. What were you planning to do when you started growing breasts?'

Ottilie let out a watery cough of laughter. 'I didn't like thinking that far ahead. Strap them down, I guess.'

Skip snorted and brushed a tear from Ottilie's cheek. 'That would never have worked.'

'It doesn't much matter now,' said Ottilie with a hearty sniff.

'You haven't hurt anyone, Ottilie. Hold on to that. They can't punish you too harshly.' Skip was a good actor, but Ottilie knew deep down she didn't believe that for a second.

They came before dawn. Skip, who had waited with her, slipped into the washroom when she heard their approach. Ottilie's wrists were clapped in iron manacles and she was ordered not to make a fuss. That would have been a great deal easier if they let her walk freely rather than half-dragging her sideways with a length of clanking chain. The disturbance caused a wave of opening doors along the hall, a sea of curious faces peeking through the gaps. Scoot was on a nightshift and, to her relief, Gully's door stayed firmly closed. He always did sleep like the dead.

A terrible thought struck her. Obviously, Gully had known all along that she was a girl. Would he be punished for lying? What would they do to him? Maybe she should have warned him – but she had been in such a state, she hadn't thought of it, hadn't wanted him to be there – to involve him – but of course, he was already involved.

Wrangler Voilies was leading the group, with Wrangler Morse to his left. A stooping, one-eyed wrangler by the name of Furdles had hold of her chain. She glared at the back of Wrangler Voilies' head. Wrangler Voilies loved Gully. Everyone loved Gully. Surely Gully would escape punishment – he was only protecting his sister. But then again, she had only been protecting him, and they were undoubtedly going to punish her.

'It's the burrows for you tonight, my dear,' said Wrangler Voilies, turning to catch her glare. 'It won't do you any good to look at me like that, you thieving little fibber.'

'What have I stolen?'

Wrangler Voilies chortled, his eyes cold. 'Our teachings, little girl. Our food, shelter and general hospitality. Our goodwill.'

'I stole your goodwill?'

'Stole it,' muttered Wrangler Furdles.

Rage curdled her stomach. Their words made her ill. She opened her mouth to argue but Wrangler Voilies cut her off. 'Another word and we'll gag you, young miss. You're already in more trouble than you could imagine.

Don't dig yourself deeper. You'll keep that mouth shut if you know what's good for you … and your brother.'

Those were the magic words. Ottilie closed her mouth tight and let them drag her in silence all the way to the burrows.

The burrows, it turned out, were in the pit below the arena where they had undergone their fledgling trials. It was arranged like a jail, with individual cells built into the walls. There were two large cages beneath the doors to the arena, with a series of wide copper pipes connected to the cells surrounding them. That was how they had controlled the release of the jivvies.

It was a dank, horrible place. There was a green tinge to the walls and the air smelled of damp and mould. Worst of all, the burrows were not empty; at least four cells were occupied. They kept dredretches down there for training purposes.

Ottilie spotted a giffersnak. Like great eyeless crocodiles, giffersnaks had wide webbing between their bodies and front legs, which allowed them to glide from treetop to treetop, ready to leap down and snap up an unwary huntsman below.

She could see an oxie, its antlers glowing, and three flares, swirling in endless circles in their prison. The last occupied cell contained a dredretch she had not encountered: an enormous crustacean, with twelve legs and shiny red pincers the colour of freshly spilled blood.

Wrangler Furdles dragged her into the cell opposite the oxie and attached her chain to a hook in the wall.

'Take off her ring,' said Wrangler Voilies.

Wrangler Furdles started scratching at her thumb, trying to remove the ring.

'Tudor, there are flares in here,' said Wrangler Morse.

The ring slid from her thumb and instantly Ottilie fell ill. The blood drained from her face to her toes. She broke out in a cold sweat. Heart pounding in her ears, she struggled to breathe.

'Tudor!'

'Pathetic,' said Wrangler Voilies. 'How many warding lessons have you had? And you are reduced to this in seconds. We should have known.'

'It'll kill her. The flar—'

'Yes, Reuben! I'm just proving a point.' Wrangler Voilies snatched the ring from Wrangler Furdles and shoved it back onto Ottilie's thumb.

Grabbing hold of her wrist and twisting it violently around, Wrangler Voilies shoved her thumb so close to her face it nearly poked her eye out. 'This, my dear, is thievery.' He threw her wrist down, bending it out of shape.

Ottilie did not cry out. She barely flinched. She would not give him the satisfaction.

26

The Directorate

'Ott.'

Ottilie lifted her head from her knees. Her neck was as stiff as an old stump and she could feel bruises forming where her spine pressed into the cell wall.

A girl was creeping towards her, one hand supporting a small tray with a plate, a cup and a candle, and the other partially covering her eyes. Ottilie crawled forwards and pressed her face right up against the bars. She shivered as her cheek made contact with the ice-cold iron. Her visitor's dark hair hung in two smooth braids. It took a moment for Ottilie to recognise her, and another to remember her name.

'Alba? Is that you?'

A flare shrilled in response to her voice and the oxie rammed its antlers against the bars.

Alba Kit jumped, almost losing her grip on the tray. She peeked out from under her hand, her gaze flickering towards the oxie's glowing antlers. Emitting a breathy squeak, she skittered sideways and snapped her hand back over her eyes.

'Don't look at them, just look at me,' said Ottilie, her voice gentle and her eyes half-closed as she recovered from the headache brought on by the whistling flare.

Alba lifted her hand again and shuffled forwards. Her eyes were wide and bright with fear. 'Hello,' she whispered.

'Are you all right?'

Alba nodded quickly. 'I just hate them.' She could barely get the words out.

'There's not a whole lot to love.'

Alba squatted down in front of Ottilie's cell and passed the cup of water through the bars, the bronze ring on her thumb glinting in the candlelight. Ottilie downed the icy water in three gulps.

'I'm not supposed to be here, but Mum sent me. She said they probably wouldn't be feeding you.'

Ottilie felt a flicker of warmth in her chest. Alba's mother was looking after her. Thinking of her.

Alba passed Ottilie a chunk of bread stuffed with cheese.

'Thank you, but you should go. If they catch you –'

'They won't. I know a secret way, and I won't stay long. How are you?'

'Fine,' said Ottilie. It was a reflex. She ripped into the bread, spraying crumbs across her lap.

'Do you know …' said Alba, her words barely voiced. 'I wondered about you, that day I met you.'

'What do you mean?' said Ottilie.

'I thought you seemed different. I just didn't know how.'

'Are you mad at me? That I lied?'

Alba frowned. 'No, of course not. I know what it's like …'

Ottilie found herself smiling, her cheeks stuffed with half-chewed bread. 'What? Are you a boy pretending to be a girl too?' she said, struggling to speak with her mouth full.

'No. I'm a Laklander.'

Ottilie choked.

'Well, about as close to a pure Laklander as you can get these days. My great-grandparents were Laklanders.'

'But you're … you don't look …'

Ottilie had never met anyone who claimed to be a Laklander, but she had a particular image in her mind. From what she had heard, Laklanders were supposed to be short. Alba was an average height. Ottilie was far shorter. Mr Parch insisted that was a myth anyway. He said Usklerians liked to remember the Laklanders as smaller than themselves.

The most renowned Laklander trait was fair hair – hair like water, a colour so pale it showed a bluish tinge. It was a shade only seen in the far west. As Ottilie understood it, it wasn't that all Laklanders were blond, but that that particular icy hue didn't occur anywhere else in the world. Alba's hair was a dense brown, thick and straight. She was the last person Ottilie would ever have assumed to have Laklander roots.

'My father's father was from north Triptiquery and my mother's mother was from the far east. So it's easy to hide. But, you know … you don't tell anyone.'

'You don't?' Ottilie felt strange. She had always thought of Laklanders as … well … they were painted as violent outcasts, vengeful ruffians. But Alba and her mother were so normal – so *nice*.

'I suppose it's not really the same,' said Alba.

Ottilie considered it. She was an imposter recruit, concealing her true identity, unwelcome in the Narroway, just as Alba was secretly descended from an ancient enemy, and unwelcome in the Usklers. However different the circumstances, both girls were hiding who they really were.

'Do you know the story?' asked Alba.

'Of the Usklers and the Laklands? Only what I've read in a book.'

'Like what?'

'Well – just that there was never peace, until the last war when the Laklands were destroyed. And the Laklanders that survived it, and came to the Usklers to live …' she paused, thinking of a way to say it politely, 'caused trouble … burned things down … hurt people …'

'Some of them,' said Alba. 'Others, like most of my family, just came peacefully, because we can't live there anymore. The thing is, you can't trust the books, because they were all written by Usklerian scholars. My mum told me a story that her mother told her, about the royal fami–'

Alba froze.

Somewhere nearby they heard the creaking of a heavy door. Scooping up the items she had brought, and snuffing out the candle with her finger, Alba whispered, 'I've got to go, but Ott, I wanted to tell you, I've been reading, trying to find out about the rule of innocence you mentioned in the library … I can't find anything, but I'll keep looking. I think it's very suspicious.'

Ottilie nodded frantically. 'Go. Go!' she hissed.

Giving the dredretches a wide berth, Alba slipped into the darkness. Mere moments later, Wrangler Furdles scuttled in, muttering to himself. Lantern light spilled into her cell and Ottilie snapped her eyes shut, pretending to sleep. She didn't know what he was checking for. That she was still breathing? That she hadn't escaped?

He left as quickly as he'd come, and Ottilie was alone again. At least now she had something other than her impending doom to occupy her thoughts. So Alba could not find any evidence of the rule of innocence. Alba, who had read every book in the library. What was this strange lie? Why did the king recruit young boys to beat back the foulest threat to his lands when he had real armies at his disposal?

Ottilie was unsure of the hour, but when they finally dragged her upstairs she caught a brief glimpse of the mid-afternoon sun. She was escorted to a circular room in one of the towers. Captain Lyre and the other two Fiory directors were there, along with the directors from Arko and Richter. They were seated in a wide semi-circle facing Ottilie, who stood alone in the centre of the room. On a raised stage there were three thrones, and on them sat the cardinal conductor of each station.

The cardinal conductor of Fiory, Conductor Edderfed, had a scrappy white beard and flyaway hair atop his head, which he had carefully combed to cover an expansive bald patch. He had a large nose and kind, crinkled eyes. Ottilie found him rather unintimidating — until he spoke.

'Please state your true name,' he said calmly, with a voice of such unexpected depth that Ottilie shivered upon hearing it.

'Ottilie Colter.'

'You are lucky, Ottilie Colter, that our full directorate was already gathered here at Fiory to deal with other matters. I am sure you would not have liked to spend another night in the burrows.'

They all seemed to be waiting for her to respond.

'No, sir.'

He studied her for a moment before turning to the others. 'Before we begin,' he picked up an orange box from the arm of his throne, 'we need to select an impartial representative of the Fiory select elite. I have taken it upon myself to remove Leonard Darby's name from this box as I think we can all agree that he does not qualify as impartial.' There were murmurs of assent from around the room.

Ottilie realised she was nodding in agreement, and hastily steadied her skull. She glanced around to see if anyone had noticed. They hadn't seemed to, but she felt her face glowing all the same.

No, Leo was certainly not impartial. She supposed she should feel relieved that his opinions on the subject would not be heard today, but instead she just felt angry. And hidden well away, masked by the anger, was sadness; she was sad that she had lost a kind of friend, and hurt that he had turned his back on her so quickly.

'Captain Lyre, if you would,' said Conductor Edderfed.

Captain Lyre rose from his seat and took the box from Conductor Edderfed. Prying it open, Captain Lyre glanced at Ottilie. Did she detect a hint of sympathy in his gaze?

Without looking at the box, Captain Lyre plucked a card from within and read out the name: 'Edwin Skovey.'

Ottilie remembered her first moments in Fort Fiory; a shepherd snarling in her face and someone gripping her elbow, helping her stand. Ned. She felt a wave of relief.

It didn't last.

Ned was Leo's best friend. Would he share Leo's view of the situation?

'Are there any objections?' said Conductor Edderfed.

No-one spoke.

Conductor Edderfed nodded to Captain Lyre, who strode across the room and opened the door. Wrangler Furdles was waiting outside. Captain Lyre muttered something to him, and Wrangler Furdles nodded gravely and hobbled away.

'Ottilie Colter, you are called before the Narroway Hunt Directorate to witness our deliberation upon your fate. Upon the arrival of our impartial elite you will be given a chance to explain your actions. It will then be put to a vote. If the majority find that you can remain in your position as a Fiory fledgling, a suitable punishment will be determined. If not, the alternatives will be nominated and put to a vote. Do you understand?'

Ottilie swallowed hard. She had not realised there was a possibility that she could remain a huntsman.

They were all staring at her.

'Yes,' she said.

There was a knock on the door.

'Enter,' said Conductor Edderfed. Ned stepped into the room. 'Edwin, you are called here to cast a vote as an impartial representative of the select elite. Do you accept this responsibility?'

'I do,' said Ned, taking a seat beside Captain Lyre.

Ottilie didn't look at him. If Leo's anger was mirrored on his face, she didn't need to see it.

'Let us begin. Ottilie Colter, it was reported to this directorate that you entered the Narroway unauthorised and took upon the guise of a recruited fledgling to join the Narroway Hunt. How do you explain yourself?'

'I —' Ottilie faltered. Her pulse quickened and she could feel a rash creeping up the side of her neck. She looked at Captain Lyre, who shot her a small smile.

'My brother was kidnapped. I found out where he'd been taken and I followed. I meant to catch up to him at Wikric and bring him home, only he'd already moved on, so ... I cut off my hair and snuck into the cell with the other boys while the pickers were sleeping.'

'How exactly did you get into this cell?' said a director with rosy cheeks and two extra chins.

'I climbed up the wall and jumped in.'

There were mutters around the room. Ottilie thought one or two of them looked rather impressed.

'You jumped in?' said the rosy-cheeked director. 'And the pickers didn't wake?'

She smiled inwardly. 'They'd had too much bramblywine.'

Captain Lyre let out a cough that sounded suspiciously like a laugh. 'And then what happened?' he said, after clearing his throat.

'They woke up the next day and moved us on to the border gate.' It seemed so long ago now, that slow trudge through the tunnels, the hunger, the fear, the anticipation of catching up to Gully.

'But what about the list?' said Captain Lyre.

'Oh ... I stole that before I jumped.' She didn't think mentioning Bill was a very good idea. She didn't want them to be aware of his existence, considering how much he knew about the pickings. 'I just wanted to find my brother. I followed along until I caught up with him here at Fiory. Then I wanted to leave but there wasn't any way, and after a time I ... well, I liked it here. I liked the Hunt. I want to be a huntsman and I don't want to be away from my brother. I only came here to find him.'

'And your brother is Gulliver Colter?' said Conductor Edderfed.

'Yes.' Why was he asking? Were they going to punish him?

'Gulliver Colter was a special recruit. Showing exceptional promise, he was picked early, at eleven years old, and currently leads the fledgling tier by fifty-three points,' said Captain Lyre. 'I believe he's your fledge, Eddy?'

'He is,' said Ned.

'But you, Miss Colter, are not a recruit,' said Conductor Edderfed. 'You are an imposter.'

Ottilie didn't know what to say. She knew she hadn't said enough. She wished she could think of something marvellous and brave to say that might help her case.

Skip would have known exactly how to put it. Skip would have explained herself better, explained about how important Gully was to her, and how important the Hunt had become, maybe used the fact that she was ranked third out of eighty-seven to argue that she was a valuable asset.

But Ottilie couldn't think of how to say all that, so she just stood there, staring straight ahead, her back stiffening from standing still for so long and her skin hot from all the eyes upon her.

'Before we vote, let it be known that Wrangler Reuben Morse has offered a character reference for

Miss Colter. We three,' Edderfed gestured to his fellow cardinal conductors, 'have decided not to hear it today, but let his offer be taken into consideration as you cast your votes.'

This was it. They were going to vote. There was nothing left to be said. No defence, no character witness, just her own meagre words and the vote.

'All those in favour of Ottilie Colter retaining her position as a Fiory fledgling, please raise your hands.'

Ottilie sensed movement to her right. Two hands were in the air: Captain Lyre's and Ned's. What would Leo have thought of that? She glanced around at the rest of the directorate. No-one else moved. It was two to eleven.

'Moving on,' said Conductor Edderfed, 'to the matter of banishment. It has been previously sanctioned that no untrustworthy persons may be permitted to leave the Narroway in possession of conscious knowledge of the Hunt. Considering deceit is the crime for which Ottilie Colter stands before us, return to the Usklers cannot be considered an option.'

Ottilie's stomach fluttered. Would they really permit her to stay?

'In situations such as this we have three courses available to us. Servitude in the Narroway, banishment to the Laklands, and death.'

Ottilie felt as if she had plunged into an icy lake.

'Deceit is a grave crime, but as there is no evidence to suggest Miss Colter has caused any substantial harm to our operation or community, I put it to a vote that we remove the last course as an option. All those in favour, please raise your hands.'

Every hand in the room was raised but for three; the two directors that sat to the left of her, and one to the right – Captain Lyre.

'Oh. Wait,' said Captain Lyre. 'Are we voting for death or against death?'

'Against,' muttered Ned, his eyes smiling.

'Oh good, because I'm for. I mean, against. Sorry Ott. *Against*. Against your death.' He thrust his hand into the air. 'I knew something must be wrong if I was voting along with Yaist.' He gestured to a sallow-skinned director with sagging features and rather yellow lips.

Director Yaist narrowed his small eyes and kept his hand firmly down.

'Motion passed,' said Conductor Edderfed. 'Death will not be considered. Moving on. All those in favour of banishment to the Laklands, please raise your hands.'

Ottilie's heart plummeted. There were more hands in the air than she would have liked. Her vision grew blurry. She couldn't count them.

'Denied,' said Conductor Edderfed.

What was denied? She looked about frantically. Captain Lyre looked satisfied. Was that good? He did seem to be on her side.

'It looks as if you will get your wish, Miss Colter. You will be allowed to remain in the Narroway with your brother. If there are no objections, I will allow you to stay here at Fiory,' said Conductor Edderfed. He paused.

There were no objections.

'And that brings us to the question of what, exactly, is to be done with you.'

Ottilie lay on the floor, watching the shadows cast by moths in the candlelight. She had not been sent back to the burrows. Instead, Wrangler Furdles had led her to one of the long communal bedchambers they had slept in before the fledgling trials.

'They told me not to lock you in, but I'm going to do it anyhow,' he'd said, as if it were the most cunning of plans.

The directors and cardinal conductors from Richter and Arko had returned to their stations. The Fiory Directorate alone would decide what happened to her now. She imagined she would join the other girls and become a custodian of some sort, perhaps a sculkie like

Skip. That wouldn't be so bad, she supposed. It was a job with room and board. She would still be helping the Hunt in a way, and she would still see Gully every day.

Someone was struggling with the latch on the door. After much clanking and muttering it finally swung open.

'Well! None of them want you, Colter,' said Captain Lyre, striding into the room.

She blinked at him, and moved to sit with her knees pulled up to her chest.

'Montie Kit said she'd take you in the kitchens, but the custodian chieftess was particularly adamant that she wanted nothing to do with you, which personally I think is something to be thankful for, but one outranks the other, so ...' He settled down onto a bed. 'That of course put us in a bit of a pickle considering your gender and all. But a vote's a vote and compromises must be made. For whatever prejudicial reason, the healers wouldn't take you as an apprentice patchie, and you're not qualified to be a bone singer, which of course left the only field with no grounds for refusal considering their entire rank is made up of discharged huntsmen.'

'I'm going to be a shovelie?'

'Hope you like shovels.' He patted her on the head. 'It could be much worse. Well, you know ... you were there. And there is one upside. They won't let you sleep with the shovelies on account of your,' he waved his cane in her direction, '… femininity. Which, considering the shovelies sleep in an annex – that's really a nice word for *barn* – is something to be thankful for. They're going to let you move into the sculkie quarters, which are inside the main buildings, and far nicer.'

She was going to live with Skip – that was a happy thought. But it was further from Gully than she would have liked. 'Is my brother all right?' said Ottilie. 'Have they … are you going to punish him?'

'As I hear it, Gulliver was initially very distressed. But I imagine Eddy will fill him in right away, and the result should calm him.'

Ottilie chewed her lip. She hoped Gully hadn't made more trouble for himself. She was desperate to see him, and resolved to find him the moment she was free.

'Wrangler Voilies has had a talk with him. He was scolded for keeping secrets, but no, we're not going to punish him,' said Captain Lyre. 'Also, I thought you should know Mr Sloch was apprehended earlier this evening. Apparently, he was trying to sneak beyond the boundary walls after your confrontation was overheard by Leonard Darby. Leo informed us of the threats he made against you, so it should give you some peace of mind to know he is in our custody.'

'He can get out of locked rooms,' said Ottilie. 'He got out before.'

Captain Lyre frowned. 'Yes. It seems we underestimated him. I would imagine that happens to him a lot. I assure you we've been more careful this time.' He got to his feet and brushed off his blue coat. 'I've got to get back to business. A sculkie will be down to take you to your new bedchamber in a bit.' He gripped her shoulder and muttered, 'Good show, Ottilie Colter,' before sneaking a smile and marching from the room.

Ottilie closed her eyes in relief. Her secret was out. There were no more lies. She could breathe again.

Captain Lyre had been gone barely three minutes when Skip dashed into the bedchamber. 'You're staying!' she cried, hugging Ottilie so heartily that she was lifted off the ground.

'Agh, can't – breathe – Skip!'

Skip released Ottilie, pulling back, but still gripping her wrists tightly. 'Well,' she said, 'what a wonderful, horrible day.'

The Newest Shovelie

Ottilie trudged towards the shovel shed. She didn't think about the way her arms swung, the length of her stride, or how she should let her weight fall. She just walked. The afternoon sun was hot on her neck and for the first time in a week she was grateful not to have to don her hunting gear. She was wearing a peculiar oversized garment that was both trousers and a shirt in one. It looked silly, but the pale green shovelie suit was gloriously comfortable, and far better suited to the warm summer afternoons.

On her first day, Mr Bote, the ancient shovel master, had handed her the suit with a twitchy wink. Ottilie had suspected it was a spasm rather than a deliberate gesture, until he leaned in and muttered, '*Magic.*'

'Magic?' Ottilie had asked, the folded suit feeling heavy in her hands.

'Invisibility.' He'd smiled a toothless smile, pointing a knobbly finger at the shovelie suit. 'You'll see. You won't have to put up with that much longer.' He'd jerked his gnarled thumb towards a group of whispering gardeners. The young custodians, with a mass of fluffy woffwoff seeds caught in their hair, had ceased their assault on the weeds to stare very obviously in Ottilie's direction.

Now, a group of huntsmen wandered past, one of them pointing at her and another laughing loudly. Rage simmered beneath her skin. What was funny? That a girl had scored highest in the fledgling trials? That a girl had been paired with their precious prize champion, Leonard Darby? But Ottilie wasn't really angry with them. She was angry with herself because, despite having all those things to be proud of, she had let them make her feel ashamed.

Ottilie only wished the shovelie suit really would help her be less visible, especially when she came across Leo by the pond. At the sight of her, his freckled face turned scarlet with rage. Two weeks had done nothing to abate his anger. She understood it to a degree; she had deceived him. He had a right to be mad. But not *this* mad.

In a silence cut only by frog song, they avoided each other's gaze. Leo glared. He stood stock still in the centre of the path, forcing her to step around him. She knew he was utterly disgusted with her, disgusted that she was a girl, disgusted that she had fooled him – and his disgust, in turn, disgusted her. She didn't think she would ever be able to look at him the same way again.

Despite the fact that his anger made her heart rattle in her ribs and her hairs stand on end, her stubbornness tempted her to stand still and force *him* to pass. Would he really hurt her? Surely not. But she couldn't be sure, not when he was acting so atrociously, and so, to avoid the possibility of a black eye or a broken nose, Ottilie stepped aside and slipped past him, forcing herself to hold her head high as she marched towards the shovel shed.

In the month that followed her dismissal, Ottilie learned what it was like to be truly unpopular. There was a lot of anger directed her way, particularly from Leo and a number of the wranglers. But some others, like Ned, seemed neutral. Scoot had an interesting journey, beginning with denial, then confusion, an odd bout of misery and finally hilarity. He found the idea that she'd fooled them for so long endlessly amusing.

Some of the worst reactions, or at least the most confronting, came from a few of the sculkies. It was in no way overt – whispers behind hands, disdainful glances and false smiles. Ottilie wasn't sure she could actually name a single girl that had said anything to upset her. It was just a sense; she could feel their animosity. And then, of course, there were the little things that kept happening.

One morning Ottilie woke to find all of her underclothes were missing. Two days later someone burnt little holes into the knees of every one of her shovelie suits, and that very night she slipped into her bed only to find great bunches of human hair scattered beneath the quilt.

Skip was irate about it. 'You know who it is?' she said the next morning as they dressed. 'It's those ranky witches, Moth and Moravec!'

'Ranky?'

'Ranky!'

'Is that some sort of Wikric street talk?'

'Ottilie, this is serious. They can't treat you like this!'

It was serious. The little acts of bullying were affecting her more than she wanted to let on. She felt unsafe in the sculkie quarters. Seventeen girls shared that cramped bedchamber and Ottilie didn't know who she could trust. She was having trouble sleeping and found herself feeling inconsolably shaken and weepy.

'I know, sorry. I just don't know what to do about it,' said Ottilie, forcing her voice not to shake.

'I do!' said Skip, rubbing her fist.

'All right, calm down. Who are you even talking about?'

'Maeve Moth and Gracie Moravec.'

'Who's Gracie Moravec?'

'The skinny blonde one Moth's always with.'

Ottilie glanced across the room. The pair were sitting in the corner, one with raven hair and intense eyes, the other blonde, with very dark eyebrows.

'Gracie's never really —'

'Call her Moravec. Suits her better,' said Skip with narrowed eyes.

Gracie Moravec was a quiet girl with a perennially faraway look in her eyes. She seemed harmless enough.

'I'd believe it was Maeve, but —'

'That's the point! No-one suspects ranky little Gracie Moravec. Moth's hideous, to be sure — can't stand the witch. But at least she's sort of upfront about it. Moravec's proper evil. Way more vicious, and dangerous, too, because she hides it all away. You think she's a sweet, innocent little thing who needs to put a bit more bread in her belly, then, BAM!'

'Then, BAM, what? She puts hair in your bed?'

'I'm not joking.'

Ottilie glanced out the window. 'I've got to go, I'm supposed to be at the shovel shed at dawn.' She pulled on her boots and got to her feet. 'Just don't hit anyone while I'm out shovelling, all right?'

'Fine.' Skip scowled.

Ottilie headed for the door.

'Bye, *Shovels*,' said Maeve Moth in her strange, low voice.

Ottilie heard Gracie Moravec's soft laugh as she pulled the door closed. 'Shovels' was quickly becoming her nickname, but she refused to acknowledge it. Shaking it off, she hurried down the winding staircase and out into the morning mist.

The grounds were shadowed in the last moments before dawn. No matter the season, the far west never lost that early morning chill. Ottilie hugged herself in the cold and hurried towards the shovel shed behind the pond. She could see the silhouettes of huntsmen jogging up ahead, and slowed her pace. With the exception of Gully and Scoot, Ottilie had taken to avoiding all contact with the boys that just a month ago had been her peers.

'Ott!'

Ottilie jumped. She was increasingly jittery of late. Infamous for her deception, she knew she was being watched by all. Worse still, sometimes Ottilie felt she was being followed. Her hairs stood on end for no reason. Her back stiffened and her ears pricked, as if sensing sounds beyond her range of hearing. She put it down to the business with the sculkies making her paranoid.

A slender figure was trotting towards her out of the dark. Ottilie thought she recognised the voice.

'Preddy?'

'Hi,' said Noel Preddy, hurrying up to meet her.

'What are you doing here?' She wrapped her arms tighter around her middle, freshly conscious of her shovelie suit.

'I arrived last night. They, um, they asked if I wanted to transfer stations.'

'Why would they do that?'

'Because, well, they didn't want to waste Leonard Darby as a guardian, now that he doesn't have a fledge to train. And I suppose Wrangler Voilies recommended me, so …'

'Oh. Right. That's great, Preddy. I'm really glad you're back.' Ottilie tried to muster a smile, but wasn't successful.

'I felt really bad, Ott, taking your place, but I wanted to come back here with you lads … I mean …'

'Preddy, it's fine, really. It's good. Of course you should have come back. We missed you! They shouldn't waste Leo. He's really good. And it's Ottilie, really, if you want.' She was being overly polite, and she didn't quite know why.

'I heard about all that. I can't believe you didn't tell us. And you were the whole time? I mean, you're a …'

'Yes, Preddy, I was a girl the whole time,' she said, an uncomfortable smile creeping onto her face.

Preddy made a strangled coughing sound.

'I couldn't tell anyone.'

'No,' he coughed again. 'And you're a shovelie now?'

'Yep.'

'How is that?'

'It's fine.'

Preddy reached forwards and hesitantly patted her arm. Ottilie didn't know what to say. She felt very small.

'I have to go,' she said, pointing over towards the pond. 'I'm running late.'

'Oh, me too!' He glanced at the paling sky. 'I'm supposed to meet Leonard Darby in the lower grounds at dawn.'

'You better get going, he won't like it if you're late – and best call him Leo.'

'Oh right, thanks. Well, it was really good to see you again.'

'I'll see you later. Good luck!'

Preddy smiled and hurried away. Ottilie stood still for a moment or two. She felt oddly jittery and lightheaded. Scrunching her eyes closed and clenching her fists, she willed herself to snap out of it. She would not feel sorry for herself. She would not feel small.

Ottilie thought she might actually be happier sleeping out in the shovelie bunks with the rest of her lot. Things were getting harder in the sculkie quarters. Skip was right. It was coming from Maeve Moth and Gracie Moravec. Maeve Moth had let her friendly facade slip entirely away. She was now downright rude to Ottilie whenever she saw her. Rudeness she could handle. It was the strange behaviour of Gracie Moravec that really had her on edge.

Ottilie woke one night, roused by movement in the bedchamber. Moonlight lit the room but her bed was cast in shadow. She looked up. Gracie Moravec was sitting upright in bed. She was utterly still, just staring across at Ottilie. It was too dark to make out her face but Ottilie had the horrible feeling she was smiling. When she went to speak Gracie settled back down beneath the covers as if nothing had happened.

Ottilie didn't tell Skip about it. She didn't know what to say. It seemed such a silly thing to be disturbed by. Even though she was quite sure Gracie was the instigator of all the horrible little pranks, Ottilie didn't know how to respond. She could have told someone, some figure of authority – that was the right thing to do. But who could she tell? The custodian chieftess, irate that Ottilie was mingling with her sculkies, didn't acknowledge Ottilie's existence. The wranglers disapproved of her and she couldn't bother Captain Lyre about something that seemed so silly compared to what the huntsmen were dealing with on a daily basis. In the end she let it go. If it happened again she would do something. That was what she decided.

As the weeks rolled by Maeve Moth became more unpleasant but, apart from a dead mouse Ottilie found in her boot, Gracie Moravec seemed to be leaving her alone.

'She put a mouse in your shoe?' said Gully, his legs dangling off the edge of a low-hanging branch.

In an attempt to avoid prying or disapproving eyes, they had gathered on the fringe of Floodwood, close to where the yicker had crawled out of Christopher Crow. Ottilie did her best to try to forget what had happened there, but it wasn't easy with Scoot flinching at every rustle and snap.

'Well, I don't have any proof. I've never caught her at it, but Skip reckons it's her,' said Ottilie, pulling her dress up over her knees as she hopped onto a log. They'd given her dresses for daywear clothes. It was strange to be back in skirts. She had never noticed before how much they affected the way she moved.

'Why are they being such rankers about it?' said Scoot.

'Who?' said Ottilie. Something had caught her eye a little way through the scrub. She blinked and found her mind adrift in a displaced memory. A figure standing between two trees. It was months ago now, and so much had happened to distract her, but she remembered it; just before the yickers attacked, she'd seen a figure standing not far off, watching them.

'The sculkies,' said Scoot, squinting nervously at a flickering shadow.

'Scoot, do you rememb–' She stopped herself. It was instinct, to hide her thoughts. She shut her mouth for the same reason she hadn't mentioned her suspicions about the rule of innocence to the boys. This secret society was exclusive, elite and, above all, a brotherhood. They weren't asking questions – not anymore. Ottilie, with her hidden identity, had always held a tenuous position within their little group, and now that the jig was up, whether they acknowledged it or not she was an outsider, and she was afraid of drifting further away.

Ottilie shrugged, considering Scoot's question. 'It's because I, I don't know ... some of them are bitter because I *dared to rise higher than my station*. That's how Voilies would put it.'

'What station?' said Gully, snapping a twig from the branch above.

'I'm a girl and I pretended to be a boy.'

'And?'

'Well, the girls here are all custodians, and the boys get to be huntsmen. I guess it wasn't fair on the rest of them that I got to do what they can't.' *None of it's fair*, she thought.

'But Skip's not mad,' said Scoot.

'No, Skip always saw it differently. She thought it was great. I think she thought that because I'd done it, maybe one day she'd be able to hunt dredretches too. So much for that.' Ottilie felt prickling behind her eyes. She looked up and willed away the tears.

Gully cracked the twig in two. He looked miserable.

The fort bell clanged, breaking the silence.

'That's me,' said Ottilie. 'I've got a shift in fifteen minutes.'

'Me too,' said Gully, leaping down from his branch. 'I better get dressed.'

Ottilie patted the soil down and whistled for the bone singers to approach. Two blue-hatted bone singers came forward, their simple grey robes blending in with the tree trunks around them. Approaching the mound of freshly buried bones, they pulled fistfuls of crystalline granules from the sacks at their belts. Ottilie assumed the dust they sprinkled was salt of some kind, although it looked like there might be a bit more to it.

The bone singers with her that day were older than Ottilie, but not by a great deal. She was working with a boy and a girl, and she knew very little about them. Shovelies, it seemed, even a notorious one like Ottilie, were of very little interest to bone singers.

'I'll go and start on that other one,' said Ottilie, pointing to a track through the wattle trees.

Their guards, two second-tier footmen, ignored her, but the female bone singer acknowledged her with a nod and Ottilie heard them begin their dulcet humming as she trekked off towards another pile of festering flesh and bone. She moved deeper into the forest, where the scrub grew thick and swamp gums towered. Ottilie stiffened. She felt strange. Beneath her rolled-up sleeves she could see the hairs on her forearms standing on end. She had the oddest feeling that she was being watched.

A pitchy twitter rang out somewhere above. Ottilie dove behind a rotting log. She knew that sound. It was a kikiscrax, a tiny blue birdlike dredretch that dripped poisonous black liquid from its feathers. Kikiscraxes were fast-moving and difficult to fell. Beakless, they seemed to have no mouth at all, but their bone-white claws stretched longer than the length of their bodies, and the tips were so sharp they could pierce a human skull. Ottilie felt for her ring. Despite its protection, she still felt a little queasy.

The kikiscrax passed over the log and disappeared into the trees. Ottilie wondered if she should call for the guards. She hesitated. It was strange. Why had it moved on? Why hadn't it attacked? She was just about to get to her feet when she sensed movement ahead – no, not just ahead – all around. Dark shapes closed in, prowling through the trees. Lycoats. That was why the kikiscrax had gone. Most of the smaller monsters stayed out of way of the lycoats – a ruthless dredretch species that resembled armoured dogs.

The pack of lycoats stalked out of the surrounding brush. Five sets of pointed yellow teeth were bared in five identical snarls. Shell-like black armour wrapped around their middles, necks and legs. Yellowish fur grew in between the armoured areas, marking narrow places where an arrow could pierce their skin. Ottilie had never faced a lycoat before. They stuck to the thicketed areas that flyers couldn't penetrate. Footmen usually took care of them.

Ottilie lifted her fingers to whistle for the guards. She knew it was pointless – they wouldn't get there in time. The guards were really for the bone singers, not the shovelies. Shovelies were failures, a disgrace. They didn't deserve protection. She would have to do the best she could with her shovel.

Less than a second before the whistle escaped her lips, an arrow shot through the trees, piercing the nearest lycoat between its armoured shoulders. The dredretch snarled and crumbled to the ground.

The pack sprung into action, one diving at Ottilie and the others turning towards the archer. Ottilie lunged to the side, gripped her shovel, and hit the attacking lycoat in the head. It fell sideways and smacked into a tree. She took the opportunity to glance at the huntsman.

It was Gully!

Gully and Ned had appeared through the trees. Ottilie froze for a moment. She had never seen Gully in action. It was horrible, like watching a child fight a wolf, but worse than that, much worse, because these weren't wolves.

Ned was practically wrestling the largest lycoat, who wrapped its jaws around his arm, breaking the skin. Ned cried out, then gritted his teeth and managed to elbow it in the eye, forcing it to release its grip. The pair rolled over three times, locked together as if in an embrace, until Ned plunged a knife into its exposed furry chest and kicked it away. The lycoat rolled over twice more and came apart mid-turn.

Ottilie's assailant was coming back for more. Holding her shovel at the ready, she braced to strike again.

'Ottilie!' Gully threw a dagger in her direction. It landed embedded in the ground behind her. Ottilie hit the lycoat again, lunged backwards to grab the dagger and, before it had a chance to recover, dived on top of it, plunging the blade into its chest. There were only two left now. Ned drew his cutlass and caught a lycoat mid-pounce, and Gully shot an arrow, taking the last.

The three of them stood for a moment, panting. Gully and Ned were so covered in dark dredretch blood it was impossible to make out their own injuries. She knew Ned's arm had been punctured, but other than that it was probably just cuts and scrapes.

Ned turned to Gully. 'They get you anywhere?'

Gully looked himself over, wrinkling his nose at the smell of dredretch blood. 'No. That's all theirs,' he said, flicking a dark clot of it off his forearm.

'How about you? You all right, Ott?' said Ned.

'Fine. They didn't get anywhere near me,' she said, holding up her shovel.

Ned looked like he might laugh, but instead said, 'Nice work with that one,' and pointed to the pile of clumped fur and rancid bones by her foot. 'We should get moving, Gully.'

Ottilie had the sudden urge to grab hold of Gully and keep him from leaving. She didn't want him out there, rolling around with dredretches.

'See you later,' said Gully.

Ottilie smiled, but didn't speak. She felt so powerless, standing there in her shovelie suit. Things had seemed so much safer when instead of a shovel, she'd held a bow.

⚜ 28 ⚜

The Hex

Montie Kit placed a steaming bowl of black bean stew onto the old oak table. 'Eat up,' she said.

The kitchen smelled of dried garlic and freshly baked bread, and the air was warm and thick, like a meal in itself. Ottilie had been taking refuge in Montie's kitchen whenever she needed an escape from the sculkie quarters. Through the steam, she regarded Montie's half-twisted face. Up close, the scarring reminded Ottilie of the patterns on the trunk of an Uskler pine. The lumps twisted around her left eye socket were like a knot in the wood.

'Eat,' Montie repeated. 'You look like you need it.'

Ottilie was no longer the underfed swamp creature she'd been when she first arrived at Fort Fiory. With the generous meals provided by the Hunt, and the extra meals Montie presented her with whenever she visited, she had gained a fair amount of flesh on her once well-starved bones. Her body looked completely different to the one she remembered. Training had hardened her muscles and although she was no longer hunting, the shovelie work was still physically demanding.

'Are you getting enough sleep?' said Montie, her good eye scanning Ottilie's face.

'I think so.' That was a lie.

Montie made a knowing noise deep in her throat. 'I know you don't think it, Ottilie, but you're better off now,' she said. 'None of you should be out there hunting. It's too dangerous.'

'None of who?' said Ottilie, narrowing her eyes.

'Don't you look at me like that, Ottilie Colter. I'm not saying it's because you're a girl. I'm saying it's because you're too young. All of them are. I don't like it. I've never liked it.'

Ottilie had been wondering about Montie and Alba. She knew that most of the custodians had chosen to come here – many, like Skip, seeking a better life. She couldn't find a way to phrase the question without seeming rude, so Ottilie had never asked, but she suspected that Montie's presence in the Narroway might have something to do with the source of her scarring.

Ottilie had just scraped the last lump from her bowl when the kitchen door creaked open and Alba slipped into the room.

'An hour and a half late, Alba,' said Montie, who was drying plates with her back to the door.

'Sorry Mum.' Alba raised her brows, meeting Ottilie's eye with a meaningful stare.

Ottilie blinked at her, tilting her hand ever so slightly, as if to say *what?*

Montie sighed and mounted a rickety ladder, stretching to reach the highest shelf. 'You're too late to help with clearing dishes, but you can place the gardener's drop in the root cellar.'

'I'll help,' said Ottilie, hopping off her chair. 'Thanks for dinner. It was so good, I'll just wash the bowl –'

'Never mind that, go on,' said Montie, without turning around. 'Go and discuss whatever it is you're sneaking off to talk about.'

Alba grinned and ushered Ottilie out the door, clearly bursting with news. 'I've looked everywhere, Ottilie,' she said breathlessly, as they slipped through the outdoor entrance to the cellar. 'There's nothing in the library. Not a word about the rule of innocence – even in the old legends from the Lore, which they say are mostly myths and fables.'

Alba lit the lamps and Ottilie jerked the door shut, hugging herself in the cold. 'So you think it's not real?

It's a lie?' She found herself whispering, even though there were only moths to overhear.

'Well. That's the thing. I've read every book in that library, and I've …' She looked sheepish. 'I've even had a look in some of the private libraries.'

'What private libraries?' said Ottilie, settling down on top of a stepladder.

'Some wranglers and directors have their own collections. I've made my way through most of them, but not Conductor Edderfed's. His security system is much more complicated than the rest of them.' An expression of deep annoyance narrowed her usually owl-like eyes.

'You've been breaking in?' said Ottilie in awe.

'They've got all the interesting books in there. The main library only has books on dredretches, but the directors have books on history, philosophy, healing … everything. I know my way around this place better than anyone, and, well, one of the sculkies taught me how to pick a lock a couple of years ago – your friend, actually, Isla Skipper.'

'You know Skip?'

'We all know each other. Who else is there to know?'

Ottilie glanced at the door. 'Does your mum know about this?' She smiled, realising Alba reminded her of Bill. Alba appeared to be a fairly timid creature, yet she was always creeping in the shadows, appearing from secret tunnels and, apparently, stealing from important authority figures.

'Do you know, I think she does. That's why she gets so mad at me when I'm off reading. She knows I'm doing the wrong thing. She never stops me though.' A twitchy, guilty grin lit up her face. 'But Ottilie, here's the thing. I've never been into the bone singers' scrolls before, and I found something. It was an unfinished collection of stories, and there was one about the king, our current king, Varrio Sol.'

Ottilie's heart began to race. 'What? What did it say?'

'It was about a hex that a witch put on him. I almost passed over it, but then I read she hexed him so that he could send *no man* to fight to defend his kingdom. Afterwards, he was left with two choices: give up the crown, or rule knowing that for his entire reign, his kingdom would go unprotected. Do you think that could be something?'

Ottilie pondered it. A hex? But the witches were all gone. They were dead and buried a long time ago. 'Do you really think there could still be witches out there?'

Alba didn't look afraid. 'It's possible, just in secret ... the same as how there are still Laklanders in the Usklers.'

Ottilie shivered and glanced at the door. 'So if he's hexed so that he can't send any man to fight ... and the dredretches started showing up in the west ... then what? He made a secret child army to deal with the problem?'

'It was the only link I could make,' said Alba.

It was a link. It fit. 'But it's just a story?'

Alba shrugged. 'I don't know, but it's the only thing I've found that comes close to explaining why they would make up the rule of innocence.'

'But, if it is true ... who knows about it? I've never heard the story before. Do you think the wranglers know?' Surely these people residing in the Narroway knew whether they were capable of felling a dredretch. Was it possible none of them had ever tried?

'I couldn't say for sure. But logically, if it is true, the king wouldn't want anyone to know. If people knew he couldn't defend the kingdom, he'd be de-throned, maybe even assassinated. I think he made up the rule of innocence to cover himself. It explains why the Hunt is such a big secret. The less people who know what's going on, the less questions are asked, and the less people there are to silence if they stumble across the truth.'

'I need some air,' Ottilie muttered.

The idea that witches were running around hexing kings was too much for her to handle that evening. She unlatched the door and shoved it open with her foot. Lantern light flooded the night, revealing three barrows of freshly harvested vegetables that they were yet to put away. 'We should probably start on that,' said Ottilie, grateful for the distraction.

'Good idea,' said Alba.

Half an hour later, Ottilie wandered back down to the sculkie quarters with a carrot in her hand and her head in a dream. Igor Thrike was leaning against a wall, talking to Maeve Moth. When Ottilie approached, he stuck out his foot to trip her. Ottilie stepped over it without so much as a glance in his direction. She had more important things to think about.

A hex. A witch had hexed the king. The dredretches were a threat to his kingdom, an invasion approaching from the west, and he could not send his armies to meet them. She knew there was little evidence to support the theory, but the rule of innocence had never sat well with her, and this seemed to fit. Ottilie wasn't sure how she felt about the story, or the lies. But as it stood, with the current, deceitful king in power, only the Hunt could protect the Usklers from the dredretches, and more than anything Ottilie wished she could be part of that again.

29

The Wind and the Watcher

The wagon rattled, bumping and jerking on uneven ground. Ottilie was being sent into the heart of the forest, in the direction of the Withering Wood. The usually docile mountain bucks were troubled. She could hear them huffing and snorting as they neared the poisonous patch of trees.

She was working with the same pair of bone singers from weeks ago, when she had been attacked by the pack of lycoats with Gully and Ned. She knew now that the girl's name was Bonnie and the boy's was Nicolai. Their guards were two fifth-tier mounts. They rode ahead of the wagon, scanning the way for any sign of trouble.

Summer was ebbing away. The days had grown colder very quickly and the mornings even more so.

The early morning sky was heavy with dark clouds. An icy wind swept through the open-ended wagon, making Ottilie's teeth chatter. She hoped they'd stop soon. At least once she started digging she would warm up a bit.

She shivered. She had that awful feeling again, the strange sense that she was being watched. She glanced over at Bonnie. Her faint eyebrows were drawn together in a frown. 'What is it?' said Ottilie.

'I don't like nearing the Withering Wood,' said Bonnie, a shadow passing over her eyes.

But the work needed to be done. They started with the bones closest to the Withering Wood and then began making their way back towards Fiory. Ottilie felt shivery and agitated and kept pausing to glance at shapes and shadows between the trees.

A warm breeze slithered into the clearing. Warm? Why was it warm? It had the stench of rancid dredretch flesh. The wind had carried the scent from the Withering Wood. Ottilie retched, her stomach retracting. She lurched down onto the ground and vomited.

She froze, her hand raised to wipe her mouth. A dark figure was standing between the trees. Hooded and cloaked, it was too far off to recognise, but there was definitely someone there, watching her. Ottilie's heart pounded in her ears. It couldn't be a huntsman. Footmen were always at least in a pair, and there was no sign of a horse or a wingerslink. Anyway, huntsmen didn't wear cloaks. A wrangler? A director? No. They would never wander, unguarded, so far from a station. She had seen this figure before. She knew it. Ottilie took a breath and clambered to her feet. She stepped towards the figure and the mountain buck behind her let out a terrified shriek.

Ottilie whipped around. A greeve, like a fanged reptilian stoat, sprang out from beneath a bramble bush and raced at Nicolai. Ottilie whistled for the guards, but they were already there, shoving Nicolai out of the way and bracing to defend him. Greeves were almost impossible to catch. They were one of the quickest land-based dredretches. It would take the guards a while to eliminate the threat.

Above the horses' snorts and bucks' shrieks, Ottilie heard a wingerslink roar – there was a flyer nearby.

The guards fired arrow after arrow at the greeve, missing by a whisker each time. Ottilie kept her shovel raised, ready to strike. Another hot breeze blew through the trees and another wave of nausea overcame her. It took all of her strength not to throw up again.

A dreadful grunting growl rolled through the clearing. Everyone froze, even the greeve. The ground seemed to shake as hooves thundered and low-hanging branches were ripped from the trees.

A scorver crashed through the undergrowth. Twice the size of the mountain bucks, the scorver had slimy, greyish skin with razor-sharp spines down its back. Its wolf-like snout was filled with four rows of pointed yellow teeth.

Despite their horrific appearance, scorvers were thin-skinned, and relatively easy to deal with – although perhaps not so much with a greeve running underfoot. The scorver snarled and rumbled. This was followed by a shrill whistling from the greeve, and more terrified shrieks from the bucks. But over all of it, Ottilie heard the wingerslink roar again.

The guards sprang into action, and the bone singers started humming and sprinkling salt around themselves while turning in slow circles. They looked like they had lost their minds. Ottilie didn't move. She heard it again. It was Maestro, she was sure of it. But it wasn't his normal war cry. He was distressed. Something was wrong.

There was nothing to be done; the guards had their hands full with the scorver and the greeve. Ottilie made a split-second decision. Clutching her shovel, she crashed back towards the Withering Wood, following the sound of Maestro's distant roars. If the guards called after her, she didn't hear them. The sounds led her to the edge of a ravine. Despite the recent rain, the water was mostly dried up so close to the Withering Wood. Puffing hard, Ottilie stumbled along the edge. Maestro roared again and this time she heard something respond; a deafening screech, like a hundred bats shrieking at once. Ottilie threw her free hand over one ear and pushed herself to a sprint.

She could see them. The ravine wound all the way to the edge of the Withering Wood. Far below, in the blackened, cracking mud, Leo was trapped on the ground, his back to a vertical cliff face. Maestro was in front of him, wings flapping wildly as he roared, standing between Leo and the most horrifying dredretch Ottilie had ever seen.

Twice Maestro's size, the dredretch looked like an enormous scaly bat. It had tufts of black fur sticking out between vast green, crusting scales. Fangs the length of Ottilie's arm stretched out of its jaws. A long, scaly tail swung behind it, lined with spines and ending in a mace-like tip the size of a small boulder.

Maestro braced and roared, swatting at the air between him and the dredretch, trying to keep it back. Ottilie noticed he was limping. The great batlike beast screeched again, hovering in the air just above Maestro. The sound made Ottilie's teeth chatter. She gritted her jaw shut and leapt, half-tumbling, half-climbing down the edge of the ravine.

She tripped and stumbled across the cracked riverbed, smacking her shin on a rock. Squawks sounded somewhere above. Her head snapped up. Jivvies. Leo must have been bleeding.

'Ott!' Leo called to her. 'I'm stuck – help me lift this!'

His leg was trapped beneath a rock. Ottilie pulled herself upright, but something froze her in place. Directly above Leo, at the top of the cliff between two blackened trees, stood the hooded figure. Watching. Ottilie's heart raced. *Witch*. She didn't know why, but it was all she could think. *Witch*.

The jivvies shrieked, circling lower and lower. Leo fired at them, missing again and again. He couldn't get the angle right from his position on the ground. Ottilie tore her eyes away from the figure and dashed towards him.

Leo fired again.

'Stop wasting arrows!' She threw her shovel aside and snatched the bow from his hand just as the jivvies dived. Firing in quick succession, she took out three in a row. The fourth, savage with bloodlust, knocked the fifth out of the air, severing its head with its beak. Maestro roared and swatted again. Ottilie shot at the last jivvie, missing its heart but piercing the wing. It was enough. She needed to get Leo out from under the rock.

'Here,' he grunted, trying to push the rock off his leg, 'help me lift it.'

Ottilie latched her fingers underneath, pulling hard.

'Where's Preddy?' she panted, realising he should have been with Leo. Had something happened to him? Was he hurt?

Gritting his teeth with effort, Leo said between breaths, 'He – had – training – not – with me.' The rock lifted just enough for Leo to pull his leg out from under it. He let out a sound that was something like a groan of pain and sigh of relief all in one. 'We need to get out of here,' Leo grunted. 'Maestro's hurt.'

That very second the dredretch screeched and knocked Maestro out of the way with its mace-like tail. Tumbling across the cracked earth, he hit the cliff face with a crunch. Leo roared with rage. He tried to stand but his injured leg couldn't take his weight.

Knees quaking, Ottilie raised Leo's bow and faced the dredretch. Its wings tucked back, snorting wildly, the dredretch charged at them on foot. Ottilie shot it in the chest but it didn't so much as flinch.

'Eye, it'll have to be the eye!' said Leo, glancing frantically back and forth between the recovering wingerslink and the advancing dredretch.

'Leo, I can't shoot its eye!' said Ottilie. The dredretch had eyes the size of grapes. The target was too small. Thinking fast, she aimed again, shooting an arrow into its fleshy foot. The dredretch faltered and stumbled. Ottilie whistled for Maestro and shot an arrow into its other foot, giving the injured wingerslink time to limp across to her. Ottilie helped Leo upright, leaned him against Maestro's side and clambered up into the saddle before reaching down and hoisting Leo up in front of her. Leo was out on his own so it was only the single saddle, but they could just fit together. His leg was useless. He couldn't grip. Ottilie helped him buckle his legs into the straps as Maestro beat his wings, lifting up into the air. Down below, the dredretch ripped the arrows out of its feet with its jaws. Shattering them to splinters, it screeched and rose into the air to meet them.

Leo couldn't squeeze both his legs so Ottilie had to take control. Steering Maestro in a wide circle, she said, 'Can we outrun it?'

'No. I don't think so.'

The dredretch folded its wings and shot at them like an arrow. Ottilie, having no idea what to do, let Maestro take the lead. The wingerslink rolled in the air and lashed out at the dredretch's underbelly with his claws. He tore a gash in its scaled stomach, but it healed immediately. The dredretch shrieked in protest, spun in the air, and readied for another advance.

'I can get the eye,' said Leo. 'Give me the bow.'

Ottilie passed it over. Nocking an arrow, Leo drew his arm back, but the saddle was too small and Ottilie's body was in his way. There was nothing she could do. She couldn't bend far enough to clear the space and still grip on with her legs. The dredretch lunged at them and Leo fired. The arrow just grazed the side of its head. Leo snarled in frustration. Maestro lurched sideways to avoid the dredretch's jaws, and Ottilie, who had been leaning away to try to give Leo room to aim, was nearly flung clean off.

Grabbing Leo's arm and gripping harder with her legs than she ever had before, Ottilie righted herself. The dredretch circled below, preparing to attack again. But Leo couldn't aim with her so close behind him.

There was nothing else to do.

Terror rattled her bones as Ottilie shifted her weight. Her fingers shook, but she locked her grip and swung off the side of the saddle. Holding onto the straps that bound Leo's good leg, Ottilie dangled below like bait on a fishing line.

'What are you doing?' Leo bellowed.

The fear was overwhelming. Her entire body seemed to pulse with the rapid pounding of her heart.

The dredretch screeched and shot up towards her feet, fangs bared.

Arm straining and fingers slipping, she barked, 'Just shoot it, Leonard!'

'Don't you dare fall!'

'Concentrate!'

Leo took aim. The dredretch tore upwards. Its jaws were an inch from her toes when the arrow struck. Leo's arrow embedded itself in the dredretch's beady eye. Without so much as a groan, its batlike wings spread wide and disintegrated into festering skeletal scraps as it plummeted down into the Withering Wood.

Leo gripped her forearm and Ottilie hoisted herself back up behind him. She glanced down and saw a steady stream of red blood dripping down the wingerslink's side.

'We need to get him home,' said Leo, stroking Maestro's pale neck.

'I left my shovel,' said Ottilie, her eyes slipping down to the trees in a daze.

Leo coughed up a bark of laughter, which was cut off immediately as Maestro shuddered beneath them. Leo tensed and buried his hands in Maestro's sweat-matted fur. 'You're all right,' he muttered, more to himself than the wingerslink. 'Come on. Home.'

30

Mending

Soaring above the trees, over the Red Canyon, across the fields, and finally sweeping down to land just within the Fiory boundary walls, Maestro didn't falter once. A wingerslink landing in the upper grounds drew plenty of attention; wranglers and huntsmen on watch duty along the wall rushed towards them, and only when Leo had been helped down from the saddle by two fourth-tiers did Maestro slump onto the grass with a terrifying growl of pain. There was too much blood, red and black, to make much sense of his wounds. But Ottilie could see a terrible gash on his left side that she thought was the source of most of the red blood.

'Back off!' Someone was trying to help Leo to the infirmary, but he shoved them away.

Wrangler Voilies trotted towards him. 'Leo, my boy, we need to get you –'

'Someone send for Wrangler Ritgrivvian,' said Leo, through gritted teeth.

'Ramona? But she's the horse –'

'Just get her. She's better with injuries than the wingerslink master.'

'I – all right, yes. Bacon, lad, fetch Ramona Ritgrivvian, quick as you can. Now, Leo –'

'I'm not going anywhere until she sees to Maestro.'

Amazingly, Wrangler Voilies closed his mouth. Leo, sensing his victory, finally lowered himself to the ground, grimacing in pain. He was very pale. Ottilie wondered if he'd broken his leg.

Wrangler Voilies turned to Ottilie. They had all been so concerned with Leo that no-one had noticed her until now, but there she was, standing by Leo's side in her bloodstained shovelie suit. Wrangler Voilies narrowed his eyes and studied her suspiciously, as if she were somehow responsible for Leo's injuries. 'Are you injured?' he barked.

'No,' she said.

'Go to the infirmary and get yourself checked over. No arguments, Miss Colter. Now!'

Ottilie scowled. He had no power over Leo and he knew it, so he was taking it out on her. Her neck muscles stiffening under Voilies' venomous glare, Ottilie stroked Maestro's neck before reluctantly heading for the infirmary.

Ottilie had more injuries than she realised. They were mostly bruises she had inflicted on herself by tumbling down the ravine, but there was also a nasty cut on her arm that needed dressing. The patchies gave her a draught for the pain. Although they said she was fine, Ottilie wasn't allowed to leave; they wanted to keep an eye on her for a couple of hours.

The infirmary was a low-ceilinged chamber lined with rows of slender beds. It was a clean, comforting space that smelled of fresh mint and thyme. Ottilie was sitting in an armchair by the large square window, gazing out into the sunlit grounds, when the blue double doors were thrown open and a heavily bandaged Leo was carried in on a stretcher. Ottilie jumped to her feet. What had happened? Had his injuries gotten worse?

She calmed the moment she saw his face. He was scowling and fidgeting. It was clear he had been forced onto the stretcher against his will. Three patchies in grey clothes and pale green caps helped him onto a bed and, grumbling, he immediately pulled himself up into a sitting position. One of the patchies looked like he was about to suggest Leo lie back, but Leo shot him a look so chilling the patchie scuttled into the storeroom instead, muttering something about tea.

'You all right?' Leo said, turning to Ottilie.

'Fine, mostly bruises. How's Maestro?'

'He'll be all right. They've stitched him up and put him away to rest.'

Ottilie felt her shoulders settle as a sigh of relief escaped her lungs. 'And you?'

Leo grunted with disgust. 'Fine. Voilies got the patchies out to treat me in the grounds so I could stay with Maestro.'

She wondered if his leg was broken, but didn't dare ask. 'What was that dredretch?' She remembered its nightmarish jaws, just inches from her feet – imagined them stretching wide to swallow her whole. She shuddered.

Leo shook his head, cringed, and leaned back against the wall, squeezing his eyes closed. 'I have no idea,' he muttered. 'I've never seen it before and I didn't recognise it from the bestiaries.'

'Could it be new?'

'I don't know.' His eyes slid open. 'Sometimes new ones pop up that they've never seen, but they're usually small. I don't know how something that big could have gone unnoticed.' Rubbing his neck, he glanced at her. 'What were you doing out there? How did you find us?'

Ottilie explained about the greeve and the scorver and how she'd heard Maestro's roars.

His eyes narrowed. 'You're out of your mind, Ott – coming after us with a shovel.'

Ottilie assumed that was his way of saying *thank you*.

'I didn't have a choice,' she said. 'They took away my bow.'

Leo looked away from her. Had she detected a hint of shame in his eyes or was that just wishful thinking? Would he go back to loathing her after today?

'Well, you did a good job with mine,' he said, still not looking at her.

Ottilie didn't respond. Part of her didn't care if he hated her again, because part of her was still furious with him. He had turned her in, and if that wasn't enough to earn her ire, his treatment of her ever since certainly was.

The door swung open and Ned strode over to Leo's bed, trailing mud behind him. 'I just heard,' he said. 'You all right? What have you done to yourself?'

One of the green-capped patchies clicked his tongue, snatching up a mop bucket and stomping off to fill it.

'Ah, sorry,' said Ned, glancing guiltily down at the mud. 'Ott, Gully's in training with the other fledges but I sent someone to tell him you're here the moment they're done.'

'Thanks,' said Ottilie.

'What happened?' he said, turning back to Leo.

'Found a massive dredretch, bigger than a barro,' said Leo.

'What species?'

Leo shrugged. 'Never seen it before. It knocked Maestro down with its tail, and we fell into the dried-up river, along with a huge chunk of the cliff. My leg got stuck under a rock and Maestro fended it off until Ott found us. She helped me get my leg out and got us back into the air, then I shot it in the eye.'

It all sounded so simple spoken out loud, so easy – especially her part.

'So. Ottilie saved the day, did she?' said Ned, grinning.

Ottilie noted the use of her full name. Ned usually called her Ott out of habit, Scoot did the same, but it was clear he'd used 'Ottilie' on purpose. He was trying to make a point.

Leo looked uncomfortable. He adjusted the strapping on his leg, frowning. 'Is it broken?' said Ned.

'Nah, just sort of … crushed.'

Ned raised his eyebrows. 'Can you walk on it?'

'Not today,' said Leo, scowling. Ottilie knew he was sulking over how many points he would miss out on if he was confined to a bed.

'I wonder how much they'll score you for it,' said Ned.

Leo shrugged. 'They'll have to figure out what it was first.' He glanced over at a patchie. 'Can you get a message to Wrangler Morse and tell him I'm requesting an urgent audience with the Fiory Directorate?'

'Right away,' said the patchie.

Ottilie sighed quietly. She was well and truly sick of Leo being treated like the Crown Prince of the Narroway.

'Ottilie! Ottilie, stop snoring!'

Ottilie forced her eyes open. The sculkies' bedchamber was bright around her. The lamps were lit. Most of the girls were still up and working, but with the help of the patchies' draught Ottilie had been asleep since the fifth bell.

'Skip, what?' she groaned. She'd been up since before dawn, lifted a huge rock, felled four jivvies, and helped take down an unknown dredretch bigger than a barrogaul while hanging off a wingerslink's saddle. She was exhausted.

'They want to see you,' said Skip, forcing her upright.

'Who, Gully? I saw him before,' she said, flopping back down.

Skip yanked her back up and said, 'Do I need to slap you awake? No, the directorate want to see you. Get up!'

Ottilie's eyes snapped open. 'What? Why?' Her breath grew short. What had she done? Was she on trial again?

Skip was scowling. 'I don't know, but you need to go.'

Ottilie clambered out of bed, wincing. Her muscles had already stiffened. It had been two months since she'd last ridden a wingerslink and her legs were not happy. The widespread bruising didn't help. She hobbled towards the door.

'Here, wait!' Skip pulled her back and shoved a clean dress at her. 'You look terrible,' she breathed as Ottilie changed, revealing her bruised and torn skin. Once she was dressed, Skip pushed her down onto the bed and ran a comb through her hair, trying her best to smooth down the curls. It was getting longer by the day, but Ottilie couldn't decide whether to keep cutting it. Finally Skip deemed her presentable. She took her arm and stayed by her side all the way to the circular chamber.

Wrangler Furdles was waiting at the entrance. He greeted Ottilie with a nasty one-eyed scowl, and opened the door without a word.

'Good luck,' whispered Skip, squeezing her arm.

Ottilie swallowed and stepped into the room. Conductor Edderfed sat on his throne. The three Fiory directors were seated below and, in the centre of the room, facing the directorate, sat Leo.

What was this about? Did they want to hear her account of the dredretch? Wasn't Leo's information enough?

'Miss Colter,' said Conductor Edderfed, 'thank you for coming, please take a seat.'

Ottilie's face grew steadily hotter as she settled into the empty seat beside Leo.

'Mr Darby has informed us of the events of the day,' said Conductor Edderfed.

Ottilie glanced sideways. Leo was looking away from her. What had he done? What had he said? Had he got her into more trouble somehow?

'We would like to commend you for the extraordinary bravery you showed today in coming to the aid of Mr Darby here, armed with nothing but a ... shovel, was it, Leonard?'

'That's right,' said Leo.

They had brought her here to commend her? That was it?

'Mr Darby has requested that we rethink your dismissal from the Hunt, and I have to say, he has made a very convincing case for you.'

Ottilie couldn't believe what she was hearing. Leo had come to ask if they would let her be a huntsman again? Leo, who had triggered her dismissal in the first place, had convincingly argued her case? He must have told the story a lot better than the way he explained it to Ned.

'We have put it to a vote,' said Conductor Edderfed, 'and the majority agrees that Mr Darby's testimony, along with a character reference from Wrangler Morse, is sufficient to warrant your reinstatement.'

Ottilie's heart leapt even as tears welled in her eyes.

Just to her right, Captain Lyre flashed the sallow-skinned Director Yaist a smug smile.

'I will write to my co-conductors this evening and, should the Richter and Arko Directorates have no objections, you will be officially reinstated at summer's end.'

***

'What – why – what did you do?' said Ottilie, walking slowly beside Leo as he struggled back to the infirmary on his crutches.

'Just told them what happened,' said Leo, 'and how Ned saw you take out that lycoat the other week.'

Ottilie was still suffering from a small amount of shock. Her voice sounded strange in her own ears. 'And what? They just changed their minds? They don't care that I lied anymore? Or that I'm a girl?'

Leo scowled. 'I convinced them that you're a wasted asset, Ott. Why are you interrogating me? You should be thanking me.'

She scowled right back. 'Thanking you? Where's *my* thank you? I got your leg out from under that rock!'

Leo looked furious and Ottilie had the sudden urge to push him over. It would only take a gentle shove to topple him.

'Look, just … get yourself back into shape, all right. I don't want you messing up again when we get back out there.'

'We? You're going to be my guardian again?' She felt an excited swooping in her stomach.

'Course I am.'

'What about Preddy?'

'They'll find someone else for Noel. He'll be happy anyway, I'm pretty sure he missed the mounts. He and Maestro didn't get on,' said Leo, holding back a smile.

'You don't think they'll send him back to Richter, though?' They had only just got Preddy back. She didn't want to lose him again.

'What? No. I don't know. Who cares? They'll figure it out. Are you going to say thank you or not?'

Ottilie stopped. 'Am I going to say thank you?' She glared at him in disbelief. 'You were the one who turned me in in the first place! Oh yes, thank you, Leonard. Thank you so much for telling them about how I saved your life today! That was so kind of you not to lie and say you did it all on your own,' she snapped.

His face turned scarlet. 'I would have got out of it on my own!'

'Oh, all right, then!' Ottilie threw up her hands. 'Thank you so much for letting me save you so you could use the story to undo the mess you made and ease your guilt for being so horrible to me just because I'm a girl!' she said in one long breath.

'I – you sound like a crazy person!'

Ottilie took a deep breath. 'I'm sorry,' she said, more calmly.

'What? For … ?'

'For lying. You didn't make the mess. I did. I didn't have a choice, but it was *my* mess. You didn't make it – but you made it worse!'

He glared at her. 'Well –'

'But thank you for fixing your mistake.' And with that she turned and stormed away.

She had left Leo well behind when Gully came bounding along the corridor.

'Ottilie!' His face shone with excitement. 'Skip just told me you had to go see them. What did they say?' His energy was infectious. And so, almost forgetting her anger, Ottilie told him what had happened.

Gully's joy smothered her bad mood immediately. Eyes alight, he did a celebratory leap before locking his arms around Ottilie's ribs and squeezing tight.

'We're both huntsmen now! Or you're a hunt … huntswoman? Huntress?' he released her.

'Doesn't matter,' she said. 'I think huntsman can be for both.'

Gully beamed. 'Let's show them, Ottilie!' he said, breathless with excitement. 'Let's win it … be champions!'

'I don't think you can have two champions in one tier.'

'We can get the same points – tie for it! I want to be great at this. I think I could be!'

She smiled and shoved him with her shoulder. 'Me too. Come on, it's late.'

'I want to be the best,' he whispered. 'Don't tell anyone,' he added, seriously.

Ottilie laughed. 'I won't.'

⟿ 31 ⟿

Summer's End

Grey skies swallowed the last moon of summer and an autumn sun peeked above the trees. It was summer's end. The directorates of Richter and Arko hadn't objected, and Ottilie was a huntsman again. She woke in her old private bedchamber to the sound of a knock on the door.

'Co—' she cleared her throat. 'Come in.'

Skip slid into the room. 'Good morning Ottilie Colter, first female Fiory fledgling.'

Ottilie half-yawned, half-grinned. 'Morning Isla Skipper, superior sculkie and secret keeper.'

Skip threw the window shutters open wide and Ottilie blinked in the light. She smiled, feeling happier than she had in a long time. She had so much to look forward to. She was a huntsman, and there was an end-of-summer festival planned for the evening, with lights, music and lots of food. It was going to be a very good day.

'This is just the beginning, you know.' Skip flopped down on the bed. 'You've got Leo on side now, and there's Gully, Ned, Preddy and Scoot.' She crawled up to the top of the bed to sit cross-legged beside Ottilie's head.

'What are you talking about?' said Ottilie, pulling herself up.

'You've got all those huntsmen in your corner. You saw how influential Leo was. The Hunt rely on their huntsmen, they're nothing without them. Get enough of them on your side and you could really change things.'

'On my side? Are there really sides, Skip?'

'That's my point – there shouldn't be.'

Ottilie groaned and flopped back down onto her pillow, squeezing her eyes shut. 'It's too early in the morning for riddles,' she grumbled.

Skip pulled her back up, shaking her until she gave in and opened her eyes. Ottilie laughed and shoved her away. 'What? What do you want? Them to start kidnapping girls as well as boys?'

Skip laughed, then frowned. 'At least if they did, it would mean they see our potential as equal. It's a start. That's all I'm saying. They've put you as an equal to all those boys, Ottilie. I don't think you know what a huge step that is.'

'But it's just me. They're not changing anything. If they had a magic spell that could turn me into a boy, they would use it.'

'Lucky for us, they don't. Like it or not, they've got a female huntsman,' she grinned.

'I still can't believe Leo changed his mind.' Ottilie ground her teeth. She was still annoyed that his mind had needed changing in the first place.

'Of course he did. There's nothing like being faced with death to sort out what's important from what's not –'

On the word *death* Ottilie remembered something: the hooded figure standing on the cliff above Leo. She tucked the memory away. She didn't want to think about it. Not now.

'– he nearly died, you brought down the dredretch together, all that rubbish faded away and whether he admits it or not, he recognised you as an equal.'

Ottilie snorted. 'I'm not sure Leo sees anyone as an equal … except maybe Maestro.'

Skip rolled her eyes in agreement. 'Even so, you're going to make a difference, Ottilie, I can feel it.' She jiggled her knees. 'We're not in the Usklers anymore. This is the Narroway. Why would they bother wasting their energy shoving us girls back into the shadows when there are real live monsters to fight?'

'What are you saying, Skip? What do you want me to do? I'm only a fledge. I don't matter to them that much.'

'Just be you. Be great. And try your best to win – make them name you champion. We'll see how much you matter to them after that.'

***

Becoming a champion, as it turned out, was going to be pretty close to impossible. The sun was just settling down to sleep as Ottilie climbed the cliff stairway on her way back from visiting Maestro. The disgruntled wingerslink may have been recovering quickly, but he was seriously displeased about being cooped up to heal.

Passing by the torch-lit raptor statues, Ottilie caught sight of a figure on crutches standing beneath the rankings. Assuming that after a week of deliberation they had finally scored Leo for felling the unknown dredretch, Ottilie wandered over to see.

Hearing her approach, Leo turned towards her. A triumphant smile spread across his face. Ottilie scanned to the top of the third-tier rankings. Sure enough, Leo was sitting securely in first place.

'How many did they give you?'

'A hundred and fifty,' he said. 'Would've been three hundred if it was at night. So still less than what Thrike got for that barro.' He scowled. Ottilie doubted she would ever be completely forgiven for ruining that shot. 'But I had enough of a lead on him before that day that one-fifty was enough to get back on top.' He looked ready to sing about it. 'They named it, too – they're calling it a kappabak.'

Ottilie frowned. Naming the monster was like resurrecting it. 'Do you think there are more of them out there?' she said.

'Don't know,' said Leo. 'Look, your name's back up.' He pointed to the fledgling rankings.

Ottilie scanned the names. 'No, it's not.'

'Look down. Lower,' he said, a little too cheerfully.

Ottilie skimmed all the way to the bottom of the eighty-seven fledges. The last line read:

87. Ottilie Colter 9

'Nine? That's my trial score.' She didn't like seeing her name down at the bottom, not one bit.

'They're discounting all the points you earned since then on account of your deceit,' said Leo, beaming.

'But I was pretending to be a boy in the trials too. Why isn't it zero?'

'You can thank Captain Lyre for that. He said your trial was so impressive you deserved to have it count.'

'What are you grinning about? I thought you wanted me to do well. Look, Igor Thrike's fledge is beating me.'

She waved at the name Dimitri Vosvolder, in twenty-sixth position.

'Everyone is beating you,' he laughed. 'Cheer up, you've got all of autumn and winter to make up the points.' He thumped her on the back, adjusted his crutches, and made to leave. Ottilie was still glaring at her nine when she heard him say quietly, 'Thank you. For last week.'

She blinked. 'You're welcome.'

'Though you wouldn't have been much help if I hadn't trained you so well. So if you think about it … I did save myself.'

Ottilie wanted to kick him, but she couldn't withhold the laugh. She covered her mouth. Leo merely grinned and hobbled on his way.

As he limped off, Ottilie thought back to that day. So much had happened, with the dredretch and the directorate, that the hooded figure had slipped from her mind yet again. What had that person been doing so close to the Withering Wood? Was it a coincidence that on the same day the strange figure had appeared, so did a completely unheard of species of dredretch?

They were unnatural. That's what the wranglers kept saying. They weren't meant to be there. They were wrong. They didn't eat, or breed. Their very presence was toxic, not only to people but to the natural world as well. If she and Alba were right and a witch had hexed the king, then could it be possible that the dredretches were being summoned somehow – or even controlled – by the same witch?

'You're welcome.'

Ottilie spun around. Captain Lyre was leaning against one of the stone arches. He had swapped his blue coat for a fiery orange jacket with black trimming, and his usually pointed beard was twirled into a neat curl at the tip.

Ottilie blinked at him, unsure of what he meant.

He threw his cane into the air, caught it, and pointed it at the rankings.

'Oh. Yes, thank you,' said Ottilie. 'For the nine.' Her tone flattened somewhat on the last word.

'I thought it might be interesting for you to know, Miss Ottilie Colter,' he strode over to stand beside her, 'that we did not assign you to Leonard Darby because of your high score in the trials.'

She looked up at him. 'You didn't?'

'We try to arrange a pairing that will be beneficial to the development of both the guardian and the fledge. Your trial revealed you to be a clever and careful thinker. We thought you might be a good influence on him.' He gripped her shoulder, his eyes twinkling. 'You're a crafty one.'

'There you are, Ottil– oh, sorry.' Preddy stopped short and flushed pink. 'Good evening, Captain Lyre.'

'And a marvellous evening it is, Mr Preddy. No need to apologise, I'm off, already running late. I'll be seeing you both in a jiff. Don't dawdle too long, you don't want to miss the music – my fourth-favourite day.' He turned to leave.

'Captain Lyre!' Ottilie couldn't help herself. 'What's your first-favourite day?'

He stopped, turned his head and raised an eyebrow. 'Your best guess?'

'Your birthday?' said Preddy, turning pink again.

Captain Lyre looked at Ottilie. 'She knows,' he said, with smiling eyes.

'I asked the question,' said Ottilie, baffled, but after a moment it came to her. 'It's the day you name the champions.'

He smiled, tilted his head in a small bow, then marched out between the stone arches.

'How did you know?' said Preddy.

Ottilie shrugged. 'I guess I'm looking forward to it too.' She frowned at the nine. 'Or I was.'

Preddy glanced at it, but didn't comment. 'We were looking for you. They've started lighting the lanterns,' he said.

The lantern festival was a tradition observed every year on the first night of autumn. Usklerians would hang lanterns on a tree to mark the end of the season of the sun, and traditionally pray to the old gods for a gentle winter – although that aspect of it was long gone. Nowadays the festival consisted of lantern hanging and lots of eating. Even in the Swamp Hollows the keeper would light a lantern in the chamber and hand out food scraps to his favourites.

'There she is!' said Scoot, appearing behind Preddy. 'Come on. I'm starving.'

Ottilie turned away from her abysmal ranking.

'Nice *nine*, Ott,' said Scoot, cackling with glee. 'I knew I'd overtake you!'

Ottilie grinned. 'Well … not for long.'

'Don't think it quite counts as overtaking,' said Preddy.

'Sure it does,' said Scoot, miming firing an arrow at Preddy's face.

Leo had been right about Preddy. He was overjoyed at the prospect of returning to the mounts. He'd had the choice to return to his previous guardian at Richter or be paired with a Fiory fourth-tier mount. Much to Ottilie's delight, Preddy had decided to stay, explaining that he had only agreed to take Leo as his guardian in the first place because he wanted to be at Fiory with his friends.

Ottilie, Preddy and Scoot approached the Moon Court. Joyful music wove and curled down the low-ceilinged passageway and Ottilie could see lights flickering through the arches ahead.

'I was looking for you,' said Gully, dashing up the passage behind them. 'Saw you're on the wall again, Ottilie.'

'Last,' said Scoot, holding up nine fingers. He flashed her a wicked grin, then snatched Preddy's eyeglasses from his nose and slid them onto his own face, smoothing his hair, standing up poker-straight, and rising to the tips of his toes. Preddy reached for them, but Scoot jerked away and sauntered off towards the lantern light. Preddy followed quickly after, and Ottilie heard him say, 'I do not walk like that!' before their voices were swallowed up by the music.

'This'll be different,' said Gully quietly.

'Than scraps of boiled bird and one sad lantern in a cave?' said Ottilie.

'Yes,' said Gully. 'Do you think she's all right? Back there without us?'

'I don't know if she's ever all right. But the keeper always kept her fed, and Mr Parch's there if she needs him.'

Ottilie stopped for a moment and pressed her fingers against the passage wall. She felt heavy yet hollow, just for a moment – an emptiness and a weight both at once. She hoped Mr Parch wasn't too worried about them. But there was no going back now. There was too much for her to do, too much to find out, what with the hooded figure, the widening of the Withering Wood,

342

the new dredretch and the idea that a villainous witch was possibly behind it all.

She would get back to the Brakkerswamp someday, she was sure of it – even if only to find Old Moss and Mr Parch and tell them her story, and to see if Bill remembered who she was. Maybe she could find a way to send Mr Parch a message, just to let him know that they were all right; that they were healthy and happy and doing something to help.

'Come on, Ottilie.' Pulling her sleeve, Gully sprang to a jog.

Ottilie hurried after him.

Waves of music and laughter rolled down the passage like a current of cheer. Ottilie levelled with Gully at the final arch. Preddy and Scoot were just ahead, Preddy laughing loudly at something Scoot had said. Captain Lyre was just beyond, playing a pipe with the band, and Skip stood nearby, tapping her foot to the beat of the drums.

Ottilie and Gully didn't linger another moment. Grinning, Gully nudged her with his elbow and, shoulder to shoulder, they stepped into the light.

THE END

Fort Fiory is supposed to be impenetrable —
yet when a wyler attacks inside, no-one is
safe. Not the Huntsmen. Not the fledges.
And definitely not the unarmed sculkies.
Ottilie and Skip are determined to change
that — but how can they train the girls when
only boys are allowed to hunt?

Ottilie and her huntsmen friends are
under attack — by something far worse than
dredretches. A witch is cursing them one by
one, making them unwilling participants in
a vengeful scheme. But what, exactly, is she
planning — and will Ottilie have to join her
to find out?

Acknowledgements

An enormous thank you to Hardie Grant Egmont and the team behind the Ampersand Prize for giving this fledgling author a chance. Thank you to Marisa Pintado and Luna Soo for your wonderful wisdom and guidance. This book became everything I hoped it would be and it couldn't have got there without you.

Penelope White, Maike Plenzke and Jess Cruikshank, you created the cover of my dreams, thank you.

Thank you to the Williams and Huck clans for your encouragement, and for just being fantastic people. And a special thank you to Trish for the books and the confidence boosts. Your belief in me means the world.

Jackaboy, thank you for the rhythmic snoring. I wrote the best chapters with you by my side. And Solly, our unsettling enactment of a certain chapter in this book convinced me this story was something special. I forgive you for terrifying me.

Matty, my first adventure companion, thank you for the good days. I'll never stop trying to write myself back into the worlds we explored.

Lucy Fry, my sister in spirit, I would have gone mad without you. Thank you for never leaving the cat alone in the dark.

Catrin, if you hadn't been there from the very beginning I might not have found the courage. Thank you for reading the roughest drafts and always just *getting it*.

To my incredibly supportive parents, I can't thank you enough. Dad, you have never let me feel unloved a day in my life, and that makes all the difference in the world. Thank you for helping me believe this was something I could do. And to my mum, you are a true example of strength and kindness. I know how to write about hope and heroes because of you.

About the Author

Originally from Taradale, Victoria, Rhiannon Williams is now a Sydney-based writer. She studied Creative Arts at university, has climbed Mt Kilimanjaro, and once accidentally set fire to her hair onstage. Her Ampersand Prize-winning debut novel, *Ottilie Colter and the Narroway Hunt*, was published in 2018 and has also been released in Germany and the Netherlands. In 2019 it was named a CBCA Notable Book, an Aurealis Awards finalist, and was shortlisted for the Readings Children's Book Prize and the Speech Pathology Australia book awards.